SECOND
CHANCE HERO

IVY JAMES

Kindred Spirits Publishing

Ivy James is the alter-ego of Kay Lyons, who now focuses on sweet/clean and wholesome contemporary romance and romantic suspense. For more information about Ivy's slightly sexier novels (or to find Kay's clean and wholesome versions of them as well as her latest titles), please go to Ivy James Author/Kay Lyons Author. Or, find her at one of the following:

@KayLyonsAuthor (Twitter)

Kay Lyons Author (Facebook)

Author_Kay_Lyons (Instagram)

Kay Lyons, Author (Pinterest)

Chapter 1

"MOM, ARE WE THERE *yet?*" Cody asked from the backseat. "Why are you going so slow?"

Skylar Mathews-Adams drove along the road toward the main buildings of the Second Chance Ranch, very much aware that the closer she came to arriving, the more slowly she drove. She'd spent three very impressionable years living on or around this ranch, and with every roll of her tires, a memory surfaced.

"We're almost there," she answered for the hundredth time, her gaze meeting her son's briefly in the rearview mirror. "And I want to be careful, too. Remember, there are going to be lots of physically challenged people on the ranch. Horses and animals, too. We can't go racing somewhere or we might hurt them."

Cody didn't answer and she wondered if he took heed of her warnings at all. Her seven-year-old son went back to playing, making sounds, his hands fisted around his dolls as they flew through the air, crashed and fought.

She stopped outside the building that served as

check-in, dining hall and game room. She felt sick to her stomach at the chaos and grief she'd left behind in New York and yet she was happy to have finally arrived. "We're here."

"Let me out! I wanna see."

Cody released his seat belt and stood between the bucket seats of the rental. He gazed up at the snow-capped mountains towering above the ranch.

"Awesome."

Cody's enthusiasm did nothing to ease the tension pulling her shoulders tight. Fifteen years ago her mother, Rissa, had uprooted Skylar from New York and moved them to their cousin's family owned ranch to help Skylar cope with her father's death and some other heavy-duty personal issues no fourteen-year-old kid should go through. Now on this sunny Wednesday afternoon, Skylar was making the same pilgrimage with Cody for similar yet very different reasons. "Pretty cool, huh?"

His psychiatrist hadn't agreed with Skylar removing Cody from his weekly sessions, but when her colleague had mentioned drug therapy as the next step in her son's medical plan, Skylar couldn't bring herself to do it.

Cody was struggling with his father's death, yes, but drugs? Her son was almost eight, and kids his age had active imaginations. Cody's fixation on his imaginary world was…acceptable for what he'd been through.

There was an issue. She knew there was an issue. But before she began feeding her child chemicals, she had to try removing him from everything and focus on him one-on-one. Montana had worked for her, helped her deal with her father's traumatic death in a car accident and the part she'd played in it, so surely it could work for a little boy who needed to find as much fun and adventure in real life as he did in his fantasy world? "I told you they made the mountains big here."

"I bet there are *lots* of vampire caves up there. See that one?" He pointed to the tallest peak. "That one belongs to the oldest vampire *ever.*"

Skylar got out and pushed the seat forward so Cody could climb out the conventional way versus plowing over the console and scuffing it with his shoes. "Then it's a good thing we won't be going up there."

Even as she made the statement, she chastised herself for playing along. But after ten days of grief counseling the teens at her high school after a student's suicide, it was the best she could manage.

They'd had a delay-ridden flight and a long drive from the Helena airport, and Skylar was exhausted. She'd already spent countless sleepless nights debating staying in New York, keeping Cody in therapy and continuing to work alongside her co-counselor to help their students deal with the loss. In the end, she had decided to stick with her original plans. The last thing she wanted was for Cody's troubles to manifest themselves like Travis Duncan's, the boy who had hung himself.

Cody's mop of silky-straight, white-blond hair lifted in the breeze that blew over the beautiful landscape. Thanks to the cowlick at the crown, Cody's hair always had a messy, fresh-from-bed look. And she loved it, loved *him*, more than life.

"But we gotta! How will I find my dad if we don't?"

Ignoring the guests leaving the common room, Skylar focused on Cody and stamped down the nerves churning within her. "Cody, we've talked about this. About how make-believe is fun, but it's not real. Remember?"

Her son's indigo eyes stared at her with mutinous intensity, his chin set at a stubborn angle she recognized from looking in the mirror. With his naturally dark complexion and light hair, he looked more like a sun-kissed California surfer than a kid born and raised in the heart of New York City.

When he didn't respond, she said, "Why don't we go inside and find Grandma Rissa and Maura? Figure out which cabin is ours? Won't that be fun?"

He lowered his head and his fingers tightened around his dolls—or rather, *action figures*—as though he wanted to sling them at her. Ignoring her suggestion, he stared at Batman as if the doll was talking.

"I know," he whispered to Batman, then heaved a gusty sigh. "Okay. We'll wait."

"Cody," she said, pulling his attention to her. "What's going on? Where are we right now?"

"Montana."

"That's right. I want you to remember that. Now we're going to see Grandma. Are you ready?"

Cody lifted his head and focused on the mountains with such longing, her heart skipped a beat. Maybe she shouldn't have brought him here. "Listen to me. Look at my eyes." She waited for him to obey her. "Honey, I know I sort of looked *like* a vampire in those pictures you and Natalie found," she said, referring to the

4

babysitter, "but I was playing dress up. I'm not a vampire, and neither was your dad."

He shook his head. "Mom, I *know* the secret."

"Cody, there is no secret. Your dad is—"

"No, he's not! He's not really dead!"

Nine months, six days. That's how long it had been since Tom had died on August 26 of last year. Nine months and six days, but Cody still couldn't accept it. "Your father is buried in Rose Mount Cemetery. We've visited his grave how many times? You have to stop making up these stories."

Cody stared at Batman *again* before he grabbed his backpack. "We don't have to go up there to find Dad."

She blinked at the sudden turnaround, but welcomed the change in topic with open arms. Talking about Tom's death wasn't easy for her, either. "We don't? Why?"

Cody shrugged.

"Cody, why?"

"Because Dad's probably asleep now, and if we go, the other vampires might be hungry. We can stay here. Dad'll find us."

She was glad Cody had changed his mind, even if she was upset because he was still pretending.

Other than a single trip to Montana when Cody was too young to remember, her son had never seen so much open land. He didn't know the dangers of getting lost, despite the number of talks she'd had with him. "I'm glad you're thinking about the risks, Cody."

"Yeah. Parker said vampires have lots of power and move really fast, like they're flying. Some are good and some are bad. Dad's a good one. When you were a vampire, could you fly?"

Never had she regretted her ultimate Goth-girl days —complete with the black fishnet, ass-kickers and too-short skirts topped by skull T-shirts—more than now. Those pictures she'd saved as a reminder of how far she'd come in her life fueled Cody's make-believe world. While babysitting him, Parker and Natalie—the teenagers next door, good, straight-A, genuinely nice kids—had loved helping Cody come up with a story to match Skylar's clothing, not realizing the depths to which Cody's dream world took him.

"How about we go get our key so we can settle in and explore? Won't that be fun?" Skylar said.

"Yeah. Can I turn into a vampire like you did?"

"Cody, *enough* already."

"Parker said they have to bite you. Does it hurt?" He then proceeded to have Batman—a vampire in Cody's mind, despite how many times Skylar had explained to the contrary—do a surprise dive attack on Robin.

What could she say to him to get through to him? Get him to understand? Get him to *stop?*

One of the horses nickered from the corral. Skylar wondered how long she'd been standing there delaying going inside because she hoped his pretending and ques-tions would end. "Come on, Cody. Let's go."

She ushered Cody up the ramp and inside, where the smell of fresh-baked cookies and bread filled her nose.

"Skylar! Rissa, she's here," Maura cried.

Maura Rowland, her mom's cousin and the chef of

the Second Chance, hurried toward them behind Skylar's mother, who'd hopped up from her chair and crossed the room in a split second.

Engulfed in her mother's embrace, Skylar noticed Grace Rowland, the ranch owner's wife, standing tall and lithe and grinning from ear to ear beside Maura, both waiting for their hugs.

"Oh, baby, welcome home. It's so good to see you," Rissa said. "I know you were torn about coming, after what happened with that boy, but we're so glad you did."

Rissa squatted to hug Cody and remark how much he'd grown since her last trip to New York.

"It's good to be here," Skylar said, while receiving Maura's hug, which smelled like the fresh-baked cookies on the counter.

"Mom, I'm thirsty. Do they have any blood?"

"Blood?" Rissa asked, her tone filled with surprise.

"Tomato juice or punch." Skylar shot Cody a hard stare of reminder. "He likes to…pretend."

"I have cranberry juice," Maura said.

He looked at Skylar as if to confirm that it was red and reluctantly she nodded.

"Thank you," he said, remembering his manners.

"You're welcome, sweetie. How about a snack, too? You must be hungry," Rissa said, at home in the Rowland kitchen from her days of working there. "You can eat while we help your mom settle in."

Barely managing to hold in a groan because she'd hoped for a little more time with Cody to get him out of his make-believe world, Skylar tried to smile, wondering what her family would think once they discovered the real reason she and Cody were here.

One thing she knew for certain, try as she might, she couldn't hide Cody's unusual behavior for long.

MARCUS WHITEFEATHER SCOWLED when he heard Oreo's high-pitched whinny. The mare didn't like being trapped in a stall, but she had a penchant for roaming. With her so close to foaling, Seth Rowland, the owner of the Second Chance, had penned the horse for her own safety.

Done teaching for the day, Marcus headed toward his van and the racing wheelchair inside of it. He had enough time to get a good roll in before Grace finished his grandfather's biweekly physical-therapy session.

A loud *thump* sounded and the wall of the barn vibrated with the force of the horse's kick, distracting Marcus from his purpose. He turned away from the van and the hydraulic ramp lowering into position, and wheeled himself into the barn to investigate.

It took a good five seconds for his vision to adjust to the change in light, but once it did, he spotted the source of Oreo's upset.

Across from the mare's stall, a child had climbed the rails of a holding pen. The boy looked to be about five or six and he had a piece of black material tied around his neck. If the boy fell off his perch and the material got caught, he could strangle himself. "Hey, kid," Marcus called softly, careful with his tone so as not to startle the child. "Get down from there before you fall."

The boy ignored Marcus, or else didn't hear, and continued making a *shooshing* sound, his arms out at his sides. As high as he was on the rail and with the material stretched out by his hands, no wonder Oreo was spooked. "Hey, you. *Kid.*" Was he deaf? Marcus waved to get his attention. "Hey!"

The boy suddenly turned toward Marcus and he wobbled before regaining his balance, his dazed expression slowly clearing. The boy stared but didn't budge.

At least he hadn't fallen. That wobble was enough to have Marcus's heart thumping out of sync in his chest. "You need to get down. You aren't allowed to play in here. Understand? The barn's off-limits unless you are with a ranch employee."

"Vampires can do anything." The boy bared his teeth at Marcus with a hiss.

Vampires? Marcus wheeled closer. "Not here, they can't. See that horse over there?" He indicated Oreo's stall. "She's ready to foal, but we don't want her to have her baby yet."

"So?"

"So, you're making her nervous."

The child turned up his nose and gave Marcus a glare. "I'm a *vampire.*" He raised his arms and the cape as though that alone should prove his point.

"Yeah, well go be a vampire at your cabin or on the playground, not here."

"Vampires like the *dark.*"

"Then play in your closet until the sun goes down. You can't play here. Now get down and try not to—"

The little *vampire* leaped from the rail to the floor

before Marcus could finish. Oreo spooked, her shriek of complaint echoing loudly off the walls as her hindquarters hit the stall.

"Damn it, I told you not to scare the horse."

The boy had landed in a crouched position, but he straightened with an ease and speed Marcus envied. As he'd discovered teaching art classes and helping out occasionally with riding lessons at the ranch, not many kids that age were that coordinated.

"You said a dirty word."

"Don't scare the horse." Marcus enunciated each word through gritted teeth because the kid's obliviousness was irritating him. "If she goes into labor right now, it could kill both of them. Is that what you want?"

The boy's eyes widened as if he finally understood the seriousness of his actions.

Marcus rolled to Oreo's stall and put his hand over the rail, waiting patiently for her to recognize his scent and approach so he could rub her nose. After she did, he reached to feel what he could of her side to see if she was contracting. "Thatta girl. Easy does it. He didn't mean anything by it. Settle down, little mama."

Satisfied she was calming, Marcus slowly backed away and swung his wheelchair to face the boy. "Don't come in here again. Not without one of the ranch employees with you. Understand? There are rules, and this is not a play area."

The boy's mouth quivered. "Is she gonna die?"

Marcus studied his face to figure out how much of the kid's attitude was sincere and how much was because he didn't want to get into trouble. "I think she'll be all right, but we can't let her get riled. If she goes into labor early, then yeah, she could die. The colt's not turned yet."

"What's her name?"

"Oreo. She's a special pet of the owners' children and we'd all be upset if something happened to her. You understand?"

The kid nodded again, not meeting Marcus's gaze. Feeling bad that he'd come down so hard on the boy, who obviously didn't know better, Marcus asked, "You got a pet?"

"No. I want a dog, but my mom won't let me 'cause we're not home much."

"That's smart. People shouldn't get pets if they can't take care of them."

The child wiped his face on the cape. "I didn't mean to scare her."

He belatedly remembered the boy was a guest with parents who wouldn't appreciate Marcus swearing at their little angel. "I'm sorry, too. For saying the dirty word." He hoped the kid understood he wasn't apologizing for ordering him about, because the boy needed to know when to listen to adults.

On a ranch with animals, equipment and dangers some wouldn't know to look out for, it was everyone's job to keep the guests safe, especially the little ones.

The boy's gaze dropped to the chair and a peculiar expression stole over his face, one fairly easy to read.

"Something wrong?" Marcus watched as the kid wrinkled his nose, but remained silent. "You sure?"

The boy shrugged. "You can't walk."

Actually Marcus *could* walk with the help of braces on his calves and feet. He was paralyzed from the knees down, but he had some feeling in his thighs, which made standing upright possible by wearing the braces and using canes. It was painful as hell when he overdid things. "What about it?"

"Don't you get tired of sitting? You can't do anything."

The rudeness registered first. What kind of parent brought a child this insensitive to a dude ranch filled with people like Marcus? The Second Chance catered to the disabled, and they'd built a reputation as one of the best.

Not all of the people who vacationed here had a handicapped person in the family. Last year, one group came simply because they wanted to show their bully of a son how politically correct they could be. The parents had quickly grown impatient with the extra time needed for some guests to perform certain tasks and they'd left before their week ended. "I can't, huh? Look, you need to change your attitude. Because you know what? I can do plenty. I'll bet I can do almost anything you can."

"Can you fly? Or climb a tree? Jump or run really fast? My dad can."

"Good for him. But you're old enough to know better than to say rude things just because people are different from you. Didn't your dad teach you any manners while he was doing all those things?"

"My dad's a vampire."

Marcus blinked at the switch back to vampires. He wouldn't have pegged the boy as having a mental disability, but what did he know? Here he was, about to give the boy a hard time about judging people, when he'd obviously misjudged. "Is that a fact?"

Maybe the vampire thing was the result of a brain injury. Or maybe the boy was autistic. They'd had a couple of autistic kids earlier in the spring and one of them had had quite an imagination. The teenager had hated riding and anything outdoors, but he'd gotten into Marcus's class on working with metal and designing small pieces of art.

"Yeah. He has superpowers 'cause he's a vampire. My mom says he's not, but I know he is. She used to be a vampire, but she's not anymore. I think it's because she doesn't like to drink blood."

Okay. He wasn't going to touch that one with a ten-foot pole. "Good for her. Come on, out you go. Let's leave Oreo alone."

The boy picked up two action figures from the barn floor before he began to meander in the right direction.

Marcus followed, watching as the child shoved the figures into his pockets before he grabbed the ends of his cape, stretched his arms out and made that noise with his mouth again.

"Hey, kid? Can you find your way to your cabin?" He was a little leery of sending the boy off on his own.

"My mom said I could explore if I stayed close."

Yeah, and look how well that worked out. What kind of mother sent a kid like that to play on his own? "What's your cabin number?"

As though he'd wised up to why Marcus was asking, the boy's mouth formed a sullen line.

They moved through the open doors of the barn, and a female voice could be heard calling a name.

"That's my mom."

"Sounds to me like she expected you to stay closer."

The woman's voice came from the group of structures to the right beyond the stand of pines.

A well-worn path cut through the trees, the lower limbs removed to allow easier access for guests. Enough remained to obscure his first peek of the woman, but he was able to make out slim legs in formfitting shorts and flip-flops. Those legs had one heck of a sexy sway.

"Well, Cody," he said, using the kid's name now that he knew it, "it was nice meeting you. Take my advice, okay? Stick close to your mom until you get the hang of things. That means no unsupervised trips to the barn or anywhere else. You don't want to wind up in trouble."

"Cody?" The woman's voice grew closer.

"Okay. But I won't get in trouble."

"And why's that?"

"Because my grandma says we belong here, and my mom used to live here."

The shock of the kid's words left Marcus rolling to a slow stop. *My mom used to live here? Grandma?*

The boy's words could mean anything, but suddenly the kid's appearance smacked Marcus in the face. The white-blond hair, his big blue eyes. That stubborn chin and a dimple the size of a small crater in his cheek.

He glanced toward the woman heading for them, able to see a little more of her lust-inducing walk. "Who's your mama?" He hated the urgent huskiness in his voice. "What's her name?" he asked, praying he was wrong.

"Her name's Skylar. There she is. See?"

The woman broke through the tree cover and stopped so abruptly little rocks scattered at her feet. Yeah, seemed he wasn't the only one surprised.

A rush of anger, fast and powerful, came at him like a three-hundred-pound linebacker. In its wake was a wave of pain and regret so massive he couldn't breathe.

"Marcus," she said, visibly dazed. "What are you doing here?"

Chapter 2

SKYLAR DREW ON every yoga class she'd ever taken to control her muscles, her breathing and get her through the next five minutes without the panic taking hold. She'd been on the ranch three hours—two of those with her mother before she had to go back to work at her charter helicopter business. Maura and Grace had helped carry in their bags before returning to work themselves. Yet in all that time, in all those conversations, not once had anyone mentioned Marcus. When was someone going to inform her?

He looked as good as ever, even with the scowl on his chiseled face. His Native-American heritage was stamped across his features, his cheekbones and facial structure that of a rugged, hard-hewn model, not the pretty boys who so often adorned magazine ads.

Marcus wore jeans and a dark blue T-shirt that brought out the intense blue of his eyes, the sleeves of his shirt straining to contain the biceps bulging below the hems.

Despite his leanness, he looked like a bodybuilder, his neck muscles thick, his chest and shoulders nearly twice as broad as the narrow, thick-wheeled chair in which he sat.

She noticed how Marcus had paled beneath his tan —his reaction to seeing his biological son for the first time.

Skylar hardened her heart against the expression Marcus wore. *Smarter, wiser, stronger.* Screw him. "Cody, we need to go."

"Seth." Marcus cleared his throat, not taking his eyes off Cody. "Seth had to let his riding instructor go at the last minute. I'm…filling in."

The news rocked her. "*All* summer?"

"More or less."

She'd spend the next *four weeks* running into Marcus? Here? In the place that was supposed to help her with her son? Supposed to be a safe place? Suddenly it was no such thing.

"No one told me." And she knew why, although that didn't stop the anger. The moment she had said she was considering a trip to Montana, *they should have told her.* "I didn't know you were living here again."

"I moved back several years ago."

Years. *Years?* No one—not her stepsister, Carly, or her mother or Maura—had thought to *mention* that fact? *You told them never to speak his name to you again. Why would they?*

"Grace is giving my grandfather physical-therapy sessions here so he doesn't have to go all the way to the VA hospital. When Seth asked me to help out with the lessons, I figured pitching in was the least I could do."

"Mom, I'm hungry."

Typical of a growing boy, Cody was always hungry. Thankfully it gave her the excuse she needed to escape and regroup. Struggling for normalcy, she managed a smile. "That's why I was coming to find you." She lay her hand on his shoulder. "Maura made you mac and cheese. Why don't you go eat? And don't forget we're going to see Grandma and Grandpa tonight."

"Yay!" Without a word of goodbye, Cody raced toward the cabins.

Skylar watched him until the moment his foot hit the ramp leading into their cabin. There were a half-dozen cabins along that side of the stand of pines. Another dozen or so were on the other side of the main house closer to the creek.

It was amazing to see how much the ranch had changed since she'd been gone. With all the memories attached to this place and all the lies that had been told, she'd avoided coming home and always urged her family to visit her.

"He…looks like you."

Some days she agreed. Others, such as a moment ago when Cody and Marcus had been within feet of each other, she thought her son's expressions very much resembled his father's.

"He's old enough for school now. He's doing well?" Marcus's voice was rough with emotions she couldn't identify.

Not that she'd try. She refused to feel sorry for him. Or angry or hurt or anything else. Refused to lower her guard where he was concerned. Period. She'd forgiven him the past, but she'd be a fool to forget it. Live and learn, right? "You saw for yourself."

He stared in the direction of the cabin. And because she wanted to make a point and make it clear, she stepped to the right to block his view. "We're not here to bother you, Marcus. We're just visiting."

"You need to keep a better eye on him. The boy was in the barn, pretending he could fly. If he'd gotten that cape snagged on something, he could've hung himself."

The warning brought an instant punch of gut-churning fear as Travis Duncan's face came to mind. She could only imagine the horror Travis's mother felt at finding her son hanging from a rafter in their garage.

Skylar had already warned Cody about jumping off things while wearing the cape, but so far nothing had stuck. And after Travis's suicide, the possibility of Cody getting hurt due to his vampire antics scared her even more. "I'll talk to him." She turned to walk away.

"Wait. What's wrong with him?"

Her breath huffed out of her chest. "Nothing is *wrong* with him." Okay, so maybe that sounded defensive, but what mother wouldn't be? *What's wrong with him?*

Marcus locked his jaw so tight she swore she heard a *pop* sound. "Skylar, it's just… He kept insisting his father is a vampire."

Of all the people for Cody to say that to, why did it have to be Marcus? "He likes to pretend. Is that your only comment having just met your son?" She kept her voice low. Thankfully the path was clear and the closest living beings were the animals in the barn several yards away. "You want to know what's *wrong* with him?"

Marcus cursed and managed to appear remorseful. "I wasn't expecting to see you. Or him. *Skylar.*"

She had taken several steps toward the cabin, when she realized Marcus was at her side. She looked at the distance he'd traveled so quickly and blinked. How did he get to her so fast?

"You have to give me a chance to catch up here."

She shrugged. Whatever. "Now you have."

He made a sound of frustration. "That day at the hospital when you told me you were pregnant, I'd just found out the injury was permanent."

"I know. That's *why* I told you. So you'd have something to focus on besides what happened in that game."

He held her gaze. "I know that now, but then? I wasn't ready. I wasn't expecting you to drop a bomb like that on me."

Unbelievable. It dawned on her that during their brief conversation Marcus had referred to Cody as *the boy* and *he* and *a bomb*, but never once by his name. Didn't Marcus have the guts to say it out loud? "The *bomb's* name is Cody," she drawled, her entire body aching from holding herself so tense.

"Cody," he said. "What's with the vampire stuff?"

"He's having some issues with Tom's death and is still adjusting to losing his father. Pretending is a natural and creative way of expression for kids his age," she said, aware that she sounded like a textbook.

She didn't think it possible for Marcus to look more fierce, but at the mention of Tom, his scowl deepened.

"Seemed like more than pretending to me. That's all I'm saying."

Because it *was* more. Not that she'd tell Marcus that. He wasn't involved in their life and he never would be—his choice. "Like I said, Tom's death has been hard on Cody. And me."

His nostrils flared and emotions flickered rapidly across his face. But surely she was wrong. Marcus had made his decision and she'd told him at the time that he'd never be able to undo it.

"I'm sorry for your loss," he murmured.

She folded her arms, but quickly lowered her hands to her hips when the move had Marcus's gaze focusing on her ample chest. Memories flooded her. All of them of better times. "Thank you. I'm sorry Cody bothered you. And I'll talk to him about the cape." She turned on her heel. "Give Ben my best," she said, referring to Marcus's grandfather.

"Skylar…"

Wondering why he insisted on dragging out what was obviously an uncomfortable moment, she tapped her foot to keep from saying something she shouldn't. She faced a ponderosa pine, fingered the needles and tried to stem the flood of memories. Making out with Marcus in the barn loft. Getting into a water fight while washing his grandfather's truck. Leaving prom early to be alone. Relishing the freedom of his college apartment.

"You said you were visiting. That's the only reason you're here?"

"Of course. My family is here. Why wouldn't I visit?"

"You haven't been back to North Star for years."

He was keeping tabs on her? Today seemed to be full of surprises. "Tom and I came to visit when Cody was one. After that, Tom was too sick to travel far."

Marcus wheeled himself closer, the special tires of his wheelchair easily able to maneuver the bumpy terrain. Marcus seeing Cody wasn't the only first of the day. She'd never seen Marcus in a wheelchair and the sight wasn't easy to stomach.

Not because she was phobic. She'd worked at the Second Chance the three years she'd lived in North Star with her mother, stepfather and stepsister, and had even considered becoming a physical therapist like Grace.

She had no qualms about dealing with wheelchairs or the various injuries and impairments that put people in them. But seeing Marcus—once a world-class athlete —in one made her heart ache, despite the overwhelming pain he'd caused her.

"Don't look so worried." She was determined to get the space and distance from him she needed. "I haven't told your secret and I don't plan to."

"Our secret," he corrected. "It's *our* secret, Skylar. I may have started it when I told you to forget I existed, but you wasted no time turning it into what it is today."

"Yes, I'm to blame for our breakup," she said drily. "It wasn't the naked woman in your apartment, in our *bed.*"

Marcus's expression darkened, his face ruddy beneath the Western-style cowboy hat he wore. "Or you marrying another man *one week* after you told me you were pregnant with my kid?"

And there they were. They'd each gotten a shot in, but neither of them seemed to feel better because of it.

Maybe she had let Cody's paternity turn into a bigger secret because of Marcus's rejection when she'd told him the news. But it was *his* fault their relationship ended.

Skylar wiped her damp hands over her shorts and tried to find peace within herself. An impossible task. She'd worked hard to put the past behind her, but seeing Marcus dredged it all up again, and she hated how it made her feel. Panicky and sick and dark inside. Angry. In an instant, she was transported to the Goth teen she'd been, the one who had hidden behind a mask of makeup and clothes because she couldn't handle the problems in her life. Even if she'd created those problems herself.

Like breaking up with Marcus, and giving him the excuse to sleep with that skank?

She'd said she needed a break, yes, but when she'd returned to his apartment a few hours later to make amends, he had already screwed the tramp. As though what he had shared with Skylar wasn't worth waiting more than a few hours. Sometimes love wasn't enough to make a relationship work. She and Marcus had been the perfect example of that.

"I need to check on Cody. But your secret is safe. I kept my promise, Marcus. I didn't tell. No one knows. I left you alone, and I raised my son—"

"With help from Daddy Warbucks." His tone was full of censure.

It took everything inside her to control her fury, but

she refused to rise to the taunt. Yes, Tom had been well-off. He'd been a partner in a very successful business. But more important, he had been a good man and a wonderful father. *And trustworthy when I needed him most.* "You have no right to judge me or any decision I've made." She struggled to keep her voice calm when all she wanted to do was scream and curse at him the way he had at her that awful day in his hospital room. "You forfeited your right to judge the moment you ordered me out of your life, knowing I faced the choice of having *a baby* or getting an abortion. Alone.

"You made your decision, Marcus, and I abided by it. I left you out of it, just like you wanted. Now the *least you can do* is abide by my wishes while Cody and I are here on vacation. You're not part of our family and you never have been, so stay the hell away from us."

"That's going to be hard to do when I'll be here a couple times a week for classes."

Her nails bit into her palms. "It's a big ranch. I'm sure we can manage to avoid each other."

She shoved the tree limb out of her way and walked in the opposite direction, every step leading her deeper into the past she'd tried so hard to forget.

Why had she thought Montana was a good idea?

MARCUS SHOOK WITH anger by the time he got to the barn. His grandfather should be finished with his physical-therapy session, but Marcus was in no way fit to face the questions he knew his mood would attract.

Spying Maura leaving the kitchen by a side door, he called to her. "Would you mind giving Ben a message?"

"Sure, Marcus. What is it?" She approached with a water bottle in her hand.

"I'm going for a roll. So when he finishes with Grace, tell him to take the van home. I'll see him there." His grandfather loved driving the specially equipped van. The hand controls had given Ben back some of the freedom he'd lost when rheumatoid arthritis had limited his movement.

"No problem. Here, take this. I haven't opened it yet and it's cold." She held out the water bottle for him. "You'll be careful?"

"Always am," he said, setting it on the van's bumper so he could pull out the lightweight racer he'd made.

Maura moved to help get the three-wheeled chair on the ground, standing by while he shifted into it.

"Are you okay? You seem a little off and— This wouldn't have anything to do with Skylar being here, would it?"

He hesitated before lifting his regular chair into the vehicle and closing the doors. "Can't say it wasn't a surprise to see her."

"I thought so. I saw you talking to her and Cody. You two have a lot of history but I hope you can set it aside for the summer. We wouldn't want to lose either of you."

"I made a promise to teach those classes. I'll do it. But she's not happy I'm here."

"What about you? Are you happy she's here?"

Happy. Pissed. Shocked. He'd always wondered

what it would be like to see Skylar and the child he'd rejected, but he hadn't expected it to happen now, *today*. His hands still trembled from the brief encounter.

Marcus fastened the straps over his thighs, one around his waist then inserted the bottle into its holder, wishing he'd thought to bring a pair of shorts to combat the heat. Wishing…he hadn't run into Skylar and their son? Was the unknown better than the known? "I'd best get going," he said, ignoring the question. He removed his T-shirt and pulled on gloves to protect his hands. Wheeling around with blisters on both hands was nothing short of stupid.

"We all make mistakes. I'm sure if you tried, you and Skylar could find it in yourselves to forgive each other. You were both so young, and very different people."

That they were. But every second he sat here and tried to pretend he hadn't just seen his son for the first time put him closer to the edge. "She tell you what I did the night we broke up?"

One glance at Maura's face left him swearing. Of course she had. Maura was Skylar's family. Technically he was the outsider here, even though he'd been around and involved with the Rowlands and the ranch a lot longer than Skylar.

"You and Skylar were the topic of quite a few discussions afterward. The whole 'is being on a break the same as breaking up' debate."

"I thought we were over." He didn't owe Skylar's cousin an explanation, yet felt compelled to defend himself. "I wouldn't have slept with that girl otherwise."

"That is the one point we all agreed on. None of us thought of you as the type to cheat. It's good to hear you say it, though." She tapped the back of his chair. "Keep your cell phone close in case you run into trouble."

More than willing to get the hell out of there, Marcus nodded and began pumping the wheels, building his speed. It took all his concentration to steer clear of the potholes lining the long driveway, but once he reached the highway, he found his rhythm and his mind focused on only one thing: Cody.

Skylar's appearance had blindsided him. But seeing his son for the very first time... He had always wondered what the child looked like. Now he knew.

His heart squeezed in his chest, and if he didn't know better, he might think he was having a heart attack. He pumped the wheels faster, not stopping until the wind whistled in his ears and the trees and grass beside the road were a blur that did nothing to wipe away the past.

Every shove of his hands against the rim propelled him forward but it didn't make him forget what he'd done. He'd been full of himself, especially once he'd landed that NFL contract. Cocky, his quarterback, multi-million-dollar ego was bigger than his brain.

When Skylar continued to sidestep his requests that she move in with him, quit school so she could travel with him, get engaged, he'd gotten frustrated and acted like a jerk. He'd pressed her for more when he knew, could see, she wasn't ready. Finally, he'd pushed her enough to say they needed a break from each other.

Fine by him. Why be with a woman who clearly

didn't want to be with him? Who held herself back? Who wasn't willing to do whatever it took to support him? In his mind, a break meant they were done and, in a fit of drunken bullheadedness, he'd brought some girl home from a bar. Even while he'd had sex with her, he knew it was wrong. But he'd been pissed at Skylar for walking away. For being *able* to walk away so easily.

For shutting him down so many times.

When she'd shown up in his hospital room eight weeks later, saying she was pregnant… *Shit.* All he could do was lie there, unable to move, knowing the damage was permanent and his career was over. That many of his so-called friends would disappear. That he had next to nothing left. In that moment, he couldn't face himself in the mirror, much less Skylar. And to bring a baby into the world? Be a father? He couldn't do it. Sending her away was the smartest decision he could make.

Cody's image appeared in Marcus's head. He tried to blink it away, shook his head hard enough the racer wobbled. Nothing removed the picture.

His kid. His son.

What kind of man became a father and didn't care?

All this time it had seemed like a bad dream. A nightmare he could set aside during the light of day while he worked and took care of his grandfather. Something he could compartmentalize. But having seen Skylar again, he couldn't set aside the truth. The pain he'd inflicted by abandoning her.

When Skylar had needed him, he'd shut *her* down. And now his own son looked him in the eyes without an ounce of recognition.

Rejecting them had been the biggest mistake of his life. One made worse when, in a matter of days, Skylar married someone else, ending all possibility of reconciliation. How could she have done that to him? Shove him away over and over, then marry someone else?

Rage burst from him, his hoarse shout echoing in his ears and sending a startled eagle into flight.

He let go of the wheels, his arms spasming, the gloves scratching his face as he buried his head in his hands and let the racer slow.

He'd abandoned them both and gotten what he'd deserved as a result. But now more than ever, he wanted to undo the mistakes of the past and be the man he should have been.

Chapter 3

SINCE THE SECOND CHANCE was overflowing with summer guests, Skylar's stepsister, Carly, had arranged for everyone to meet at the Circle M Ranch, which belonged to her husband's family, later that evening. It was a massive property consisting of a hundred thousand acres that bordered the Rowlands'.

Skylar wasn't sure which of the three brothers—Liam, Brad or Chance McKenna—was in charge of what, but they all seemed to get along fairly well. She was impressed by the dynamic. She'd spent the past seven years working as a family counselor for the court system, then as a high-school counselor, and she'd seen how wrong things could go. Too often, people argued over the slightest things. She could only imagine how hard it was to keep perspective when it came to owning and operating something as vast as the Circle M.

Carly had married into a strong, unique family, and Skylar couldn't help but be a little envious.

Even so, her face hurt from the effort it took to keep

a smile pinned on. Looking around the crowded dining room, she was glad to be momentarily left out of the various conversations taking place. All three of the McKenna brothers, their spouses and kids were there, as well as Skylar's parents, Maura and Jake and their three children. It was all a bit much at the moment.

"Lex, I'm not going to tell you again. Put it away or I'm taking the phone." Jake's tone indicated how exasperated he was with his seventeen-year-old daughter's habit of texting during a meal, even though she tried to hide her activity under the table.

"I will, Dad, just a second."

"Now."

Sitting beside her, Skylar saw Lexi's thumbs flying over the keyboard before the girl shoved the phone under her thigh so that she'd feel it if it vibrated. Skylar couldn't help but compare her with Travis Duncan, who had been close to the same age. Like Lexi, his phone seemed to be his primary means of communicating with his friends. He'd been bound for an ivy-league school and obviously hadn't felt up to the weight of expectation on him. Skylar prayed Lexi didn't feel the same sense of despair as she prepared to head for college.

The room was filled to the brim with noise and people, yet nothing seemed to drown out Cody's statements about it getting dark outside—and how his father would be joining them soon.

Whenever Cody embarked on another tangent about vampires and caves and blood, Skylar talked over him and changed the subject to something more appropriate, asking her new brother-in-law, Liam, about his job as a deputy working for her stepfather, or one of the other McKenna brothers about ranching. Everyone responded and kept the conversation light, but she could feel their curious stares on both her and Cody.

By the time dinner was over and Carly announced that dessert would be served on the porch, Skylar's nerves were frazzled, and she didn't have a shred of hope left that her mother or Carly would let Cody's behavior pass without comment.

Lexi made a dash for the door, phone in hand, and the kids raced outside. The men excused themselves to head for the porch, while Carly's sisters-in-law, Gabriella and Jenna, moved into the kitchen to collect pies and coffee, leaving Skylar to face her mother and sister. "I'll gather up these dishes," she said, desperate to escape.

"Stop," Rissa ordered. "And sit down."

Skylar forced herself to meet her mother's worried gaze. "Mom, it's fine. He's pretending."

"Sky, honey, Cody is not okay. He thinks Tom is still alive? A *vampire?*"

How many times was she going to have to have this conversation today? "Cody went to the funeral last year, and we've visited Tom's grave since. He knows Tom is dead. He's just having some trouble adjusting."

"It is a bit much, Skylar," Carly said softly.

"Exactly. That is way more than having some trouble," her mother insisted. "When did this start? Has he seen someone?"

Slumping into the chair, Skylar fidgeted, folding and refolding one of the linen napkins. "Yes, he has. But before we get into that, let me say it's normal for kids Cody's age to fantasize, but given the…frequency that he does it, the issues are being addressed. His therapist and I have noticed that he's more prone to the behavior when he's nervous or uncertain. It's a coping mechanism he's developed. We're trying to teach him to cope with things another way, but the process takes time."

"That's all understandable, but how long has he been doing this? Tom died *nine* months ago and you've said nothing to us?"

"It started after you left New York, after Tom's funeral, and I thought Cody would come out of it. I didn't want you to worry."

"But he hasn't stopped," Carly said.

Her mother rubbed her hands up and down her arms as though the news gave her a chill.

Skylar felt their combined gazes on her—felt the judgment and wounded emotions—and struggled to maintain her composure. If she let them see her own unease, this situation would escalate. "Like I said, we're seeing a counselor and we'll continue the sessions once we're back home."

"Should he be missing his sessions?" Carly asked.

"You can't counsel him," Rissa added. "You know you can't be objective."

"I know."

"But you came anyway, which means… You're scared, too," Rissa said. "Oh, Sky."

"He'll be *fine*," Skylar said. "He needs some fresh air and time out of the city and away from the memories. North Star got me out of my Goth funk, so it might work for him, too." She fingered the edge of the napkin. "I didn't know I'd be facing Marcus, though."

"I'm sorry," Carly said, her expression hesitant. "We wanted to tell you but thought if we did, you might change your mind."

"And why shouldn't you come? You and Marcus have been over a long time," Rissa added.

That they had. As far as her family knew, the only reason for her to change her plans to vacation in Montana was if she still had feelings for Marcus—other than the standard *you suck* kind of feelings after a breakup.

"He's only at the Second Chance a few days a week. Don't sign up for his classes and you won't see him." Carly tilted her head to one side. "Please don't be angry. We really wanted to see you guys. You haven't been home in years and we didn't want anything to keep you from coming."

"It's fine. I was…surprised."

"Call it mother's instinct, but there's something going on that you're not saying." Rissa's gaze searched Skylar's face. "I'm right, aren't I?"

You have no idea. "Mom—"

"Don't lie to us. We're your family. We're the people you can trust to help you. Tell us."

Skylar stared into her mother's face and faltered. Rissa's strawberry-blond hair was starting to show the slightest tinge of gray at the temples—and as a teenager Skylar had done her best to give her mother gray hair. She'd made her mother's life hell.

Through it all, her mother had been there for her,

and, later, Carly and her father, Jonas, had been, as well. They'd formed the typical blended family with his and hers but none of the *step*whatevers mattered. They were family, and they were hers, and the guilt she felt at lying to them all of these years was taking a toll on her, even if it was the right thing to do.

Skylar wanted to relieve her mother's worries and express her appreciation that Rissa hadn't given up on her when things had gotten really bad. How do you tell your mother you're sorry for causing such pain? *Even the pain she isn't aware of.*

"Okay, so I'm scared. If this visit doesn't work to pull him out of the fantasies, I'm going to have to consider his counselor's recommendation for drug therapy. And while that works for a lot of people, I can't do that to Cody until I'm sure I've exhausted all other avenues."

Rissa rounded the table, tears in her eyes. She dropped to her knees in front of Skylar and drew her into a long hug. Skylar could feel her mother trembling. "Mom, stop, please. It will be fine. You'll see."

The trembling worsened and a sob tore out of Rissa.

Skylar looked to Carly for help, only to find Carly's eyes bright with tears. What on earth?

"I'm sorry," her mother whispered, struggling visibly to rein in her emotions. "I didn't mean to cry when you're being so strong about everything."

"We're all a little tense and tired. It's okay, Mom."

"No, it's not. You've been handling all of this alone. We should be supporting you, holding you, not the other way around. I'm so sorry. If you'd only told us— I understand why you needed to keep the news to yourself. You needed time to cope and come to terms with things, but we could've *helped* you. We're here for you," Rissa insisted softly. She palmed Skylar's cheeks. "Oh, baby."

Something about the conversation felt off, as though she was missing a piece.

"Sky, we know about the genetic link for Tom's disease. Mom read an article about Alpha-1 Antitrypsin Deficiency and we researched it." Carly paused before continuing. "We know the odds of Cody developing it."

"This isn't great welcome-home dinner conversation, is it?" Rissa smiled sadly. "But we wanted you to know we're here for you."

Oh. Oh, no, they thought—

"You don't have to put on a brave front. Not anymore. Has Cody's doctor said anything? Has he begun to show symptoms?" her mother asked.

Skylar floundered, so shocked by the rapid turn of conversation she could only focus on the disaster.

She and Tom had waited until a year before his death to finally break the news to her parents that his condition was deteriorating. They had told her family the basics and little else. She had believed her family had taken her reassurances that Cody was fine at face value, never dreaming they would dig deeper. "Mom…Cody's okay."

"They've tested him?"

Feeling the hole she'd made swallowing her whole, she fought the urge to blurt out the entire truth and let Marcus deal with the fallout. But how did you tell someone the past seven years, her marriage to a man *willing* to claim a child he knew wasn't his, *everything* had been built on a lie? "He's fine," she repeated. "You do *not* need to worry about Cody."

"Dessert is ready!" Jenna called from the other room.

"We'll be right there." Carly wiped her eyes.

"You'll tell us if something changes? When Cody's tests show signs of the disease?" her mother asked.

Skylar nodded, knowing she couldn't let the lie continue but unable to speak up now. She'd been twenty-two when she'd gotten pregnant, and thoroughly unable to handle it on top of the breakup with Marcus, and the extent of his injury. Tom had been a friend and his solution had been a godsend. She'd married him knowing he was sick, getting sicker.

Maybe marrying Tom hadn't been the best decision but it had been right for her at the time. The right thing to do for two very lonely, very scared people. Break-throughs in medicine had given him four years longer than they'd expected. Four years in which she'd fallen in a different kind of love. Not the hard, fast, instant love she'd felt for Marcus, but something more tender and pure, inspired by friendship and mutual caring. Tom asked nothing of her *but* friendship, yet she had learned to love him in ways she never thought possible.

Still, Carly was correct. Had Cody been Tom's son, the odds were high that Cody would eventually develop the disease, even if he hadn't shown signs of the genetic abnormality at birth. As Skylar wiped the tears from her mother's cheeks, she knew what she had to do. Tomorrow morning, she'd pay a visit to Cody's father.

The lie they'd told would end and she'd face the consequences of her actions. It was only fair to warn him she would be breaking her word.

Some promises couldn't be kept.

MARCUS WAS WELDING A long strip of metal to the base of his latest sculpture when the door to his workshop opened and closed with a flash of sunlight. Granddad often came in, a diversion from watching television.

Heavy metal played over the speakers. Some days rock music was the only appropriate soundtrack, other days country was. Every piece he'd ever created had its own set of tunes.

He finished joining the piece, cut the torch, then flipped up his helmet to check his work. It was coming together nicely. Not bad progress, but he needed to pick up the pace to make his upcoming deadline.

"When did you become an artist?"

He twisted in his chair, surprised to see Skylar. She was dressed too fancy for Montana, in khaki shorts that skimmed the top of her knees and a deep purple sweater that hugged her chest and made her pale skin look like porcelain. Her blond hair was loose, falling over her shoulders and slightly curled at the ends.

By comparison, he was sweaty and dirty, his head and neck covered in grime. It reminded him of the very first time he'd set eyes on her. She'd been sitting on the porch with Lexi, playing cards. Despite the Goth clothes and attitude, she'd looked cool and untouchable. The difference between that girl and this woman was astounding. Yet at the same time, she maintained the same air.

After eight years and a mountain of pain, her fancy clothes didn't change the fact he preferred seeing her in his football jerseys and nothing else. The image fixed in his head and it was all he could do to think straight.

He wheeled himself from the workbench. "You're not following your own advice." When she gave him a blank stare, he added, "You said you wanted us to stay away from each other."

"Yeah, I know but— Marcus, I need to talk to you."

He'd gathered as much. Why else would she make the trek to his place so early in the morning? "I need to talk to you, too. You've saved me a trip."

He'd come to a decision yesterday, on the road, baking beneath the sun, tears streaming down his face at the ass he'd been. He thought of going to see her immediately, but he'd needed to pull himself together, figure out a game plan.

He didn't like to think of himself as a coward, but in light of his behavior, the word fit. Maybe he was being opportunistic, but the way he saw it, Skylar's presence in Montana was his chance to right the wrong and get to know his son. He had to take advantage of it. If he didn't, he knew he'd always regret it. The way he'd spent the past eight years regretting sending her away.

She looked curious, but shook her head. "No, I—I need to say this and it isn't going to be easy. I have to break my promise." She took a breath. "I have to tell my parents about Tom not being Cody's father because

Mom believes he could develop the disease Tom had. And I can't let her go on worrying about something that can't happen. No one needs to know about you."

"I understand. It's fine." Her expression made him smile wryly. Yeah, she hadn't expected him to say that. "Your family has been decent to me and they've gone out of their way to help Granddad over the years. You *should* tell them. But I have conditions."

She tensed. "What conditions?"

He wheeled to the refrigerator and pulled out a water bottle, offering her one.

"No, thank you. What conditions?"

Conditions you won't like. To buy himself time, he asked, "What do you think of my work?"

Her face softened slightly. "They're unbelievable. I had no idea you did this." She stopped by a piece he'd titled simply *Free*. She smoothed her fingertips over the mustang's mane, along its nose, over the shoulder.

Marcus was proud of the piece, identified with it when he was in the racer and in the zone, chasing the wind. "I started working with metal in rehab. Seemed to have a knack for it."

"You have a gift, not a knack."

All he knew was that working with metal had saved him, literally and figuratively. Lying on the thirty-yard line after that tackle, staring at the lights and the faces hovering over him, he'd known something was wrong. Something big. Something bad. When he'd hit the ground, he'd felt the *pop* and the immediate change in his body. Then to find out the damage was permanent…

After losing everything that mattered to him—football, his career, Skylar—everything he'd identified with, he'd latched on to the new hobby with passion and determination. Desperation.

It was while going through his rehab that he'd come to appreciate all that Seth had accomplished. Seth had sustained a spinal-cord injury when he fell from a horse and it was after that experience that he'd converted the Second Chance into a resort dude ranch for those with disabilities.

In his arrogance prior to his own injury, Marcus had pitied Seth and those guests, glad he would never be one of them. Then suddenly, in a life-altering moment, he was. He hadn't accepted the changed circumstances easily. Focusing on metalwork had given him purpose, a new life.

One he could share with his son?

"You make your living this way?"

"Yes." Anxiety knotted his gut. How do you convince someone to let you be a part of her life after having shoved her away?

"Wow." She zeroed in on another piece, his project for the Montana statehouse. The bear reared on its hind legs, its right front paw outstretched above her head.

She raised her hand toward the bear's, her fingers not even coming close to the tips of the claws.

"That's life-size," he said.

"It's amazing."

He looked at her standing there, tall and beautiful, her hair falling down her back as she tilted her head for a better view.

Before the accident, before Skylar had demanded

they take a *break*, he'd dreamed of them getting married. Like some teenage girl, *he* was the one with images in his head of Skylar wearing white, of his grandfather standing by his side as his best man.

He knew he should have been in Cody's life from the beginning but it wasn't possible then. In the chaos that was his brain following the injury, he'd had the presence of mind to know he wouldn't have been good for them. He'd had to fix himself first.

So it was possible now. And he couldn't wait any longer. Maybe he could only be a long-distance dad, maybe he and Cody could spend some summers together, a holiday here or there. They would have to figure out the logistics. However they arranged it, he longed to know his son the way a father should.

Besides, his grandfather wasn't getting any younger and neither was Cody. Once he was older and other parts of his life became more important, would he want to know the man who had abandoned him?

After a few long pulls from the water, Marcus doused a rag and wiped the grit from his face. "I agree that you need to tell your family," he said, wondering what hell Jonas would dole out on behalf of his stepdaughter. Whatever it was, Marcus knew he deserved it. "But when you tell your mother and Jonas, tell them the truth. Tell them everything."

She stared at him in surprise, her hand slowly lowering to her side. "You don't mean that."

"I do. I'm Cody's father. It's time I acted like it."

Chapter 4

SKYLAR STOOD CAPTIVATED by the beauty of the sculptures, and wondered if she'd ever really known Marcus. She hadn't known he was capable of such artistry.

How did a man shift from being a football star who lived and breathed pigskin to...*this?* She couldn't recall him drawing in high school or college. But there was no denying his talent.

There were beautiful gates that should be hung on gallery walls. A massive security door with ironwork scrolls and designs the likes of which she'd only ever seen in coffee-table books. A bed frame that looked like a tree from a fairy tale, the head and footboards rising from the floor, twisted and gnarled like trunks, then narrowing to form a crown with branches and foliage, the leaves on delicate wire stems allowing them to move. And the *sculptures*...

He seemed to prefer horses, but there were bears,

coiled snakes and a mountain lion, as well. All beautiful in their frozen metal details.

Each piece expressed emotion and intensity. The flare of the horse's nostrils as it charged forward, the wind separating the long strands of its mane, the glide of muscle as it galloped.

"Skylar?"

She blinked, the cold metal warming beneath the heat of her fingers. "These are beautiful."

"Did you hear what I said?"

Of course she'd heard him, although the words hadn't sunk in at first. "No." She didn't bother turning around. "I won't tell them it's you."

"I want you to. He's my son."

The rush of fury came so fast, from so deep within her she was momentarily blinded. That was the biggest insult of all. "No, he's not. Cody is *my* son."

And because Marcus was obviously going to argue DNA, she forced herself to face him. No more running from the room the way she had that day at the hospital.

"I have a say in this, Skylar."

Unbelievable. She'd expected Marcus to argue about exposing even part of their secret. Maybe even be ashamed—as he *should*. But she had never expected him to ask for more. In her mind, Marcus didn't *have* that right. Not after ordering them from his life.

In the hours she'd tossed and turned attempting to plan this very conversation, she'd always assumed he wouldn't want the truth to come out. Knowing he'd abandoned them would further tarnish Marcus's image in her family's eyes, in his own grandfather's eyes, especially since he'd cheated on her.

But this wasn't *his* opportunity for redemption. Stepping in now, attempting to *fix* Cody by trying to be a father when he wasn't one. Not going to happen.

"Cody is *my* son. You made that very clear when you gave him up. And not once in all these years have you tried to contact me about him. You can't just change your mind."

"I have."

"No. *No!* I am telling my family the truth about Tom to end their worry. Nothing else changes."

"Telling them changes everything." He yanked the protective clothing from his shoulders, revealing a muscle shirt that had her eyes widening.

Yesterday she'd noticed his massive biceps, but this shirt showed how cut his torso was. Not even at his peak on the football field had Marcus looked like this.

"As soon as you say the boy isn't Tom's, everyone will assume he's mine. Not telling the entire story will make it worse." He held up a hand. "And I know what they'll say about me—to me. It's nothing I haven't already said to myself."

Because he regretted his decision? The news left her floundering for a second before she strengthened her resolve. No, he would not do this to her. To Cody.

"I didn't handle things well. I know that. When you told me you were pregnant... Skylar, my career was over, my life as I knew it was *over.* I was pissed off and freaked out. The only thought I had was that no kid deserved me for a father."

She felt for him. The rational, adult part of her understood. The counselor in her empathized with what he said. But the hurt, irrational woman who he'd rejected so harshly? "Did you think I was ready to be a *mother?*"

He swore. "No. But I think you were in better shape than me. You were the kid's best chance at having a happy life. Maybe if you had let me think things over instead of running to your sugar daddy—"

"Screw you! How *dare* you? You have no idea what Tom and I were to each other and you do *not* have the right to speculate on it. You should be thankful he was there and able to do what you couldn't, that Cody had a father and that I had someone I could count on."

A muscle ticked near his mouth. "Thankful? I don't think so. The only thing I ever wanted to do to your *husband* was strangle him for stepping in and taking over before I could get my head on straight."

She folded her arms over her chest. She wouldn't let him mess with her head, insinuate that things might have been different, that she'd been in the wrong. Not after what he'd done. "It wouldn't have mattered. You still cheated on me, then kicked me out of your life."

"When you came to me, you said you could forgive me for screwing up. You weren't lying, Skylar. I only wish to God I hadn't pushed you away."

"I know I said I could forgive you for taking that skank to bed but—"

"Had I not been lying in the hospital bed, you wouldn't have said it? You ended things, Skylar. Not me."

"I said we needed *a break*. That's not breaking up!"

"That's a moot point at this stage, isn't it?"

He was right. But now that she had that memory in her head, she couldn't let it go and her anger boiled. "Saying I needed time—to breathe, to think—after you proposed and I turned you down may have been poor judgment. But that in no way excuses you having sex with some girl *hours* later." Yeah, she was still bitter.

Like the Elizabeth Barrett Browning poem, Skylar had loved Marcus with the depth and breadth and height of her soul. She'd completely lost herself in him. And the moment she saw that girl in his bed, not bothering to cover herself, a satisfied smirk on her ugly beautiful face, those depth and heights had crashed over Skylar, burying her. Completely.

She had continued to go to work but otherwise didn't leave her apartment, didn't eat. Didn't sleep. Didn't care. Six weeks passed. Tom returned to Dallas for another round of treatment. Marcus was on the receiving end of that tackle that still appeared in television sports reels. And the stick had read *pregnant*. The worst was Marcus throwing her out like yesterday's trash.

"I have to go." She couldn't handle this anymore.

"No, wait. Skylar— It was wrong. I regretted what I did. But every time I asked for more, you backpedaled. I got tired of not being able to break down the walls."

"There weren't any walls."

"Are you kidding me? No matter how many years we were together you stayed vaulted up like Fort Knox, and when you said no…"

His voice followed her toward the door. Why had she wandered so deeply into the workshop? What if he made it to the door first?

"Damn it, how was I supposed to feel? You'd sleep with me but you wouldn't let me get close, wouldn't accept that I wanted our relationship to go deeper. You wouldn't marry *me*, but you sure as hell couldn't marry him fast enough. What was I supposed to think?"

She wasn't going to do this. Marrying Tom was the only right decision at the time, the only one that kept her from having to endure her family's interference and suffocating, emotionally charged *help*.

As to his accusations of her being vaulted up... She'd thought the sun rose and set with Marcus. He was perfect. But she'd admit—only to herself—that time and again she'd found herself struggling to find her place in his world of fame, sports endorsements and the ever-present public eye. What he could never get enough of was too much for her.

Skylar absurdly wished she'd worn better shoes, because she couldn't exactly make an exit when her flip-flops *flopped* every step of the way.

She wasn't going to do this. Wasn't going to fight with him, wasn't going to replay the past, wasn't going to feel guilty about making the best choice for *her* child after Marcus had selfishly done the same. "You made your decision, Marcus. I will not let you come into my son's life only to wreck it." *The way you wrecked mine.*

"I have legal rights. I made that decision under extreme circumstances. Any judge would see it that way. Some might even say you took advantage."

That stopped her in her tracks. She whirled to face him, her palm itching to strike out, to hurt him as bad as he hurt her. She'd worked so hard to change her self-destructive behavior, to become worthy of being Cody's mother. But faced with Marcus's threat, she reverted to that bitter, angry girl. The one who always screwed up, who made bad choices. The one who never felt good enough.

"Cody was *Tom's* son. To tell Cody otherwise now will thoroughly destroy that foundation he has. I will not be forced into admitting your role. I'll say I had a one-night stand before I married Tom."

He rolled toward her, every muscle taut. "Skylar, do you know what it did to me to see you in that hospital room? To know you were willing to forgive me and work things out—and I was hooked up to tubes and machines? That everything that defined me was gone?"

"Telling Cody now will only confuse him and hurt him when he's already upset over Tom's death. Telling him wouldn't be looking out for *his* best interests, only yours." She shook her head, denying the possibility that Marcus could somehow wind up a permanent fixture in their lives. *Not going to happen.* "I won't let you hurt him when you've already proved yourself untrustworthy multiple times."

The words were hateful but they had to be said. She couldn't hold them in, couldn't stifle them when he threatened her, threatened her *family*.

Finally she made it to the threshold, but Marcus called out to her one last time.

"I regret what I said to you that day. But you and I

both know it will be easy to find an attorney to take my case and argue that you took advantage of my accident and emotional state to keep Cody for yourself."

"You would *do* that?" What happened to him wanting her? Caring for her?

"Only if I have to. You either tell your family, or I will. That's a promise."

"WHAT HAPPENED?" CARLY asked the moment Skylar got out of the car. "Where did you go?"

Carly, Maura and Rissa sat on the shaded porch of the gathering room, tall tea glasses on the tables beside them. Maura would have to head inside soon to prepare dinner for the guests, so Skylar didn't have long to say what she had to say.

Just blurt it out and be done. It's not like it's ever going to be easy.

She braced herself. Driving to the Second Chance, she'd broken every speed limit in an effort to get away from Marcus and the past. But all that had done was bring her face-to-face with the women of her family before she'd found the courage she required.

"You look pale. Are you feeling okay? You want something to drink?" Maura asked.

Maura grabbed the pitcher of tea and poured a glass before Skylar had a chance to say no.

"Where's Cody?" She did *not* want him to overhear.

"He's playing with Riley and the twins." Carly referred to her adopted son and her sister-in-law's kids.

"Skylar, did something happen? Why are you looking at us like that?"

Skylar couldn't ignore the growing worry on their faces because, once again, she was the cause. How many times was she going to screw up? She'd thought—hoped —she was past this behavior.

"There's something I need to tell you. But first I have to apologize. I didn't mean for it to get out of hand. I thought it would be easier," she said, her throat growing raw and raspy. "Everything would have been if you hadn't found out about the genetic part of Tom's disease. I know you're concerned about Cody, so I can't let you go on believing that he might get sick."

"Sky?" Her mother moved toward her. "Honey, come here. Sit down."

"No. I have to get it out. Cody isn't at risk for Tom's disease because he…isn't Tom's son."

Carly gasped and clamped her hand over her mouth —the only visible reaction to Skylar's announcement. Rissa and Maura stared, a myriad of expressions flickering over their faces—shock, horror, hurt.

Skylar tried to calm the tumultuous pace of her heart, sliding her hand over her stomach because she felt like she was going to be ill. "It's a long, complicated story I really don't want to talk about. But after last night, I knew I had to tell you."

"You *lied* to us," Rissa said. "All of these years? *Skylar…*"

"I'm sorry." Skylar held her mother's gaze for as long as she could. "I didn't know what else to do."

"You couldn't tell us the *truth?*" The pitch of her mother's voice revealed her increasing upset. "Wouldn't *that* have been the thing to do?"

"Marcus is Cody's dad, isn't he?" Carly asked softly.

This time Maura was the one gasping. She and the Rowlands had been friends with Marcus long before Skylar had moved to Montana.

"Yes, he is." The one conclusion she'd reached while driving was that she would confess everything. She wouldn't allow Marcus to hold that power, to have that control.

Maura shook her head in disapproval. "Skylar, I know you had your issues with Marcus after your breakup, but keeping something like this from him—"

"I *knew* it," Carly said. "I knew that whole story about turning to Tom for comfort couldn't be true. How could you do that to Marcus? You have to tell him. He has a right to know. Cody's his son and he's missed *everything.* Cody as a baby. His first words—first *steps.*"

A husky laugh emerged from Skylar. How like her family to lay fault with her rather than someone else. Things were such a mess. And, yes, she knew she'd made that mess, but she hadn't made it alone.

"It's not funny!" Carly continued. "Yes, Marcus messed up, but keeping his child from him is *wrong.*"

"Marcus knows." Skylar was more than a bit bitter that her own family immediately assumed the worst about her. "He's *always* known." Her kick of satisfaction as she watched the news sink in was petty. Still, she felt somewhat vindicated. "Yes, I lied. But I told your saintly Marcus at the time, and he wanted nothing to do with us. And Tom *did* comfort me. Say what you like, but you can't blame me for wanting to give my son a better life than a father who didn't want to be one. And before you think I duped a dying man—" She yanked open the car door "—Tom knew. He knew I was pregnant when he married me. And for the record, we didn't lie. When I announced my pregnancy, you all assumed Tom was Cody's father."

"Because you rushed into marriage." Carly looked thoughtful. "Did you know Tom was dying?"

Oh, there was another million-dollar question.

Skylar's skin prickled though she wasn't sure if it was the heat of the sun or her family's censure. "Tom was a father in every way. Say what you like about me but I don't ever want to hear any of you say a negative word about him. Our relationship was loving, and that's more than a lot of people can say. It was most certainly a lot more than Marcus offered."

Her mother sank into her chair, pale and visibly shaken. Maura and Carly appeared as shell-shocked as Skylar had been after Marcus had ordered her out of his hospital room.

She didn't care about their reactions, though. All the emotions from the past were bombarding her, and she couldn't handle the building anger. Their outrage at *her* for doing what she'd had to do was why she hadn't told them the truth back then. "I'm not going to tell Cody, and I expect you to respect my decision."

"But *Marcus* is his father and he's very much alive," Carly said. "Skylar—"

"*Tom* was Cody's father. That's all Cody ever knew,

all he *needs* to know. The truth would only confuse and upset him. And as you have already discovered, he has enough to deal with. This is not up for discussion."

"But what if telling Cody he has a father ends the fantasizing?" Carly argued.

Skylar wasn't happy to see her mother and Rissa nodding in agreement. Marcus would have support here if he carried through on his threat to take legal action. The thought weakened her resolve.

No. Marcus would change his mind. Again. At any point in the ensuing years, he could have reversed his decision. He hadn't. It wasn't until he saw Cody that Marcus decided he wanted to be a parent. That told her he was using access and opportunity to "play" at being a parent. He had no burning desire to be a father. And when things got tough, or he got tired of Cody pretending his father was a vampire? What then?

If they told Cody the truth, and Marcus decided parenting wasn't what he thought it would be, Cody would wind up more hurt and devastated than he was by Tom's death. Losing two fathers could impact him profoundly. Maybe drive him deeper into his fantasy world. Maybe cause him to turn his hurts inward until he ended up the way Travis Duncan had.

Marcus had made his decision years ago. He needed to stick by it whether he liked it or not. He couldn't play with a child's mind, a child's feelings.

"I have to go," she said, her voice smoker-rough.

"Stay," Rissa said. "We have so many questions."

So did Skylar. But she didn't have answers and she

needed some time to herself. "Not now. Maura, could you ask Lexi to watch Cody?"

"Where are you going?" Carly asked. "Let me come with you. We can talk."

Skylar was done talking. The matter was closed. For now. It was wishful thinking that her family would let the matter be. She got in her car and headed for her cabin, where she changed into running gear.

Eight minutes later, she'd completed a mile. Jogging was one of the many things she'd discovered during her three years on the Second Chance. Grace ran to stay in shape and one day she'd asked Skylar to tag along. Skylar had been running ever since. She'd jogged with Marcus while they dated. And with Tom as part of his cardio therapy to help maintain lung capacity. Nothing diminished the way she felt when the only thing in her head was the sound of her shoes hitting the pavement.

As she finished mile five, she spotted something on the road ahead of her, approaching quickly. It wasn't an animal, car or motorcycle. Finally, when it was close enough, she realized it was a wheelchair racer. She knew her peaceful run would not be interrupted given the speed the racer was going. The person wasn't out for a leisurely roll.

That reassurance died the moment she recognized Marcus. After he'd sped past her, she heard the racer slow and it wasn't long before he caught up to her.

Keeping pace for a solid thirty seconds without saying a word, he finally broke the silence. "Can we agree to have an adult conversation? Talk without it turning into a shouting match?"

She didn't break her pace but she was beginning to tire, yet having Marcus beside her looking as though he could roll all day kicked her pride into overdrive. She couldn't slow down now. "No," she said honestly. This talking more, especially to him, was the last thing she wanted to do. She needed all the space Big Sky country had to offer.

"You didn't used to be a hypocrite," he drawled.

"Me?" She called him nasty names in her head, wished she had the breath to say them out loud.

"You've made mistakes, too, Skylar."

"I've never cheated on someone."

"Maybe not, but you've been involved with someone who did," he argued, bringing up the biggest mistake of her entire life.

At fourteen she'd committed the ultimate in stupid. She'd allowed herself to be seduced by a friend's father who was separated from his wife and looking for revenge sex, not that she'd known that at the time. She'd thought Rick cared for her, that they—oh, this showed how pathetic she'd been—could *be together* once the divorce was final.

"You said you'd never hold that against me." She stared straight ahead, doing her best to ignore the burn in her chest, caused by keeping the pace and the humiliation she felt to this day over her actions.

The incident had taken place at a time when her parents' marriage was ending because her *father* was cheating on her mother—with Rick's wife. Rick's interest in her fourteen-year-old self made brutal sense.

But stupid or not, she'd wanted to feel as though someone cared.

Now she realized Rick had picked up on her pain, taken advantage of it, used her. Then her father had found out. He dragged her to the car, determined to confront Rick. There was a thunderstorm, yet he raced along the busy highway, weaving in and out of traffic, cursing both her and his friend. One wrong move and they had wound up upside down on the asphalt, her father bleeding beside her. The look in his eyes…

"I don't hold it against you. I'm saying you, of all people, should know not to throw stones. I've already admitted I screwed up. Now you have to admit you gave me damn good reason when you turned down my proposal and walked out."

She'd admit nothing. Technically she might have broken things off with him before she'd left his apartment, but she'd come back to talk and he was already *screwing* someone else. In a matter of hours.

It was over. You know what you said to him, how you said it.

"That's all in the past. We have to move on for the sake of our son."

That was rich coming from him. "My. Son."

"You're as stubborn as a mule, you know that?"

"We each have our goals." Marcus could go sit and spin. He wasn't going to change her mind.

"You know, I honestly can't tell if you're mad at me or if this is because you hooked up with an old man who died on you."

Skylar stopped running and bent at the waist to

catch her breath, listening as Marcus turned the air blue with curses because he had to stop and swing the racer around to approach her again.

She held up her hand, her heart pounding hard in her chest with exertion and anger. Where did he get off saying something like that to her? "Don't you dare say *a word* against him. When I needed you, *Tom* was there. When I was hurling into the toilet at all hours of the day and night, he was *there*. Not you. It's not *my* fault your skank didn't stick around to help you recover."

"I told you it wasn't like that with her. It was just sex. And it never would have happened if—"

"Don't you *dare* blame me. And, trust me, I could tell what it was. Her naked in your bed wasn't that hard to interpret. Did you even change the sheets beforehand?"

Marcus dragged both gloved hands through his hair. "See it for what it was. I got drunk off my ass and did something insanely stupid because the woman I loved didn't *love me back*."

"If you loved me, you wouldn't have slept with her. You would've given me the time I needed."

"I agree." He said the words softly, with no hint of the previous frustration. He held her gaze with an honesty she couldn't deny, no matter how hard she tried.

"What?"

"That's what I should have done. But I didn't, and I've regretted what happened every single day since. My only excuse is that when you said you needed *a break*, I reacted because it hurt like hell. It felt like you'd ripped my heart out. I'm sorry I did that to you, Skylar. Damn it, I'm sorry."

She took a step back, unable to deal with his words or the emotion behind them. He'd say anything, *do* anything, because he wanted to be in Cody's life. For now. "It's too late to be sorry now." She turned to head toward the ranch. "Eight years too late."

Chapter 5

MARCUS MADE IT TO THE HOUSE BY dinnertime. His granddad liked to eat early so, after a shower, Marcus fired up the grill and headed into the kitchen, their chocolate Lab, Cassie, following behind in an obvious attempt to bum some people-food.

After they ate and his grandfather settled into his recliner with the remote for the evening, Marcus could head to his workshop and the piece he'd left behind when his frustration had overruled everything else.

On the deck of their specially designed house, he layered the rack with chicken kabobs and closed the lid, his thoughts on the only woman who had ever mattered to him.

"Mighty pretty day. How far'd you go? You were gone quite a while," Ben said.

"Out past the Second Chance."

He whistled. "Long way to wheel."

That it was. Marcus's hands had taken a bit of a beating, but thankfully his arms had held out.

"The home nurse said she heard Skylar was back."

Because he and Skylar had dated throughout high school, college and the start of his NFL career, she had become the granddaughter Ben had never had.

Despite the breakup, Ben and Skylar's mother had remained close, in part because Rissa had bought his helicopter business and started a charter service after he was no longer able to fly. To this day, all he had to do was make a phone call and Rissa took him flying. What would they think when they knew the truth?

"She is," Marcus replied.

"That her car I saw leaving here this morning?"

Marcus lifted the lid to turn the kabobs, unable to face his grandfather. "Yeah. It was."

"What'd she want?" Ben shuffled along the deck, assisted by his canes.

The docs, nurses and even Grace had warned Ben another fall would be serious, given his age and condition, but his grandfather was determined to stay out of a wheelchair as long as possible. Honestly, Marcus couldn't blame Ben. He was the toughest, smartest, kindest man Marcus had ever known, a man who had turned his life upside down to care for Marcus after his parents had died in a gas-station robbery.

He didn't know what he would do if something happened to Ben. More than anything, after seeing Cody, Marcus didn't want Ben to pass from this world without meeting his great-grandson. He'd denied his grandfather something special by avoiding his responsibility as Cody's father.

Skylar might claim his reasoning selfish—maybe it

was—but now that he had his life in order, he couldn't help but think he had more to offer Cody than a make-believe vampire. Couldn't she see that?

"She needed to talk to me about something."

"Oh? Last I heard, you two didn't talk. It's a shame, too. Thought you'd get married there for a while."

"Yeah. Me, too." Marcus flipped the meat one more time. "She's, uh, here visiting with her son, Cody."

"That's right. Rissa mentioned having a grandson. Has a picture of him in the helicopter."

No doubt she did. Grandparents and great-grand-parents did that sort of thing, kept pictures close by. The same with parents if they were worth anything.

The fact he had nothing to prove Cody was his, not even a photograph… "Cody's seven, almost eight, and — Granddad, he's mine. Cody is my son, your great-grandson. He was born the summer after my accident."

Ben sucked in a sharp breath. "That's why she was here? She told you that today?"

The moment of truth was at hand. "No. She told me when it happened. I've known all along he was mine. I just didn't do anything about it."

A weighty silence followed.

When Marcus couldn't take it anymore, he lifted his head and looked into his grandfather's eyes. They were red and damp. Full of censure and disapproval, and, worst of all, love. Ben might not approve of the situation or Marcus's actions, but his grandfather still loved him.

The lump in Marcus's throat grew difficult to ignore. He hated disappointing the one person who had never disappointed him. "I'm sorry. I know I'm not the man you raised me to be. All I can say is that I wasn't in my right mind then. I am now, and I'm working on fixing things. I told Skylar today that I want to know my son—I want you to know him. I want things to change."

"That would be nice. I'd like that." Ben wiped a shaky hand under his nose. "I'd like that a lot. Almost eight years old… Am I gonna be able to meet him soon?"

"I hope so. Skylar doesn't trust me much, and she's insisting I stick to what I said back then. The boy was raised to believe the man Skylar married was his father. Now the man's dead and…it's complicated." How well would Cody be able to understand when Marcus wasn't so sure himself how everything had gone so wrong?

"It sounds like it. But you can't blame yourself when she up and married another man like that."

He wanted to let Skylar take the blame but he couldn't. "Granddad, I haven't told you everything." He'd never really discussed the specifics of the breakup with his grandfather because his injury had overshadowed it. Owning up to what he'd done by sending her away wasn't easy, but he managed to do it.

"Well, I suppose she has reason to be afraid after that. A man's only as good as his actions."

"I know."

"But that doesn't mean we can't fix our mistakes. How long is she here for?"

"I'm not sure."

"It's not going to be long enough, so I wouldn't wait to get to know…Cody, is it?"

"Yeah, Cody." His *son*. A kid who believed his father

was a vampire and had wrinkled up his nose at Marcus's wheelchair.

"Don't burn those, son. This old man is hungry."

Marcus realized Ben had forgiven him, just like that. His grandfather obviously didn't approve of how he'd handled the situation, but he wasn't going to stand in judgment.

It wouldn't be easy. Not with Skylar's family or Skylar herself. He had to acknowledge that it was his decision that had sent Skylar into Tom's arms and set the stage for their hasty marriage. As Skylar had said, Tom had been there for her.

But now? Marcus wasn't giving up without a fight.

Question was—what would he say to Cody when the boy finally knew the truth and wanted to know *why?*

SKYLAR GOT OUT OF THE SHOWER and smiled when she heard Lexi laughing in the other room. She'd texted Lexi and asked her to bring Cody to the cabin while she got ready. She figured a field trip to show Cody a town the opposite of New York City was the most effective way to avoid her mother and Carly.

Skylar could take Cody to get some ice cream or go visit Porter at the diner. She planned to come home late enough that she could go straight to bed.

In short order she was dressed, hair dried and makeup on. She'd chosen jeans, a simple loose blouse that matched her blue eyes and cowboy boots that hadn't seen the light of day since Halloween two years ago.

She checked her cell phone, frowning at the call she'd missed while in the shower. With a press of a button, she called her co-counselor at work, who answered on the third ring. "Hey, Nina, what's up? Something wrong?"

One of the most horrifying realities they faced was that a teen suicide often spawned more deaths in the peer group. That's why grief counseling was so important.

"No, nothing. So far so good but I knew you would want an update."

Relief poured through her. "Definitely. No other issues?"

"Honey, there are always issues," Nina said with a laugh. "But nothing major. How's Cody?"

"Fine. We're going exploring in a few minutes."

"Good. Try to have fun and stop worrying. Your son needs you. Focus on him."

"I know. I'm trying."

"Good. That's all I wanted. To make sure you arrived okay and to hear you say you're doing fine. Go explore and meet a hot cowboy. Better yet, bring one home for me."

At one point in time Marcus had been her *hot cowboy*, both literally and professionally as a member of the NFL team. "I'll do my best."

After ending the call, she pinned a smile on her face as she headed to the living room. "I'm ready. Thanks for watching him for me." She grabbed her purse and pulled out some cash. "Here, take this."

"Ohmigosh, that's too much."

"You've watched him all day and I appreciate it. Take it." She pressed it into Lexi's hand. "Besides, I remember what it's like to be a poor student."

"Hey, no problem. I'll babysit anytime."

"Good. I'll remember you said that."

"Um, Skylar? Can I ask a favor? I don't want to be a pain, and Mom would kill me for imposing, but would you mind if I ride into town with you? Some of my friends are seeing a movie and I'd really like to go. It's one of our last chances to hang out before we pack up for college." Lexi didn't sound nearly as excited about the prospect as Skylar had at that age but she blamed the lack of enthusiasm on nerves.

"You sure your mom and dad won't mind me dropping you off and leaving you?"

"Oh, no, it'll be fine. My friend lives a few miles down the road. If I can get a ride there, she'll drop me off tonight."

That seemed simple enough, there was no reason to refuse "I don't mind. Come on, Cody. We're going on an adventure."

With the radio blasting the only station that played pop music, Lexi sang along. Cody was in the backseat, and while he piped up every now and again with a question about something, he played with Batman and Robin the entire way to town.

North Star had changed very little since Skylar had been gone. It had gained two more gas stations, a florist shop, a sit-down steak house that looked to be giving Porter's diner some competition and a few other businesses. Nothing about the town's atmosphere had altered. It was still quiet and cozy, with all the action of the summer night focused entirely around the movie theater for the younger crowd and, if memory served, the Wild Honey for the older crowd on the make.

"Thank you so much." Lexi climbed out. "I'll see you tomorrow."

"Where's your friend?" Skylar peered into the crowd.

"I think I see her. The pink shirt."

Skylar spotted the girl immediately. There was no missing that shade. "Gotcha. Text me if anything changes. Cody and I will be in town for a while."

"Okay. See ya!"

"Have fun."

Lexi took off into the crowd, her blond curls swinging low on her back. So young and a knockout. Especially in those shorts. Skylar pulled away from the curb and stopped at the red light farther down the street. In the rearview mirror, she was able to spot Lexi. Instead of heading toward the movie, she crossed the street to a truck parked on the opposite side. The big smile indicated she knew whomever was in the vehicle.

"Apparently very well," Skylar murmured when the girl stood on tiptoe to return a kiss. Interesting…

Lexi seemed levelheaded, but if she was anything like Skylar at that age… Skylar'd been all about getting out of the house to meet Marcus to *do* things.

Heat rushed into her face at some of the things she'd done on the bench seat of his truck. On dark country roads, there were a lot of places for two teens to disappear for a while, and once she'd turned sixteen and they'd dated for a year, well, there had been no holding them back. The parent in her thought of Lexi, and even Cody when he was older, and cringed. At sixteen, she'd been through so much more than most kids her age, and was more mature because of it. But Lexi had lived such a sheltered life. Maura had set Lexi straight on sex and dating and men, right?

A car horn honked behind her and Skylar realized the light had changed. She accelerated, acknowledging she could make herself insane worrying about things beyond her control. There were plenty of things on her plate to deal with. She glanced at Cody. "Hey, bud. How does going to eat the best piece of pie in the world sound?"

Batman was attacking Robin's neck again. Yeah, she definitely had other things to occupy her time than Lexi's love life. "Cody? Hey? Do you want a piece of really good pie?"

"I haven't had dinner," he said, visibly distracted.

She blinked at his reminder, wondering how he could focus to such an extent he didn't hear her, yet remember little facts like dinner or the lack thereof. "Well, I don't want you to think we can do this all the time, because we can't, *but* what if we have dessert first? Then if we're still hungry, we'll get dinner?"

That had him forgetting all about Batman. "Really?"

Obviously, distracting him was a must. "Really."

"Okay!"

Skylar headed toward Porter's Diner. When they'd first moved to North Star, her mother had waited tables there and worked at the Second Chance cleaning the cabins and helping out to make ends meet. And while she hadn't appreciated it at the time, Skylar now understood how hard it must have been for her mother to go from being a well-paid helicopter pilot to a coupon-cutting, penny-pinching member of the minimum-wage army. Or what might have happened if her mother *hadn't* done all she could to get Skylar out of the funk she'd been in.

"Here we are." She parked in front of the library, wondering if Mrs. Keenan was still the librarian. That woman could smell food, spot a drink and hear a whispered conversation from the back room. "Leave Batman and Robin in the car."

"Why? What will I play with?"

"We'll come up with games of our own. Ever play Thumb War?"

"No, but—"

"Leave them, Cody. Come on, there are lots of things we can do. We can talk about what you want to do on the ranch. Or to the people inside the restaurant."

"I'm not supposed to talk to strangers."

"That's right," a male voice said from the curb. "You shouldn't talk to strangers, but your mama can introduce you to some friends."

Skylar tensed at the sound of her stepfather's voice. She turned, hoping against hope he was on duty and therefore unable to linger. But while he was still dressed in his uniform, her mother stood beside him, looking as though she'd had a hard day while Jonas appeared... well, in a word, *pissed*.

"Your mother's joining you for dinner," he announced. "Be sure you drop her off at the house afterward."

In other words, no matter what was said, she was responsible for getting her mother home. Period.

Skylar swallowed and held Cody's hand a little tighter. Her mother had obviously told Jonas. "Where are you going?"

He raised a thick eyebrow high. "Where do you think?"

Chapter 6

SKYLAR AND RISSA SAT ACROSS from each other in a red-and-white vinyl booth inside the diner, with Cody beside his grandmother. The silence stretched as a waitress took their order and her mother helped Cody with a placemat puzzle. Once Cody was engrossed in coloring the cowboy drawing, Skylar knew the time had come.

"So, what are your plans now?" Her mother used a conciliatory tone that wouldn't draw Cody's attention.

"No new plans. Nothing's changed."

"Nothing's—" Rissa glanced at Cody, her expression worried. "We need *people* in our lives."

Meaning Cody needed Marcus? Did Cody really need Marcus when the odds were that Marcus's heart wasn't invested? Skylar didn't doubt seeing Cody in person had made Marcus *think* he wanted to be a father. He'd always been the type of guy who usually did something because he "should"—the day in the hospital being the notable exception. "Only if those people are good for us. If not, they do more damage. How's Grandpa?" she asked casually, but was determined to make her point. "Is he still married to Morgan? Oh, wait, it's Betsy now, isn't it? No—Linda?"

Her mother shifted. "He's with…Kandi."

Uh-huh. Yeah. Her grandfather had a roving eye that was a source of contention between him and Rissa. Growing up, Skylar had seen her grandfather only a handful of times because he had always put his latest conquest ahead of his family. Before her mother could give advice on paternal relationships, she really needed to fix her own. "Cute name."

"You can't compare the two situations."

"I think I can. Sometimes our first response to a situation is our gut response. It's the *right* response. Mar— uh, *people* choose their path and they follow their gut, making the best decision for all involved. Rethinking it later only causes problems."

"Some problems can become *opportunities.* New directions. Just because a decision is right at the time, doesn't mean it's right later. New feelings emerge and goals change. People change."

"Or people *think* they've changed. But they haven't so the problems get bigger once they change their minds yet again. Sometimes it's best to leave things alone."

Her mother pinched the bridge of her nose and smoothed her fingertips under her eyes as though to rub away the lines. Some would attribute those lines to her mother's hours in the cockpit, flying into the sun, but Skylar knew she was responsible for most of them.

"Some decisions cannot be made overnight. I think

time is needed here. Time to think, so you don't make another mistake."

And there it was—her mistakes, past and present, brought to the forefront again. Oh, she knew she'd made plenty over the years—some major and life altering. But it wasn't as though she could ever forget some of the stupid things she'd done. Bringing them up—repeatedly —wasn't necessary.

"First, my decision wasn't a mistake. Second, I didn't decide this alone. Third, some things aren't anyone else's business. And fourth, a certain someone's fascination will pass in time. My focus, my attention, is on protecting someone who can't protect himself. Wait— there's a fifth point. No matter what decisions I make, they are mine, Mom. Not yours."

"They are mine, too, because *you* are mine. And knowing a secret has been kept all these years while…" Rissa glanced toward a thankfully still-occu-pied Cody and shook her head slightly, as though over-whelmed.

Once again Skylar was making her mom cry. Just like during her teenage years. It was doubtful Skylar could feel worse than she did right now. But what did they want from her? Marcus had abandoned her and Cody, not the other way around. Suddenly all should be forgiven? Really? It didn't work that way. If it did, her mother's relationship with *her* father wouldn't be quite so rocky.

The waitress delivered their meals and a group of women sat in the booth behind Rissa. Because this was a small town where gossip spread faster than colds, she and her mother forced themselves to break the uncomfortable silence and talk of less personal things.

When Cody finished eating, Porter stopped by to see if Cody wanted to be a chef. As Porter led Cody into the kitchen, the conversation between Skylar and her mother remained strained.

Skylar was exhausted by the time she drove her mother to the house Rissa had purchased from Ben Whitefeather at the end of their first summer in Montana. Cody was in the backseat, sound asleep, thanks to a full stomach and lots of playtime with his cousins earlier in the day.

"I love you." Rissa leaned over the console to hug Skylar. "But I don't agree with what you're doing."

Skylar pulled away and put the car in Reverse, more than ready for the night to be over. "I know you don't."

"I wish you'd—"

"I'll do what's best for Cody. Like you did what you thought was best for me. It's late, and I'm really tired. Good night."

"Jonas will want to talk to you."

She closed her eyes, imagining what Jonas said to Marcus. She was on edge thinking about it, so the last thing she wanted was to go inside and wait for Jonas. "What's left to say? It's done, Mom. We go from here."

As Skylar drove, she turned off the radio and let her thoughts drift, hoping a solution to her current situation would appear.

At the cabin, prodding Cody awake took some time but he was too big for her to carry. Inside, she ordered him to brush his teeth and change while she put the leftovers from the diner in the fridge.

"No messing around. We've got a big day ahead of us tomorrow. I'll be in to tuck you in soon." She locked up, then headed down the wide hall. She entered his room, but Cody wasn't in the bottom bunk. Instead he'd climbed to the top bunk and lay looking out the window into the night.

"You change your mind about sleeping up there?" Skylar climbed the ladder and ran her hand over his back, smiling at the glow-in-the-dark designs on his pjs. Tonight was dinosaurs. But when he continued to lie there, unmoving but drowsily awake, she frowned. "Is something wrong? Too much ice cream?"

"No. I'm okay."

"Why so quiet?" She smoothed her fingers over Cody's hair, loving its silkiness. His infant and toddler years had been precious to her and she'd relished every moment of them. He had grown so fast that she finally understood why her own mother had lamented the loss of Skylar's younger years.

She recalled Carly's outrage today that Skylar had *taken* Cody's baby years from Marcus. Yes, he'd missed them, but that was his fault. She wasn't sure how they would have managed had Marcus not rejected them.

So much was at stake. And if Marcus was serious about wanting to introduce himself to Cody, *everything* would change. Her child wouldn't be only *her* child anymore. She would have to share him again. And she knew sharing him with Marcus would be different from sharing Cody with Tom.

He had always let her take the lead when it came to parenting, because he'd accepted that eventually she would be the one raising their son. Tom had been there from Cody's first breath, and understood when to step in, or when to back off. Her husband had known Cody inside and out. How Cody's mind worked, how tender-hearted Cody was....

Marcus understood none of that. And if he tried to force the issue... Oh, what a mess. Then there was the thought of visitations. Holidays, weekends, summer vacations. Dear God, why had she ever thought coming back to Montana was a good idea?

She wanted to scoop up Cody and race to the airport, whisk him far, far away. He was hers. Only hers. She would not let Marcus hurt her baby. Once he knew his father hadn't wanted him...

Panic rushed through her and even though as a counselor she recognized it for what it was, the feeling didn't change. This was true fear. The kind that any mother felt when faced with being separated from her child.

Marcus had said any court would understand what he'd faced at the time and she'd sat in on enough court hearings to know that was probably true. But would Marcus try to take Cody away? No judge would side with Marcus after so long...would they?

She had to make Marcus see the potential damage that could be done to Cody's emotional state. What if Marcus didn't give Cody the time he needed to adjust? Rushing things wouldn't help on the "my father's a vampire" front. "Did you have fun being a chef?"

Cody yawned. "I guess. I wanted to chop stuff but Porter wouldn't let me use the knives."

"I'm sure you did great."

"Do you think Dad will come tomorrow?"

Skylar fought her frustration with Cody's singular focus. "I think you need to go to sleep, because we've got a big day ahead of us. The twins are going to introduce you to the other kids staying here, Maura's doing a cookie-decorating class and Seth is taking everyone to the creek on a hike. That'll be fun, won't it?"

Cody shrugged. "I guess. But what about—"

"You'll like playing with the other kids."

"Maybe."

"Why maybe? Did something happen?"

"Riley asked where my daddy was," Cody murmured. "He said his real daddy died but his new daddy is a *cop*."

Her heart tugged at the way he repeated the news. She was sure Riley had voiced the question out of curiosity and an effort to get to know his long-distance cousin, but she could guess how it had made Cody feel. Then again, the two boys had both lost their fathers. Maybe it helped having a friend go through the same thing? "I know he is. Your uncle Liam has handcuffs and everything. What did you say when Riley told you that?"

"I said my dad died, too, but now he's a vampire."

Disappointment flooded her. "Oh, Cody."

"He is." His voice dropped to a low, drowsy level. "I know it. When you were in the shower, me and Lexi walked to the place where they eat and I heard Maura telling Grace that she wouldn't be surprised if my dad came to see me tomorrow. I *heard* her."

Skylar's stomach tightened into a knot. No wonder he'd been quiet tonight. He was smart. And despite all his talk about a vampire dad, she knew he was aware that Tom had died.

But what he had overheard had probably also scared and confused him. Because why would the adults be talking about his father coming to visit if he *was* dead? "It sounds to me like you were listening to a conversation you shouldn't have been listening to." This was exactly what she was afraid of. But what could she say to counter that? She couldn't blurt out the truth.

Cody snuggled into the mattress, Batman clutched to his chest. The doll's black eyes gleamed in the light of the moon shining through the window.

"I want Riley to meet my daddy. A vampire is better than a cop."

Skylar found herself at a loss for words. As much as she didn't want Marcus thinking he could barge into their lives, she couldn't continue to let Cody go on believing Tom was his only father.

She closed her eyes and tried to think of what to do. She didn't want to confuse Cody more, and the news had to come from her because she couldn't risk him overhearing another conversation and finding out about Marcus that way. Somehow she had to prepare Cody, so that when the time came—

But not tonight. Tonight he needs to sleep and not worry about things even the adults in his life can't handle.

He was so fragile. Beyond the fact Tom wasn't his

father, how *did* you explain to a child that his biological father chose to stay out of his life until now? No matter how she sugarcoated it, Cody—any kid—would think he wasn't wanted. Was unworthy. Somehow to blame.

She sighed, but it did nothing to release the tension. She lay her head atop the pillow, her nose and lips in his kiwi-scented hair, and stared at the moon.

She gently massaged her son's back, knowing by the sound of his breathing that he was relaxing into sleep.

Outside she saw headlights slowly driving toward the entrance of Jake and Maura's driveway. The headlights switched off and the truck continued in the dark. Not quite halfway to the house, the truck stopped.

Lexi had apparently made it home. But why didn't the friend take her all the way to the door?

Skylar wasn't able to see much, but after a few moments the interior truck light came on as though someone had climbed out. Minutes passed, then the porch light at the house flashed on and off three times. In response, the truck reversed down the driveway, still in the dark. The headlights didn't come on until the truck was able to turn into the main parking area around the buildings.

Interesting. What was Lexi up to? Better still, what had Skylar inadvertently gotten involved in by giving the girl a ride to town?

HARD ROCK PULSED THROUGH Marcus's workshop as he pounded at a piece, molding the metal with the hammer and shaping it into the curled leaf he wanted. A flash of light outside the open door snagged his attention and he frowned, wondering who was paying a visit.

Marcus wheeled himself closer to the gun cabinet, just in case. Then he spotted Skylar's stepfather exiting the sheriff's cruiser. And there was only one reason for Jonas Taggert to visit.

He tried to brace himself, knowing this conversation wouldn't go nearly as smoothly as the one with his grandfather. Marcus positioned himself by his design desk and waited for Jonas to enter, glad he'd left the double door open so it wasn't as stifling as it had been.

"Evenin'."

Jonas's gaze was cold as he stalked toward Marcus. A man on a mission. When he stopped in front of Marcus and grabbed hold of his shirt, it wasn't hard to guess what was coming.

"You *knew?*"

"Yes, sir. She told me. And I sent her away."

Jonas drew his arm back. Marcus made no attempt to block the blow, even though Jonas gave him plenty of time to do so. The punch to the jaw lobbed Marcus's head hard to the right and his wheelchair rocked up on one wheel. He saw stars for a second, then blinked his eyes to clear them.

Jonas stalked away, looking around as if he'd suddenly found himself in the middle of a maze. He didn't speak. His heavy breathing and the fists he kept clenched said it all.

Marcus rubbed his jaw knowing that, come morning, chewing would be painful. "I'm sorry."

"You should be. Damn it, Marcus, I always liked you." Jonas glared. "You were a good kid, a solid kid. You had dreams and goals. Obviously you still do."

He did. After the accident, he'd wondered if he'd ever be able to do anything again. Now he wondered if there was enough time to do all the things he wanted. Racing, travel. Being a family man. "I can explain." The claim seemed ridiculous because no excuse would ever be good enough.

"Can you? Because I'd sure as hell like to hear it. How could you let her marry another man, knowing she carried your *kid?*"

Marcus forced himself to hold Jonas's gaze. He'd be lying if he said he wasn't embarrassed to face a man he respected, given what he'd done. But it was time to step up, then move forward. "I was wrong. I know that. One of my biggest regrets is denying Cody and Skylar."

"Regret doesn't cut it."

"When Skylar told me she was pregnant, I didn't know my head from my ass. The accident had just happened and I'd been told the damage was permanent. I couldn't take care of myself, so how the hell was I supposed to take care of them?"

He hated it that Skylar had felt so desperate she'd married Tom. Because how could Marcus hold that marriage against her after abandoning her? As much as he didn't like it, he had to accept that Skylar had done what she'd thought best. Even if it killed him to think of her with someone else. Then. Or now.

"You want to be in Cody's life. You think you're ready?"

Honestly? He didn't have a clue. All he knew was that he couldn't turn his back on them again. "I want to know my son."

Jonas stopped at the chair positioned to the side of the desk. It was a tattered recliner used as a comfortable place for his grandfather to sit whenever he visited.

After Marcus had made it to the NFL, he'd built his grandfather a wheelchair-accessible house, replacing old furniture with new. The two-story house had a finished basement and was large enough for his grandfather to putter around in without getting too bored, every part of it accessible with ramps and an elevator.

Jonas ran a hand over the top of the old recliner, a deep scowl on his face. "What you want and what's best for my grandson may not be the same thing. How are you going to explain the fact you haven't been around for the past eight years?"

"I'll tell him the truth."

"Are you sure you have the balls to handle it? Because once Cody knows, there's no going back."

Marcus's hands tightened into fists. Being Cody's dad was something he'd thought about over the years but denied himself because Skylar had given her son a father. Maybe Marcus couldn't ever make up for sending them away, but he could try. *Had* to try. He wanted to be more than a DNA donor to his son. "I know that."

"I don't like getting involved in the personal lives of my daughters. But anything you do or say from this point on concerns my grandson and that *is* my business. You let Skylar and Cody down once. It sure as hell better not happen again."

He didn't know what to say, what to do, to convince Jonas or Skylar or anyone else that he was ready to be the man he should have been. "I have a lot to make up for. But I'm pretty sure I can do better than an imaginary vampire," he said with more confidence than he felt.

Jonas straightened, his expression grim but filled with wary acceptance. "Let's hope you can. Because we'll be watching. This time, you'd better treat them right or you'll be answering to all of us."

Chapter 7

CODY STOOD ON THE VERY TOP of the jungle gym when Marcus rounded the main dining hall. He couldn't hear what the kid was saying, but from the expressions on the other kids' faces, it wasn't hard to guess they weren't amused. Like the first time he'd seen his son, Cody had the black cape clutched in his hands. Only, this time the plastic action figures were there, as well.

Holding the cape high, Cody jumped off the structure. Marcus's lungs squeezed into his throat, but Cody landed on his feet and straightened, a triumphant smile on his face. Barely a second passed before he climbed the structure again.

Marcus watched his son for a few more minutes before rolling into the building. If Cody was playing out here, odds were Skylar was inside or somewhere close by. He tried not to think about the arguments they'd already had but maybe the fourth time was the charm. He could only hope.

Jonas's last comment before leaving last night had been for Marcus to remember that Skylar had every right to not make it easy on him but that some things were worth the fight.

After a sleepless night, he'd made a decision. The one he should have made eight years ago.

"What are you doing here, Marcus?"

It took a moment for his eyes to adjust to the change in light. Skylar's question came from behind him and he turned to see her sitting alone at a table, wrapping utensils in paper napkins. "I was hoping you were talking to me today," he said, trying to keep things light.

Her mouth flattened as she continued her task. "Are you here because of Jonas?"

"No. That visit was long overdue." He would have helped with her chore, but his hands were dirty from his class. "But I will admit I was afraid I'd show up this morning to hear you'd left town."

"I thought about it," she said, glancing toward the entrance as though to make sure Cody wasn't around.

The round metal grips of Marcus's wheels dug into his gloved hands. "I'm glad you didn't. I know we've got a big divide between us, Skylar, and I hate it, but surely there's a way we can work through it. For our son's sake."

The silence stretched before she said, "What happened with Jonas?" Her gaze zeroed on the bruise gracing his jaw. "He *hit* you?"

"Like I said, it was long overdue. For what it's worth, I don't think your stepdad is normally the type to hit first and ask questions later. We talked, and cleared the air about some things."

"Meaning, me and Cody?"

"What else?" He watched as she continued to stare at the bruise with an expression of remorse, and wondered if there had ever been a time when he didn't want her.

"Did you blame me?"

"No. I cowboyed up, and admitted I made a mistake. I hope when the time comes, you'll do the same."

A bitter sound escaped her, but he still thought she was one of the most beautiful women he'd ever known. Her blond hair, blue eyes and curvy form were quite a combination. But what sealed the deal for him was her skin. She'd always reminded him of a doll, all perfect and pretty and cool to the touch. The thing was, he knew how fiery she could be. "I thought you'd be spending time with your mom."

"She has a few charters today. She's going to take off as much time as she can, but it's her busy season. It's fine, though, considering everything that's going on."

"Are things tense between you?"

"What do you think? I'm still waiting for the fallout. Cody was with us last night and we were at the diner so, yay, me. I have that to look forward to."

He winced even as her sarcastic drawl brought a smile to his lips. "Can I help?"

"No."

He leaned his arm on the table. "I'm sure Rissa will come around."

Skylar paused in her task, her long lashes hanging low over her eyes. "You should've seen her face, Marcus. I could tell she'd been crying and you know my mom doesn't cry over stupid stuff."

No, Rissa wasn't the type. Nor was Skylar. They were cut from the same cloth, two strong women with strong beliefs. They'd had a rocky relationship but while he and Skylar dated, things had seemed to calm a bit. He wasn't happy to know he'd caused another uproar.

"You didn't answer my question," she said abruptly. "Why are you here? Because if you're here to say I have to tell Cody, I won't. It's too sudden."

"I understand. I know it will take time but I hope we can work toward telling him soon."

Skylar shook her head.

"Skylar, both of us want what's best for Cody. I'm not trying to hurt you. Either of you."

"But it does hurt. You think changing your mind about being a parent doesn't *hurt* me? How am I supposed to explain to my son I *lied* to him? He trusts me. Even if the only reason I lied was because—"

"I sent you away? That's not true," he said softly. "You could have told Cody and everyone else the truth about me but you chose not to because it was easier to pretend Tom was Cody's father."

"You *know* what they would've done," she insisted. "It's what they're doing now. Jonas hit you, Carly thinks I've deprived you, and my mother… Everyone is at odds with you and I, and we're not on the same side. It's a mess when all I wanted was a vacation."

Yeah, she had gotten a lot more and so had he. "The

deal with Tom was not my doing, Skylar. I won't let you hold it against me."

"Would you really take me to court?"

Marcus faltered. Did he want to do that? No. Never. But what would he do to be part of Cody's life? "I want to know my son. I don't want this to get ugly. I don't want to put any of us through the hassle of attorneys or the court system. So surely we can come to some kind of compromise that doesn't involve anyone else."

"How? Cody's not going to understand. He's a *little boy*. He's not capable of comprehending such a thing as *why* a grown-up—someone who is supposed to love and care for him—didn't want him. Look at how he's coping with Tom's death. It's put Cody in an extremely fragile state where he soothes himself by pretending. Who knows what telling him will do? How it will make him feel? Do you think he'll simply accept you?"

Every point she made stabbed him in the heart. "We don't have to tell him right away." Making that small concession wasn't easy because, now that he'd made his decision, he wanted to move ahead as quickly as possible —but not at his son's expense.

He was a stranger and until Cody knew him, Skylar was right, he wouldn't understand. "When he gets used to me, gets used to having me around, he'll be more accepting when we tell him the truth."

She looked away. Following the direction of her gaze, he realized she had a bird's-eye view of the action on the playground outside. Cody looked like his mother, although Marcus could see traces of himself in skin tone and bone structure. He tried to imagine the boy in five years. Ten. Cody had lived nearly that long already. Half of his childhood gone unobserved by Marcus.

If he wanted any part of his son's life, it had to be now. Before Ben's health got any worse, before Cody got older and realized what an ass his father had been. "What do you want me to say, Skylar? Do? Tell me what I need to say to be able to look my son in the eye with him knowing I'm his father. You and I may have our differences, but where Cody is concerned, I think it's clear where I…sit," he said deliberately, his tone wry.

She fiddled with the etched edge of one of the forks. When she looked up, her pretty blue eyes were sad but full of determination. "Parenting isn't easy, Marcus, and *you* have already bailed on us once. Why should I trust you? Why should I believe you truly want to know Cody, and this isn't about your recovering from some embarrassment because people now know the truth? That this isn't about your pride and your ego and maybe a little bit of that competitiveness that runs so deep inside you?"

There were a lot of hard questions packed in her little rant, all of them needing answers. "I have my share of pride. And I broke your trust. But I want to build that trust again."

"How do you propose to do that?"

"Spend your vacation with me."

"What?"

He glanced around and saw Maura and the other workers across the room. They eyed them with blatant curiosity but he didn't let them deter him.

Skylar noticed, too, however, and in response to their

perusal, she crossed the room to the window. He followed, not about to let her escape. "Skylar, our son wants a father so bad he's making one up in his head. Like it or not, I'm it."

"For now."

"*Forever,*" he corrected. "When it comes to Tom Adams, I know I tend to say the wrong things. I've never understood why you couldn't marry me yet you could marry him. Cut me some slack for getting tripped up on that."

Skylar glanced at him over her shoulder. "I guess we both have our pride."

"Look, I know I have a way to go before you're ready to believe I can handle being Cody's father. But let's not make this any harder than it's already going to be. Please." The expression on her face said his words had finally gotten through to her. "I won't say anything to Cody about being his dad. Not yet. Not until we're all sure he can handle it. But let me spend some time with him, as much as I can while you're here. Sound fair?"

"No attorneys?"

The twist in his gut eased a bit. "Not if you meet me halfway. We'll take it a day at a time." He watched her face for some sign of forgiveness, acceptance. "I'm done with the riding class for the day but my art class is coming up. Actually, it's almost time to start."

"You teach art here, too?"

"Twice a week. It's the original deal I made with Seth and Grace in exchange for Ben's therapy. I'm only covering the riding until they find someone else." Absurdly nervous, he brushed the back of his fingers down her forearm before taking her hand in his. "I was hoping you and Cody would join me. It's a basic drawing class—no torches or hammers. He can draw or finger paint. After, maybe I can show him how to draw those toys of his."

Skylar looked away, the line of her mouth firming.

Waiting for her response took patience he didn't know he had.

"Fine. We'll go. But I don't like this and if you do anything to push Cody or *hint* that you're more than just the art teacher, I'll hit you the way Jonas did."

He couldn't stop the smile. Skylar had taken her first step toward compromise grudgingly, but he'd take it any way he could.

He squeezed her fingers again. "Understood."

A HALF HOUR LATER, SKYLAR SAT beside Cody beneath a large covered picnic shelter near the main building, and wondered how she was going to handle all the changes she saw in their future.

Marcus had kept his promise not to say anything overtly fatherly and simply taught his class, explaining what they were going to do, what supplies were available and, if they agreed, that their art would be displayed inside the dining hall until the end of their vacation.

The students ranged from young to old. Some had disabilities, some didn't. And while she would have thought it too difficult to conduct a class with such a diverse group, Marcus's patience made her sit up and pay attention. Because this was the Marcus she remembered. The one who captured her heart so long ago. Patient, funny, kind. He was wonderful. Gentle in his instruction, firm with a few of the rowdier kids.

Today's project was a self-portrait. And as Marcus explained at the beginning, the images could be anything. They could draw their face and body, or how they viewed themselves or the world, or those objects that represented them. There was no wrong or right answer, only the vision in their heads.

One of the older women had sketched a very simple cross in the middle of a heart. In the heart, she had written names, presumably those of her family.

One of the kids in a wheelchair worked on a picture of a boy running toward a house, the sun at the top of the page big and yellow with streaks of orange.

A girl around twelve or thirteen, who'd attended the class with her disabled father, was quite good. Her self-portrait consisted of a stack of books, a stethoscope and a girl standing beside a man in a wheelchair, helping him stand. The depth and emotion portrayed in the picture had her father struggling to hold back tears.

Cody hunched over his paper, drawing furiously. He'd made her promise not to look until he was finished.

"What about you?" Marcus asked, rolling to a stop at her side. "You haven't started."

No, she hadn't. Her piece of paper was blank, and to be honest, her mind was as blank. She could draw a school and stick-figure children to represent those she'd helped over the years. But that seemed like taking the easy way out. And having done that more times in her life than she cared to admit, something kept her from doing it now. Self-portraits were supposed to be personal. Revealing. Still, this wasn't where she wanted to reveal her true inner self. "I came for Cody."

"You don't have to put it on display," Marcus said. "Draw whatever you like."

Realizing some of the others were looking at her because she wasn't drawing, she nodded her agreement and picked up a charcoal pencil, while Marcus rolled away to work on his own picture.

Once more, her gaze was drawn to the older woman and the contented, happy smile on her face. She'd added more to her drawing, printed words like *peaceful, faithful, joyous* around the heart. Her husband looked on with pride, and Skylar felt her heart pinch when the two exchanged a loving glance.

She picked up one of the hardback art books from the center of the table, placing it in her lap and her sheet of paper atop it. If she was going to do this, she needed more privacy.

How *did* she see herself?

Unable to fudge the sentiment and draw a happy house with a curlicue of smoke, smiling sun and child-like joy, she found herself making long strokes, the shape of a face. Eyes, a mouth. Nose. Hair. But once that was done, her gaze zeroed in on the face and she knew it was wrong. So she blacked in the eyes and lips, gave the cheeks a sharp slant of color.

With a shallow inhalation, she acknowledged the fact that after all these years she still felt like that Goth girl, wearing a mask of paint to protect herself from the pain of knowing she'd disappointed her mother and Jonas, Carly. Ben. Everyone. Protecting herself from the pain Marcus's sudden reappearance had unearthed. The pain of knowing how the truth would hurt Cody.

"It's not done yet," Cody said.

With a start, she realized Marcus had asked to see Cody's drawing. She shifted the book and paper to hide her pictorial and waited anxiously for Marcus's comments. The frown forming on his face concerned her.

"You did a good job. That's you?"

Skylar leaned forward and tried to see what Cody had drawn. She wished she hadn't. He showed a man in a black cape. But even more frightening was the boy in a black cape next to him. They were flying, with each of them holding one arm up to lead the way. Like mother, like son?

Skylar found Marcus watching her response. She quickly blanked her features, cleared her expression of worry and fear, and tried to smile. "You are a very creative kid." She focused on the positive because there was nothing else to do.

Cody beamed in pride.

"What did you draw?" the older lady asked.

He held up his picture. "Me and my dad. He's a vampire. I'm going to be a vampire, too. When he kills me and sucks my blood."

Skylar couldn't contain her gasp. Marcus's gaze was hot on her as though Cody's words were all the proof Marcus needed that he was right to change the rules.

Maybe he was right. At this stage, she honestly

didn't know what else to do to stop the vampire-father fantasies.

Yes, there were emotional risks to telling Cody the truth. He'd be hurt, and probably angry, but for the first time since her arrival, she saw the potential in him getting to know Marcus so his attention could shift from fantasy to reality. Maybe her son truly needed the reality check Marcus could provide.

The flip-flopping of her thinking process gave her an instant headache. She'd always known parenting was hard but she'd never imagined this.

An hour later, class was finally over and the shelter quickly emptied of students.

"Cody, would you mind helping me clean up?" Marcus asked.

Skylar looked up, more than ready to make an escape, but Cody shrugged and agreed.

"Sure. Sometimes I help my teacher at school, too."

"That's good. Means you're experienced," Marcus said. "Why don't you gather up the stuff and put it in the bins?"

She left her drawing facedown on the table and helped Cody sort the charcoal pencils, markers and crayons. Once the supplies were away, she and Cody turned to see Marcus had stood Cody's action figures up on the tabletop to study them.

"I'll move them," Cody said.

"They're not in the way," Marcus said, his voice gentle. "Would you like to learn how to draw them?"

Cody scrunched up his face. "Really?"

Teaching him to replicate the action figures that

were "vampires" to Cody didn't seem smart if she wanted him focused on reality. "I don't know if that's a good idea."

"But, Mom, I want to. Please?"

"Actually, since Grandma had to work, I said I'd help Maura prep for dinner this evening. We should probably get going."

"But I want to draw. Drawing is fun," Cody said.

Marcus tousled Cody's hair. "I agree. Since you'll be working, how about I keep an eye on Cody? We'll stay right here and draw and I'll bring him to you when we're finished."

Panic flooded her veins. "Oh, I don't—"

"*Please*, Mom?"

Skylar crossed her arms, aware it was a defensive gesture but unable to stop herself. Marcus was encroaching on her territory, and even though she'd mentally agreed that telling Cody the truth might be beneficial, she wasn't prepared for the emotions bombarding her because her son wanted to be with Marcus instead of her. "Cody—"

"Can you show me how to draw a real vampire?" Cody asked. "Like him?" he said, pointing at the Batman doll.

Frustration got the best of her. "Cody, that is *enough* about the vampires. Will you please—"

"Tell you what." Marcus clearly saw the source of Cody's fascination. "How about we take off his hat and I show you how to draw a man instead? You can add on the mask later if you like. Sound like a plan?"

"Yeah."

"That work for you?" Marcus asked Skylar.

Skylar nodded, unable to express her gratitude at having someone side with her. By having Cody focus on the man, Marcus would help Cody see past the mask. "Thank you," she mouthed.

She felt Marcus's gaze settle on her lips, the sizzle of heat rushing through her having nothing to do with the warm afternoon and everything to do with the man.

She turned to go, desperately needing to escape. She glanced over her shoulder when she was about to step out of the shelter and into the sunlight, and that split-second look left her trembling because it was such an in-her-face reminder of the sweet, patient Marcus she remembered. The one who existed beneath the driven, passionate, competitive man also within him.

How could the attraction still be that strong? That powerful? It scared her to death. The gentle Marcus was the man she'd lost herself in. He was also the one who had broken her heart, her spirit. The one who had forever altered her.

She had to stay far, far away. But how could she give her son what he needed and protect him at the same time? From the same man?

Chapter 8

"I'M GLAD YOU'RE BACK," Maura said to Skylar the moment she stepped into the kitchen. "I need to talk to you."

"If this is about me or Marcus or keeping Cody's paternity a sec—"

"It's not. That's not to say I don't have concerns, but it's none of my business. I'm fighting the urge to be nosy, but you were of age when you made that decision."

Skylar sensed something behind the statement. "Thanks. It means a lot that you respect my privacy."

Maura sighed as she wiped her hands on her old-fashioned apron—ruffled and dotted with bright red ladybugs on sunflowers.

"I hate to bother you with this but the other night when you dropped Lexi off, did you see her friends?"

Remembering exactly what she had seen, Skylar shifted uneasily. "I had her point the girl out to me," she said carefully.

"Were there any boys there?"

"Maura, there were kids Lexi's age everywhere. What's going on?"

"Nothing. At least, I hope it's nothing. She's just acting differently. Secretive."

Skylar couldn't stop the half laugh that erupted from her. "Sorry. If she hasn't acted out already, you've been lucky. She's a good kid. I'm sure it's nothing. Typical teenage stuff and her anxiety over starting college."

Maura shot Skylar a look that made her inwardly cringe. *No, no, no, don't ask me—*

"Can you talk to her? See if something is going on?"

And what would she say if there was? Skylar couldn't get Lexi to confide in her, only to break her trust by telling her parents. "Can't you talk to her? You've all heard my take on doling out advice for friends or family. I don't do it, because it really puts me in a sticky spot. It's hard to be objective when I'm invested in the person."

"I know. And I hate to ask, but Lexi tells me what I want to hear. With you, she seems more free. She likes you. She always has, even when she was little. Remember how she always asked you to play cards?"

That first summer in North Star, Skylar bet she'd played a thousand games with Lexi. "She likes you, too. It's probably nothing more than anxiety over college."

"I'm still worried. It's probably only that she's met a boy and doesn't want us to know because she thinks we'll grill her about him. Jake gives her a hard time about dating. He still wants her to say she won't date until she's forty."

"Fathers are known to do that to their little girls." As sheriff, Jonas had been horrible about meeting her and Carly's dates at the door and giving them the third degree. He'd even made his daughters take self-defense lessons to fend off any unwanted advances.

"Exactly. But she's become so quiet. I know you have your own issues right now but I thought since you counsel kids for a living, you'd know what to say, how to get her to open up. Rissa brags about the awards you've won, the good you've done with the kids at your school. So, will you? Just make sure she's okay?"

How could she refuse a request like that? From one mother to another? "Okay. But I can't tell you what she says. You know that, right?"

Judging by her expression, Maura didn't like that, but she nodded. "Okay, fine. So can I ask about Cody? Where is he, anyway?"

Skylar plucked a cookie from the nearby plate and nibbled at it, relishing its deliciousness. Cookies were her crack. She could so give the Cookie Monster a run for his money. "Cody's with Marcus. They're drawing a picture." Which reminded her she'd left her self-portrait behind. Damn. Maybe Marcus and Cody hadn't noticed it. Maybe she could run back, get it and check on them.

Marcus will think you deliberately left it.

Who cared as long as she got it before Marcus saw it? Her talent left a lot to be desired but she was loathe to let Marcus see she still identified with the Goth girl.

"Really? You mean, you told him?"

"*No.* We haven't told him anything yet and please do

not discuss it in public," she said, telling Maura about Cody overhearing her conversation with Grace.

"Oh, no. I'm so sorry."

"Marcus agreed to keep quiet for now. They're getting to know each other and after that, we'll see."

"Why don't you sound okay with it?"

"Would you be completely okay? Marcus pushed us away, and now he wants more? Where was he when Cody was teething or running a fever?"

"He did wrong," Maura agreed, "but he's not the same man he was then."

"So he says. Forgive me if I need a little action to back that up." Still, she had to believe him. If she didn't, the whole situation became even more impossible. "I need to run back—I forgot to get something."

"Wait, don't go yet. You don't believe Marcus is telling the truth? I'm not taking up for him," Maura interjected. "I just can't imagine knowing I have a child but not being a parent to him or spending time with him."

"By *choice*."

"Bad choices can sometimes be corrected and wrongs made right." She began lifting the cookies from the baking sheet with a spatula. "Some things take time."

Remembering how Marcus had looked at her before she'd left the art class, Skylar grabbed another cookie. "Time can't fix everything. Marcus might be different, in a better place emotionally than he was when I told him of my pregnancy. It doesn't change the fact that we had broken up before then."

"It all happened years ago, Skylar. If forgetting is impossible, maybe you have to decide to put those feelings in a box and move on. Start fresh." Maura smiled wryly. "It's not healthy to dwell on anger and pain, and while it's a bit cliché, this is the Second Chance. Maybe this is yours."

"WHY DON'T YOUR LEGS WORK?" Cody asked.

Marcus stared at the bent head of his son and reminded himself that kids and curiosity went hand-in-hand. It wasn't the first time he'd been asked that question by a child. Here on the ranch, whenever a new batch of guests arrived the question popped up.

He'd begun including that bit of information when he first introduced himself to a class, keeping it simple and stating he'd been injured playing football. Some of the adults recognized him or his name from his days as one of the Cowboys. The recognition or lack thereof didn't matter, since these days, he'd much rather build his name for his art—or, better yet, make a name in wheelchair racing.

But in response to Cody's question, Marcus recited his practiced speech.

"I thought you don't get hurt if you wear the helmet and stuff." Cody blinked at him, the pencil lax in his hand.

"The helmets and gear do protect you but not completely. People get hurt all the time, in lots of different ways." He pointed to the paper in front of Cody. "You did really well."

"You did most of it."

"I only helped you. You did the real work. Practice like I showed you and you'll be able to draw him on your own in no time."

"Can I add the mask now? Give him fangs and a cape?"

"If you want. But first tell me what's with this vampire thing? Why do you say your dad is one?"

"Because he's awesome. He can run really fast, and fly and climb trees."

Marcus felt a stab of unease as he watched Cody alter the picture. What would Cody do when he learned his dad couldn't do those things?

"What's your dad like?" Cody's words were mumbled as he concentrated on making Batman's pointy ears.

"My father died when I was young. Younger than you. I was five."

Cody lifted his head. "Were you sad?"

"Very. I think I made up a few imaginary friends to make me feel better." He paused. "Do you really believe your dad is a vampire?"

Cody bit down on his lower lip but he didn't answer.

"I'm asking because when I made up those friends, I had to finally accept they weren't real. But for a time, they helped me feel less alone. See, my parents had left me to stay with my grandfather while they took a trip. I wasn't used to being there and I didn't know him very well. Plus he seemed really old. But when my parents didn't come home from the trip, I had to stay with

Granddad permanently. That meant leaving my friends, school and our house. Everything. My imaginary friends kept me company, kind of like—" He made eye contact with Cody. "—Your stories about a vampire dad."

Cody shifted on the chair and looked away.

"Why do you think he's a vampire? Why do you want him to be one?"

He shrugged.

"Come on, it's got to be more than him being able to run fast and fly."

The boy stared at his picture. "My daddy was sick."

"I know." Marcus rubbed Cody's back gently.

"He used to try to run with me but he couldn't. He couldn't breathe right."

"So you pretend he's a vampire now because…?"

"Vampires don't get sick. My dad is big and strong and he can run and jump and play with me. And he's *real*, not pretend."

Marcus was at a loss for how to respond. As he searched for words, he noticed a sheet of paper where Skylar had sat. It appeared to be blank, but he'd seen her drawing something. Had she left it behind on purpose, for an excuse to come check on Cody? Or by accident in her bid to get away? "Have you ever been rolling?" he asked, hoping a change in subject would put the boy's mood to rights.

As he waited for Cody's response, Marcus wheeled toward the end of the table to snatch the sheet.

"No. What's that?"

"Racing in a wheelchair." He flipped the paper over.

"You can't race wheelchairs."

"Sure you can." Somehow he managed to disguise his shock at Skylar's self-portrait. "I'll show you sometime."

The image was roughly drawn. The edges fuzzy yet distinct. It brought back a slew of memories from when he'd first met Skylar, so angry and bitter and scarred from her mistakes that she had hidden from the world. Why draw a Goth girl now? Did she feel like hiding again? Feel like that girl? Was *he* the one making her feel that way?

"That's okay, I'd rather run," Cody said. "My dad's going to teach me how to run really fast."

Marcus glanced from Skylar's picture to the one Cody had drawn. He tried not to take offense at Cody's words, but how was that possible? Between the mother and son, he felt like the ultimate jerk.

"That's mine," Skylar said.

As though she'd been conjured from his thoughts, he lifted his head to see Skylar stepping into the shelter, looking stiff and uncomfortable. "So it is."

She held her hand out for the sheet of paper and he reluctantly handed it over.

"Goth?" he asked softly, studying her expression, watching the way her mouth trembled slightly.

Skylar didn't acknowledge his question. "Cody, are you finished?"

"Yeah. See, Mom?"

Not only had Cody made the man into a vampire, replete with red crayon "blood" dripping from his teeth, but also he'd added bite marks on the child's arm.

"I see," she said. "We should go. Carly's on her way here with Riley so you guys can play. You need to get a snack first."

"Okay." Cody put his pencils and crayons away and gathered up the sheets of paper he'd used.

"Bye, Marcus."

"Goodbye, Cody. I hope to see you soon. Have fun playing with your cousin."

"I will. His dad is a cop and Riley said he's going to take us for a ride in the police car. It goes really fast."

Marcus watched Cody join his mother and the two of them left, Cody breaking into a run as soon as he stepped into the sunshine.

"Mom, race ya!"

Skylar didn't hesitate. She chased after him, keeping up but always staying a wee bit behind.

Marcus didn't move until they were out of sight, then rolled to the supplies for a piece of paper and charcoal.

Absently, he sketched. A woman's slim body. Medium-length hair tumbling down her back, gently rounded hips, her hand extended slightly away from her thigh and held by a boy as they walked in the distance. Every detail of their hair and clothing came easily.

For once he was glad Skylar had insisted they not tell Cody yet. Marcus wasn't ready to face Cody's disappointment when his son realized he wasn't the dad Cody wanted.

To his sketch, he added a man, his legs bent, his feet sitting on footrests, his hands on the wheels. Always lagging behind as the mother and child walked on without him.

THAT SATURDAY EVENING, SKYLAR exited the dining hall and walked to where her mother leaned against the porch railing, staring out into the night. "You've been busy. I've seen you flying several times the past couple days."

"You know how it is. Lots of flights this time of year," her mother said lightly. Too lightly.

"Yeah, I know. Carly and Riley came over yesterday afternoon and stayed for the campfire."

"I heard. Riley told me all about the giant s'mores."

"They were good. Actually, I thought I'd see you. You know, since you don't fly at night unless it's an emergency. Is the fact you didn't, my hint about how angry you are with me?"

Rissa brushed her hair away from her face and tucked it behind her ear. "I'm sorry. I meant to drop by but— I honestly don't know what to say about all of this, Sky. I'm at a loss for words. I thought some time to ponder might be in order."

The weight on Skylar's shoulders sat heavier with her mother's words. "Say what you feel." Skylar tried to brace herself. "Seriously, Mom, just say it."

"Okay, fine. Why? *Why* would you do such a thing? Why would you turn to a stranger for help instead of your own family?"

"Tom wasn't a stranger. I knew him." When you're in a hospital setting, under the pressure of tests and procedures and potential terminal diagnoses, you got to know people quickly. You cut through a lot of the social bs.

"How well? Better than us? Me? That story you told us when you got engaged—was that true? Or was it another lie?"

She winced at the reminder. When she and Tom had flown to Montana to announce their sudden engagement, her mother had pulled her aside, asked if she was rebounding with Tom.

Skylar had waxed poetic about falling in love instantly, like magic. How Tom had swept her off her feet. Every tired cliché had passed her lips. "It was the way I wanted things to be."

"Am I supposed to understand what that means? Because I don't. Or maybe I do." Rissa moved to the ramp. "I can't tell you how much it hurts that you wouldn't come to me. Really, Skylar? After everything we went through together?" She referred to Skylar's affair with Rick and the fatal accident.

Skylar followed her mother, the fresh night air cool against her too-hot cheeks. The bright exterior lights faded as they walked a familiar path toward the small cabin where they'd lived while on the ranch. "Mom, I know you don't understand, but if you'll hear me out, maybe I can change that."

Rissa remained quiet and Skylar took that as her cue to continue.

"I *know* I could have come to you. But I didn't want to."

"*Why?*"

"Because I was tired of screwing up. I didn't want to be that girl who made you cry. The girl who acted out and ruined things. I did that enough growing up. And since Carly and I were out of the house, you and Jonas were finally able to be alone. You practically glowed you were so happy. Had you known, you would have expected me to reconcile with Marcus or move back here so you could help me. Maybe even move in with you. Right? I couldn't do that."

"So you lied to all of us instead? That was your answer?"

"No. I mean— It just happened that way. I thought if you knew Marcus was Cody's father, you'd interfere in something that was definitely *over*. After what he'd done with that girl, after he rejected me, I couldn't stand the thought of being forced or *guilted* into doing something I didn't want to do."

Rissa stopped walking and swung to face her. "Forced and guilted."

"You know what I mean."

"Skylar, what you and Tom had wasn't a marriage, it was a business arrangement."

"It was what we wanted. You don't have to understand anything more than that. Accept it. Tom was wonderful. He was a good man and a better father, and he deserved the life he dreamed of but couldn't have for fear of a biological child developing his disease."

"I understand that but, even if Marcus didn't want to be in Cody's life, did you ever stop to think about Ben? He's my friend, and how am I supposed to look him in the face knowing you've kept his great-grandson from him all these years? Robbed him of Cody."

"I know." That was one of the things that had always made her feel guilty. Ben was a nice, gentle man who cherished his family—what little he had of it.

She'd cheated Ben of Cody. But she couldn't give Ben access to Cody without the secret getting out, and without encountering Marcus again. And she hadn't wanted to face him. Ever. The wounds had been too raw, ran too deep. They were even now. "You have no reason to feel guilty. If Marcus had wanted to tell Ben the truth, he could have at any time."

"How could he? Anything he said would destroy the life you'd created. You think Marcus would have done that to you?"

"You act as though Marcus is totally innocent in this." Unbelievable. Even now, after her mother had had time to think about things, she still took Marcus's side?

"No, Skylar. I know Marcus has his flaws but I also know, deep down, he loved you like nothing I've ever seen before. You tied his hands, because the only way he could have his son was by revealing your deceit with Tom."

"And that brings us right back to how he cheated on me," Skylar said drily. "Was that Marcus showing his love for me? Oh, but wait, you're on the 'we'd broken up' side of the debate. You supported him then, too."

"Don't." Rissa shook her head.

"How can I not, Mom? This is exactly what I mean. Yes, I told a lie. I told a lie!" Skylar yelled to the woods surrounding them, lifting her arms to the sky. "But now you know the reasons *why* I lied." She lowered her voice again. "There were extenuating circumstances, and I made the best decision I could at the time. Is it too much to ask that you support *me?*"

"Oh, Skylar. I'm not taking sides. But if I was? I'm on Cody's. That little boy needs help to cope with what's happened to him."

A rough laugh escaped. "You mean, to deal with what happened because I married Tom."

"You *knew* he was dying. How am I supposed to overlook that? You had to know losing the only father he'd known would be devastating."

In that, her mother was right. Skylar had known and still married Tom. "Yes. I did. I married a man who loved and supported us when Cody's biological father wouldn't even acknowledge us. I don't regret it. Cody is hurting now because he had seven wonderful years with a man who was a *great* father, who loved him uncondi- tionally, which is more than Marcus has ever offered. You're blaming me, and even Tom, but what about Marcus? He knew, Mom, and he chose to do nothing until now."

"If you had only waited, given Marcus time—"

"What are you saying? You would rather I had waited around in the hope that he *might* change his mind? What about my self-respect? Dignity? Mom, are you serious?"

"I'm saying, had you not been so hasty, maybe Cody wouldn't have the problems he has."

Hurt seared her, making it hard to breathe. She took several steps back, fighting the urge to scream. "Yeah, you're right about that. I guess I should feel bad Cody got attached to his father because Tom outlived his prognosis. I'm sorry Tom didn't die quick enough for you."

Chapter 9

THE NEXT AFTERNOON SKYLAR was dozing on a lounge chair outside the indoor pool when screaming jerked her awake. Immediately, she recognized Cody's out-of-control wail. "Cody?"

She sprang from the lounger and tried to shake the cobwebs from her brain as she ran around the corner, her gaze searching for and finding her son rolling on the ground with another child. "*Cody!*"

Skylar jumped into the fray of kicking, screaming, flailing kids, grabbing Cody and yanking him off the child—a girl. "Cody, stop it. Stop."

Adults converged on the group, questions flying. The little girl's chest heaved, angry tears streaming down her face as a woman patted the girl's back.

"What is going on here?" Skylar kneeled between the two children. "What happened?"

"He's a liar! He's telling lies," the girl said.

"Am not!"

"Are, too. And when I laughed because he said his

daddy was a vampire, he jumped on me." The little girl began to sob.

"Cody, is that true?"

This wasn't the first time it had happened. When Cody began fantasizing and telling his friends stories about his father and they'd made fun, Cody had gotten so upset he'd pushed a boy down at school. But to get so upset—and with a girl?

A man rolled toward the scene, the electronic motor propelling the chair buzzing as it crossed the lawn.

"Brianna, are you all right?"

"Daddy!" The little girl ran to him and threw herself against him, burying her head against his legs, fresh sobs emerging from her.

Keeping a firm hold on Cody's hand, Skylar turned toward them. "I am so sorry," she said. "Cody, apologize right now."

"She made fun."

"That's no excuse to *attack* someone." She nudged him when he didn't speak to the girl.

"Sorry."

"Brianna, what do you have to say to him about making fun?" the man asked.

The girl sniffled, glared, her pout growing bigger as she stuck her lip out. "I'm sorry for making fun, but you're still *mean*."

Gathering what was left of her nerves, Skylar ordered Cody to sit on a chair on the porch and wait for her. "Don't you dare move from that spot." Once Cody was on his way, she knelt by the little girl. "Sweetie, are you all right?"

"I think she'll be fine," her father said. "But if your son has issues with violence, you shouldn't let him play unattended."

"It won't happen again. Is there anything I can do?"

"Brianna." An older version of the child hurried toward them. "What's going on?"

So many people were crowded around them. Skylar kept her focus on the girl and her parents, unable to face anyone else. "I'll talk to him."

Straightening, she ignored the comments and headed for Cody, remembering how she'd gotten into a fight in the North Star library because a girl made snide remarks about Carly. Skylar had been older than Cody, fourteen, but the librarian had called the police and Jonas had arrived to break it up, her mother hot on his heels.

This was payback for that incident. Karma. Whatever you wanted to call it. She was embarrassed by Cody's behavior, angry and upset. All the things her mother must have felt so many years ago.

All the things her mother felt regarding the latest development sprung on her?

"Come with me," Skylar said sharply, the words emerging in a tone that had Cody looking at her in surprise.

She grabbed his hand and tugged him along, needing to escape the many disapproving expressions watching their every move.

"Where are we going?"

"To the cabin."

Cody had to run to keep up with her hurried strides.

They took the path to the parking area between the main house, gathering area, barn and garage, and kept going.

"Mommy? Mommy? Mom?"

"What?"

Cody put his head down. "Marcus wants you."

It was only then that it registered Marcus had been calling her name. She'd vaguely heard him but completely ignored the call, so intent she was on getting to the cabin. "Go to the cabin and wait for me. Make no mistake, we *will* be discussing your behavior. Go." She released his hand.

Skylar stayed where she was, taking deep, blood-pressure-reducing breaths while she waited for Marcus to catch up.

"What went on back there?"

She couldn't stand still, needing to vent yet not wanting to discuss Cody's behavior with Marcus of all people. Like she hadn't done everything possible to avoid incidents like that. Like she needed her parenting skills critiqued.

"Are you going to tell me, or do I have to ask the crowd?"

"He got into a fight— No, that's not true. He attacked a little girl for laughing at one of his vampire tales." She swung to face him, hating that he could look so calm when she felt so torn up inside. "What? No comment?"

"It's time to tell him."

All the air gushed from her lungs. "Absolutely not. This is the worst time to tell him. Marcus, he's already confused. Do you really think telling him *that* would make the fantasy go away?"

"Calm down."

"I *can't*." The tragedy with Travis loomed along with her failure to save him. "Do you know how this makes me feel? I worked so hard to learn how to talk to kids, to *help* them, yet here I am. I can't help Cody and he's my son."

"Ours."

"Every time I turn around something else is falling apart."

"You're keeping secrets from him. He needs to face the truth, Skylar." Marcus swung his wheelchair toward the cabin. "I'm telling him."

"Don't you dare." She stepped in front of him.

"Skylar, the boy needs to snap out of his fantasy world. You know that as well as I do. Stuff like this is going to keep occurring until he does."

"And then what? His fantasies aren't going to magically disappear if we tell him. And what about afterward? We pretend to be a happy family? We're *not*."

Something shifted in his expression. A flash of pain, maybe need. Definite want.

Want?

No, that had to be wrong. Had. To. Be.

"We'll be like most of the families today. Don't look like that. We'll work something out. We'll even include Cody so he doesn't feel left out."

"No."

"Telling him is better than letting him continue. At least I'm something tangible he can deal with."

It sounded good. In theory. It was a step, even if she couldn't say it was in the right direction. But what about Marcus giving Cody time to get to know him? Allowing Cody to adjust? "And if I say no?"

"If you have other options, I'm willing to listen."

She didn't. And that was the point. "You're determined to do this? Even though you don't know what it's like to be a father? Even though we haven't discussed any of the custody details?"

"Even though," he said simply. "It's time, Skylar. I wised up too late last time. You were gone, *married*, and I was the chump who screwed up. That's not happening again. I'm not letting you put this off until it's time for you to go back to New York. I'm right here, and I'm not going to change my mind. You can count on that.

"I know exactly who is to blame here and I'm *sorry*. I spent months in the hospital, months in rehab. After that, I was still in a fog for a good year or two more, banging on metal to release the anger because I'd had a plan and things weren't unfolding the way I wanted them to. Not a day went by that I didn't think about you and the baby and regret what I said. I didn't want to hurt you more than I already had."

She didn't know what to think. What to do. How was she supposed to respond?

"It's time to set this right." He brushed his leather-covered knuckles against hers.

Marcus had always been a physical boyfriend. Touching, hugging, holding. Kissing.

Through the black leather of his gloves, heat sizzled, unfurling inside her in that crazy way he'd always made her feel. But she couldn't focus on that now, so she pulled her hand away, and rubbed it against her shirt to get rid of the tingle.

She couldn't get caught up in the residual chemistry they had shared. Marcus might want to be a father to Cody, but that did not mean she would open herself up to rekindling their romantic relationship. She was not going down that road again. "No matter what we do, Cody's going to be hurt."

"We can ease into it. Take it slow. Let him process."

She hated this—all of it. The tension and confusion, the hurt she knew Cody would feel, the fear and dread of what the future might bring. *Hated it.* She'd set all of this into motion yet felt like she'd been swept up into a tornado, twirling round and round, and she couldn't get out. What waited for her if she did manage to escape? A long, hard fall into reality. "I know it has to be done. But I don't know what to say. How do you explain something like this to a child?"

"I don't know. We'll figure it out."

MARCUS WHEELED TOWARD THE PORCH, not so much nervous as palms-wet, heart-thumping, yellow-streak terrified. Now that the time had come to explain, he battled the voices in his head. The one agreeing with Skylar that they should wait until he and Cody knew each other better. Another voice pointed out all the time he'd already lost and the longer they delayed, the less time he had to be with his son. Those pending custody discussions wouldn't be easy because Skylar wasn't about to simply hand Cody over for some father-son time.

"Cody? We need to talk to you." Skylar walked ahead of him to where Cody sat on one of the porch chairs.

Cody's gaze shifted to Marcus briefly before moving back to his mom. "I said I was sorry."

Skylar snagged Cody's wrist and pulled him over to the two-person swing to sit. Marcus was thankful she didn't set the swing in motion so he was able to get close.

"I know you did. But the *reason* you attacked that girl concerns me."

"They all laughed at me, but she laughed the most," he said, more than a little defensive. "She *made* them laugh!"

Marcus watched as Skylar swallowed, then brushed her fingers through Cody's hair. "You do not have the right to *harm* someone for laughing at you. I know it *hurts* to be laughed at, but you should have come to me, not attacked her."

"I just wanted to tell 'em about my dad." He sniffled when his nose ran. Two big tears trickled down his cheeks. "'Cause they were all talking about their dads."

Skylar glanced at Marcus quickly, worry and fear readily apparent in her eyes.

"Your father is not a vampire. Honey, listen, I have something I need to explain to you. If I say something you don't understand, I want you to stop me and ask questions. Okay?"

Cody nodded and drew his knees to his chest, looping his arms around them.

"We've talked about how playing pretend and imagining a vampire dad isn't— Well, you think it's fun, but you know it's not real, right?"

Cody reluctantly nodded but there seemed to be a lot of hesitation in the effort.

"Honey, you had a daddy who loved you very much but he—"

"He got sick." More tears welled in his eyes.

"Yes, he got sick. But, Cody, you're old enough now to know something else. You see, before I married Daddy, I—" She glanced at Marcus, her gaze pleading. "This is impossible."

"Cody, what your mom is trying to say is that *I'm* your father. I'm your dad," Marcus said, voicing the words Skylar struggled to express. Okay, the truth was out there. Now they could answer Cody's questions.

But Cody didn't ask questions. He sat, pale and red-eyed, and stared at Marcus as though he had two heads.

Marcus cleared his throat and tried again. "Tom, the man you called daddy, was your stepfather. Do you know what that means?"

"It's another daddy. My friends at school have step-daddies."

"That's right." Skylar sounded breathless. And above Cody's head, Marcus saw her trembling hand close into a fist.

"Tom was your stepdaddy," Marcus said again, "and I'm very sorry he died. He was a good man. But all this talk about vampires, and you getting into fights needs to stop, because the truth is I'm your daddy."

Seconds ticked by. The silence was broken by the chirp of birds and loud outside voices of play.

"Cody?" Skylar whispered. "Do you have questions?"

"I like my daddy better."

Marcus accepted the news as best he could. "I'm sure Tom was a good father, but he's in heaven now."

"No, not him. *My* daddy. I like my daddy better because he's a vampire, and he can fly, and—"

"Cody."

"My daddy can do anything 'cause his legs *work!*"

"Cody, stop it," Skylar said.

His legs shot out as he jumped off the swing and ran toward the door.

"We're not through talking, Cody. Come back here," Skylar ordered.

"No! I like my dad. I want *my* dad. I don't want him!" He turned the lever to open the door, but it was locked. That's when he lost it. He began pounding on the door, hitting, kicking the wood, screaming to be let in. Chanting *"my daddy can fly"* as he sobbed. *"My daddy can run. You're not my daddy."*

Marcus knew it was the temper tantrum of an overwrought seven-year-old, but every scream stabbed him in the heart. Kicked him in the gut. He'd felt the same way when Skylar had told him she was pregnant. He'd been so deep in misery he'd known the kid was better off without him as a father.

Over time, his thinking and attitude had changed, but hearing Cody spout those very sentiments?

"Cody, stop. Stop." Skylar pulled the key card out of her pocket and opened the door.

Cody took off, his stomping footsteps and wails easy to track through the cabin.

Skylar stood at the threshold, her expression as torn and ripped to shreds as his insides. "I'm sorry."

Marcus gripped the wheels of his chair until the pain streaked up his forearms. "Me, too."

He stayed put until the door closed, then rolled down the ramp, wishing he could run, tackle something. Fly. Anything to be the man his son wanted him to be.

Five feet from the cabin, he heard Cody scream *no*. The sound of his son's wail and Skylar's low voice stilled his hands.

If he wanted to be Cody's father, the first thing he had to be was *there*. That meant sitting locked outside the door and listening to every wail, every word. Everything he deserved for not being there for Cody in the first place.

THE SUN HAD SET BEHIND the mountains by the time Skylar emerged from Cody's room. Calming him had taken longer than she'd anticipated and she wondered if Marcus had waited or given up and left.

He had to be upset about the things Cody had said in his tantrum. Could she repair the damage? She'd antici-pated his anger and confusion, but had never expected the rejection because of Marcus's legs. Her heart broke seeing the instant flash of pain and humiliation on Marcus's face.

The door opened with a bit of a squeak. She winced and hoped the noise didn't wake Cody, then stepped through.

So Marcus had waited.

The air was charged with his emotions, and she could see what waiting had cost him.

Their eyes met, locked, and her pulse thudded hard the way it had years ago when they'd dated. Would that ever go away?

She wished it would.

Wished it wouldn't.

Wished…

"How is he?"

She tucked her fingers in her back pockets and shrugged. "Restless. He'll probably sleep most of the night, though, and wake up really early in the morning. I think it's best if he gets some rest. We haven't stuck to a schedule since we've been here and he's been up too late, not sleeping enough. It's no wonder he had a meltdown."

"I'm sure realizing his father is a wheelchair user didn't help."

Skylar moved toward Marcus with the intention of sitting on the swing, only to pause beside him and lean against the railing.

Guests roamed the area, going to or returning from dinner. Through the lower limbs of the ponderosas, she saw a fire blazing in the pit, heard the strains of instruments being tuned for the night of music listed on the events calendar.

"Marcus, you have to remember he's seven. He

didn't mean the things he said earlier. He just needs time. You really didn't expect him to come running into your arms, did you?"

He wiped his hand over his face. "No, I didn't expect that. I'm not sure what I expected."

But he'd clearly hoped for more. To be honest, so had she despite her fears. "You wanted him to know."

Marcus's blue eyes gleamed in the remaining light of day. "Wouldn't you?"

The naked longing on his face eased some of the worry she felt over Cody's reaction. Time had passed for Marcus, too. She wasn't the same person she'd been then and she had to remember that he wasn't, either.

She gave into impulse and reached out, waiting for Marcus to take her hand. He did. It took a deep breath to ignore the *zing* of electricity that traveled up her arm. "We talked and I told him that he was born after your accident and that we felt it best not to stay together. Some kids in his class have divorced parents, so I think he understood." Marcus's gaze narrowed on her, so much so she fought the urge to squirm. "What?"

"You took up for me? You didn't tell him what I did? What I said to you?"

His hand tightened on hers, making it impossible to pull away. "No, I didn't. I've seen the damage done when parents drag kids into custody battles. I won't do that to Cody. I hope you will always show me the same respect, no matter what happens between us."

"You have my word."

She tried to free her hand but Marcus wouldn't let go. "Marcus…"

"Come here." Without warning he tugged and she stumbled forward. He snagged her around the waist, guiding her onto his lap. His wheelchair didn't have arms, so her knee bumped against one wheel and she winced. "Ow."

"Sorry."

She sat stiff in his arms, as far away from his body as she could get considering his arms were made of steel. "Marcus, what are you doing?"

"You're giving me a crick in my neck from looking up at you. I'm giving you a seat."

Skylar barely dared to breathe. He smelled like wood and fire and the spice of cologne, the scent of the outdoors. But more than anything, she was aware of the changes in his body. He was bigger and broader than when they'd been together, his strength undeniable. "I'll sit on the swing."

"Why? You're already here."

"Marcus—"

"I like your hair like this." He slid his fingers through the length.

When they were together, she'd worn a short bob, but Marcus had always preferred her hair longer.

"You look good, Sky."

She swallowed at his husky tone. Knew if she spoke, he'd hear exactly how much his touch affected her.

They were in the deepening shadows at the end of the porch, in their own little world. And staring into his eyes, the heat of his body seeping into hers as the air cooled, she could almost...*almost*...forget the way she'd nearly drowned in him.

Even though her mind screamed at her to run, when Marcus stroked his knuckles against her cheek, she allowed him to brush her mouth with his. She heard a sound escape but wasn't sure if it came from her or him. All she knew was that the slight touch of their lips wasn't enough as their past swept over her.

Her lips parted, let him inside. She felt the press of his hand against the back of her head, positioning her so he could deepen the kiss until every thought fled, chased out by the awareness of what was happening now. The intensity was there. The rush of a wildfire, the frantic flow of white water on a river, rolling and tumbling, churning as it raced.

Marcus's hands shifted to her waist, pulled her closer. Up, over her ribs, stopping just shy of her breast. Another sound escaped, this one undeniably hers.

"People are coming," he whispered against her mouth. "Shh…"

He tried to follow the words of warning with another kiss but she used the dose of reality to scramble off his lap. He couldn't protest too vigorously because they were very much public.

"Skylar, wait. Invite me in so we can talk about this." He turned his chair to follow her dash for the door.

"No. Good night, Marcus."

"It's still there," he said, his tone low and full of desire. "That's amazing, don't you think? That after everything we've been through, it's still there."

She'd always gotten the shivers whenever he spoke in that bedroom voice. "I have no idea what you're talking about."

"You can't deny it, sweetheart." He flashed her a grin. "You're still into me."

The assertion of ego brought her fighting spirit to the forefront. "You're the one who dragged me down for a kiss. If anything, that makes you into me. And don't think for a second I believe you kissed me for any reason other than you suddenly want to be a part of Cody's life. What, do you think this is a two-for-one deal?"

"I won't deny still being into you," he said. "I always have been. As to why I kissed you, trust me, sweetheart, Cody had nothing to do with it."

The answer left her reeling. "What are you doing?"

He gave her a leisurely once-over. "I'm doing what I should've done that day in the hospital. I'll be back tomorrow to see Cody." He paused, then added, "And you."

The husky sound of his voice sent her mind down dangerous memory-laden paths. She crossed the threshold and locked the door firmly behind her before collapsing against the cool wood. Not hearing anything from the man on the porch, she bit her lip and glanced through the peephole to see what he was doing.

Marcus hadn't moved. He sat staring at the door. Seemingly right at her.

Finally he turned, his whistle sounding way too smug as he rolled off into the night.

She twisted and slid to the floor, her back against the wood. How had things gotten so turned around? Out of control?

Marcus had kissed her. Said he was into her. But why? Because of old times? Or because he'd decided he wanted Cody and was willing to do whatever it took to get him? Marcus was competitive. Smart.

Either way, the thrill surging through her body was undeniable, leaving a lot of questions about what she would face in the coming weeks given Marcus's whistling departure. "Oh, *crap.*"

Chapter 10

SKYLAR WOKE UP TO THE unmistakable sensation of something crawling into bed with her.

"Mom?"

She smiled and rolled over, appreciating the feel of Cody snuggling close. "Good morning. You're up early."

He nuzzled his face into the material covering her shoulder as he always did before settling against her side. "It's late. I'm dressed. See?"

Opening her heavy lids wider, she realized sunlight blazed behind the window coverings and the bedside clock read nine-thirty-four. "Wow, it is late, isn't it?"

They never slept this late at home. Usually they were up, fed and out to work or school or day care before seven. But sleep had eluded her and she'd spent more time pacing around the small cabin and thinking of every possible worst-case scenario than sleeping.

"What are we doing today?"

She knew what she wanted to do. Pack. Go home to New York. Leave the tension with her mother and her confusion over Marcus's kiss behind. But for Cody's sake, she couldn't. And the truth was she didn't want a relationship with her mother like the one Rissa had with her father. "What do you want to do today?"

"I don't want to go back to the art class."

In other words, Cody didn't want to have to see Marcus again. As much as she wanted to indulge him, she couldn't. The decision had been made. *And Marcus said he'd return.* "Art class is only twice a week. We don't have to worry about that today." She smoothed her hand over his back, feeling the little-boy sturdiness that would change into manly strength.

Children were young, *babies,* for such a short amount of time. Growing and learning so fast you couldn't keep up. One minute a newborn, the next a toddler, the next in kindergarten. However they arranged custody, she'd miss some of the precious time with Cody—long weekends, holidays, summer vacations. Her whole body ached at the thought. "Don't forget your father said he'd come see you today."

Beneath her hand, Cody tensed. "My daddy's a vampire."

She'd have to be deaf not to hear that the statement carried less conviction than before. "Cody, I know you're confused but remember what I said?"

"He's not my daddy. He's not!" He yanked away and scrambled for the edge of the bed.

Skylar grabbed him before he could get away and hugged him. "Shh. Listen to me." Her breath stirred the hair by his ear.

Cody's shoulder lifted as he rubbed at the offensive puff of air. "No."

"Everything is going to be okay," she said, speaking slowly and calmly. "I promise. Have I ever promised and not kept it? You'll see. It's going to be all right."

"No, it won't. He can't walk, and he can't fly. He can't do *any*thing. I want somebody else."

Her heart tugged at the bare emotion in Cody's tone. At the same time, it broke on behalf of Marcus. Even though Cody's words last night could be overlooked because of his age and distress, nothing could erase the pain they caused and she knew it. "We don't get to choose our family, Cody. But Marcus—your father—is *real*. That means more than an *imaginary* father who flies. Focusing on the fact your father can't walk or do those things is hurtful. He knows he can't do certain things and he probably misses doing them. You pointing that out is not nice."

Cody remained silent at her admonishment but his stomach growled long and loud, drawing a giggle from him and a smile from her. Ah, the short attention span of a child.

"I'm hungry."

"I can tell," she said, laughing and squeezing him, blowing a raspberry into his neck, and letting the heavy subject drop for the time being.

Giving Cody bits of information and letting him process it a little at a time was worth the frustration she felt at the situation. "Get up, go watch TV so I can get ready then we can feed that hungry belly."

"Okay."

She released him and he bounded off the bed and out of the room, as if the conversation had never taken place.

Later Skylar and Cody entered the dining area to find her mother and stepfather there with Riley in tow.

"Hey. This is a surprise. What's going on?" She was more than a little leery considering the last conversation she'd had with her mother.

"I thought I'd take my grandsons for a ride in my squad car this morning. You can each have a turn blasting the siren," Jonas said, smiling at Cody.

"Cool. Can I?" Cody asked.

"Actually, I was hoping Cody would hang out with me after my riding class."

As one, they turned to see Marcus behind them, his expression unreadable.

Skylar attempted to smile. "We, uh, told Cody that Marcus is his father yesterday."

Realizing her mother and Jonas were both gazing at Cody with concern, Skylar glanced down and saw Cody had hidden himself behind her and glared at Marcus. His hand snuck into hers.

"I wanna go with Grandpa."

Skylar swallowed, knowing this was the first of many instances like this. "Cody—"

"I want to go with *Grandpa!*" Cody screamed, his voice, his expression, pure panic.

"Let him go," Marcus said. "It's fine. Have fun with your grandpa, Cody. I'll come by and see you after you get back, okay? You can tell me all about it."

Marcus's expression indicated the situation was

anything but fine and Skylar was torn between not wanting to rush Cody more than necessary, and wanting Marcus and Cody to bond.

Marcus's confidence from last night seemed noticeably absent, and in its place was a man divided between wanting to spend time together yet not wanting to be the bad guy by insisting Cody do that.

"Mom, I don't wanna go with him. I wanna go with Grandpa!"

Marcus nodded once, sharp and hard. "I've got to get to class." Marcus wheeled away.

Despite the noise of the diners, the silence among them was deafening. Worse, it stretched, as though no one knew how to fill the gap Marcus left.

"I'm not hungry," Cody said abruptly. "Grandpa, can we go now?"

Skylar had to give her stepfather credit. He was the sheriff, a guy's guy. The first one to act or make a decision. But instead of immediately answering Cody's question, Jonas looked to her.

"Growing boys need food. Grab a waffle or granola bar. You can't come with that stomach of yours growling the whole way."

She released Cody's hand and nudged him toward the counter before turning her attention to Jonas. "Are you bringing him back here, or should I pick him up?"

"You'll be picking him up," her mother answered. "My charter canceled so you and I are going to Mandy's spa for an official mother-daughter day with Carly."

A mother-daughter day? Time to mend some bridges.

Skylar thought about protesting, because she suspected things would get testy at least once, but a glance at her parents told her it would be futile.

"It's my way of saying I'm sorry," Rissa said. "I shouldn't have said what I did. Will you forgive me?"

Relief poured through Skylar. "Of course. I'm sorry, too. I shouldn't have reacted the way I did. A spa day sounds great."

"Do you want to get something to take with you?" her mother asked.

Remembering Marcus's expression as he'd exited the building, her appetite fled and she shook her head. "I just need coffee."

The sooner she was off the ranch the better.

MANDY'S WAS NORTH STAR'S ONE and only salon and spa combination. It offered almost every service a NYC salon could offer at a fourth—maybe even a sixth —of the price.

"Feeling better?" Carly asked, smiling at Skylar from her chair. Five of her toes sported bright, coral-pink polish.

"I've melted," Skylar replied, settling in beside Carly for her manicure while Rissa shuffled into the massage room, carrying her cup of green tea. "This is awesome. When did this open?"

"A little over a month ago. Remember Mandy Blake from high school? She owns it. It's her brainchild."

"What?" Mandy had tormented them both in high school, and, more than once, Skylar had gotten in a fistfight protecting Carly from Mandy's cruelty. The fight in the library had started because *Mandy* had trash-talked Carly. "What the hell are we doing here?"

Carly laughed, drawing attention Skylar didn't want. "I knew your reaction would be priceless. Too bad she's not here to see it. She's said several times that she hoped to be around when you discovered we were friends again. Oh, Skylar, stop glaring. Mandy's changed, believe it or not."

"Not," Skylar said firmly. "Please tell me you haven't fallen for whatever crap she's spouting."

"She's *changed*," Carly said. "Hasn't she, Sarah?"

Skylar blinked, realizing the woman painting Carly's toes was also from their high school. Then again, anyone in town around their age would have gone to the small school, and she shouldn't be surprised at all.

"Definitely. That girl was paid back tenfold for all the drama she caused in high school," Sarah said.

"How's that?" Skylar asked.

"Her daughter." Carly exchanged a sympathetic look with Sarah. "She was bullied in school, even by her stepbrother, and Mandy experienced it all through her daughter's eyes. It gave her an entirely different perspective, humbled her. Now she's nice, and means it."

"I'll believe it when I see it." Skylar sincerely doubted someone could change that much. Go from mean, nasty evilness to kindness? Still, she felt sorry for Mandy's daughter.

"You'd better start believing it." Sarah grinned. "Because all your services today are free. Mandy's order. She called to check on things and when she heard you were here she ordered us not to take a dime in payment."

"What?" Carly said. "No, that's too generous."

"Hey, I'm under strict instructions. She said if you had a problem with that to swing by her house and talk to her yourself."

"She's pregnant and on bed rest," Carly explained.

"She still comes in every now and again," Sarah murmured. "We shoo her out as soon as we see her but I think she's lonely and wants some company. You should go see her. She'd enjoy that—especially seeing you." She grinned at Skylar, then gathered her supplies and instructed Carly to stay put.

After she walked away, Carly released a throaty laugh. "You look so freaked out right now."

"It's a lot to absorb."

"Yeah, took me a while to accept it, too." She lowered her voice. "Mom said you told Cody about Marcus."

Skylar glared at her sister, silently reminding her to keep quiet. Nothing traveled faster in this town than gossip—and having been the subject of those rumors many times as a teen, she knew this better than anyone. And everyone knew salon gossip traveled at ten times the speed of light. The most unassuming woman with her head crowned by a dryer could be listening with CIA intensity. "Keep it down."

"Do you think they don't already know?"

"We only told Cody last night."

"But Marcus told Ben the other day and the locals have seen you three together on the ranch. I've been fielding questions for days from my clients at the office."

She leaned her head back and groaned. "No wonder everyone got quiet when we walked in here."

"Well, that and the fact they don't often see New York chic. I'm having serious clothes envy and plan to raid your suitcase before you leave. Still, hard as it was, you and Marcus did the right thing. You've made Ben so happy—there's a spring in his step I haven't seen in years." Carly took a sip of her Diet Coke. "Besides, given the way you and Marcus were such an item, it's not like there weren't rumors all along."

That was not what Skylar wanted to hear.

"So how *are* you handling things?"

"Did Mom put you up to the inquisition?"

"Like I need Rissa's urging to be curious," Carly said. "What's going to happen? Have you and Marcus come to any agreements yet about visitation? Are you going to move here?"

"I have no idea. No visitation plans worked out and definitely no on moving here."

"Oh." Her sister's disappointment was visible.

"Carly, please don't start on me right now."

"I'm not starting anything. Yeah, I'd love to have you back. I *miss* you. And it would be so nice for Riley and Cody to be able to play together and be friends, grow up together. But I promise, I'm not starting in on you."

"That's not going to happen. I'm still not convinced telling Cody was smart, and I really don't want to fight with you when I've finally made a tentative truce with Mom, so can we change the subject?"

She knew how much her family liked living in North Star. While she could appreciate the town's charms, and certainly many of its inhabitants, she much preferred to live somewhere that provided more opportunity and potential experiences. Not to mention the anonymity of living in a big city. If she wanted to go to the store in her sweats, no one cared. Here it would be a sign that she was depressed or had given up, and six people would be waiting on her doorstep to intervene.

"What about the vampire thing? Has it helped with that?"

So much for changing the subject.

She thought of how Cody had crawled into bed with her, how he'd gotten quiet when she'd reminded him that Marcus was real, not make-believe. "It's too soon to tell. But the behavior isn't likely to change or disappear overnight."

Sarah headed toward them, pushing a cart full of nail-polish bottles. "What color are you feeling like today?"

Staring at the rows, Skylar picked up several colors only to put them down again when something else caught her eye. Finally she settled on a light purple color that matched her mood. "This one."

Sarah took the bottle from her and rubbed it between her palms. "Not many people pick this one. Dazed and Confused, it is."

MARCUS WENT TO CHECK ON OREO after his riding class, using the time to get his emotions under control—he'd barely held it together for the riders. While stroking Oreo's nose and whispering to her, he heard a noise in the loft above him and turned to find Lexi climbing down the ladder.

"Oh, hey, Marcus."

He eyed the loft again and listened closely but didn't hear anything else. "Hey, yourself. What are you doing out here at this time of day?"

She held up a book. "Reading. The twins wouldn't leave me alone. Guess I'd better go help Mom, though." Her expression was sheepish because her responsibilities on the ranch ranged from child care to food prep beneath her mother's talented tutelage, neither of which could be done in the barn loft.

"Guess so."

Lexi headed toward the door, but Marcus saw her glance up at the loft as she left.

Long seconds ticked past without a sound from the loft. "You can come out now. It's not like I can climb up there to get you."

Nothing. Not even the scratch of a mouse or the ranch's cat prowling for food. He might have almost thought he was wrong, except that the silence wasn't quite natural. "Suit yourself."

He gave Oreo the carrot he'd brought, and noted that she'd be foaling in the next day or so. No doubt Seth was aware of the change in Oreo's condition but Marcus would make a point of stopping by the house just in case. It would give him an excuse to hang around the ranch a bit longer in case Skylar and Cody returned.

He swore under his breath. Cody didn't like him and

he wasn't making any bones about it. How was Marcus to overcome that? He had to be honest, with himself at least. Cody's rejection stung, but things weren't going to get better without some effort on both their parts.

And when he thought of Skylar leaving and going back to New York, taking Cody with her…

Patience. You waited this long, a few more days isn't going to kill you.

He shook off the thoughts and forced himself to focus. What could he do to encourage Cody to spend time with him?

First, he needed to check if Seth had found another instructor, so he could free up some time for Cody. Hanging out on the ranch as much as he had in the past few days had put him behind on his commissioned pieces. With training, too. There was a marathon coming up in Washington State that he wanted to enter, but he wouldn't be able to if he got too far behind on his work.

Wheeling himself out the barn he looked back in time to see a bit of hay fall from the loft. He smirked and shook his head. Some things never changed. But in too many ways…nothing ever stayed the same.

Twenty minutes later, he'd tracked down Seth at one of the storage barns. He was scowling into its recesses.

"Something wrong, Seth?"

"Have you seen the portable air compressor?"

"No." Marcus wheeled closer. "Isn't it by the pool?"

"Should be, but it's not. Makes me wonder if O'Donnell made off with more than we thought," he said, referring to the riding teacher Seth had fired because he'd been stealing. "I was hoping someone had stuck it in here."

Seth shut the oversize doors, adding the padlock intended to keep any unauthorized visitors out. "I hear congratulations are in order."

Marcus shook the extended hand. "Thanks. Actually, that's why I wanted to talk to you. Skylar's here only three more weeks and I want to spend as much time as I can with Cody. I was hoping you'd found a riding instructor."

Seth took off his hat and wiped his forehead on his sleeve. "Not yet, no. But if you need to cancel a few of the classes, I understand."

"Thanks. Appreciate it. I've lost enough time as it is." Marcus debated bringing up the other topic that had him in knots. He trusted Seth, who had experienced so many of the same issues around his disability as Marcus had. Still, was it cool to talk to another guy about this stuff? "Seth, can I ask you something?"

"Never hurts to ask."

That hot session with Skylar last night had been the bright spot on what had turned out to be a crappy experience. He definitely wanted a repeat performance with her. What about the next step? He was a confident guy, but certain things had changed.

"Was it hard for Grace to accept that you were… different after your injury?"

"I take it you and Skylar are working things out?"

Marcus shook his head. "No."

"But you'd like to."

"It would be the easiest way of settling the whole

custody issue about Cody," he said, unable to admit it would mean a whole lot more to him than that.

"Is that the only reason? Because of custody?"

He couldn't meet Seth's gaze. "No." Definitely not. Kissing Skylar had been a reminder of how good things could be between them.

"I didn't think so." Seth paused. "It wasn't as hard for Grace as it was for me. Grace was just like her name. Turned out I had the bigger issues. In a way, it was like going through how the injury changed who I thought I was all over again." He indicated the wheelchair with a sweep of his hand. "You think Skylar can't handle it?"

"I don't know. It hasn't exactly come up but…"

"You want to be prepared if it does."

A man could dream, couldn't he? Despite his anger that she'd married someone else, despite his fury that another man had raised his son while he'd let it happen, his feelings for Skylar were as strong as before. Undeniable.

Yeah, he had a boatload of regrets and issues to work through but it didn't change certain things, one of which was that he wanted them. Both of them. But he didn't want Skylar thinking the *only* reason he wanted her was because of Cody.

Marcus looked up when Seth's hand landed on his shoulder and squeezed.

"I know things between you two are rough right now, but Skylar has never struck me as a woman who couldn't look beyond the surface."

Swallowing, Marcus nodded but wound up staring at his shoes for his next question. "I guess the real question is how do I get her to trust me again? Not only for the other girl, but by turning her away when she was pregnant? What kind of man does that?"

"I did the same thing. I pushed Grace and everyone else away because I couldn't handle what happened. I figured they couldn't, either."

"How did you get them back?"

"I found myself, as stupid as that sounds. I had to learn to be the man I'd become before I could move on to anything else. And I fought for them. Took some convincing with Grace, let me tell you. But in the end, it was worth all the hoops she made me jump through. She had some stuff to work through, too—things that happened to her before we were together. Things that made her afraid to believe I could love her the way I do."

Seth's words reminded Marcus of all Skylar had been through. How she'd pushed him away, and when she'd finally come to him he'd done the pushing. Between the two of them they really were a mess, weren't they?

If he let Skylar set the pace, he knew she would be back in New York without a single close encounter between them. But remembering how she had kissed him back last night... Granddad had always told him every man needed a mission, a goal to set his sights on, so he didn't find himself wandering around lost.

Marcus's mission? To fight for the family it had taken him eight years to be brave enough to embrace. And the first step was reminding Skylar of how good they were together.

Chapter 11

"CARLY AND RISSA FINALLY let you escape?"

Skylar looked up from her cell phone to find her brother-in-law, Liam, heading toward her outside the police station. He was fresh from his patrol and looking a little worn at the end of the afternoon but she certainly saw the reason Carly was attracted to him. The man was hot, and from what she remembered of him in high school, not a bad guy. "Had I known the destination you probably would've had to come rescue me from Carly's trunk."

He chuckled at the news, not something she thought he was prone to do all that often.

After their appointments at the salon, Carly had insisted they grab some food from the diner and visit Mandy. Her mother had left them to head home. And because Mandy *had* given them the day at the salon free of charge, how could Skylar say no to a visit Carly promised would be short?

The experience was…surreal. Good, once the ice

was broken and things weren't so awkward, but weird, too. Skylar had never thought she'd spend an afternoon in her high-school tormentor's company that ended in an awkward hug rather than a right hook.

A wry smile formed. It just went to show how much people could change—if they tried. No doubt she fell into that category, too, but she'd like to think she'd never possessed Mandy's viciousness toward other people. The principal at Cody's very pricy private school frequently talked about how we're often the first to point out other's flaws but the last to see them in ourselves. He'd probably get a kick out of the story. Today definitely went down in history as a very unusual day.

"Surprised?"

"Totally." Skylar wondered how long it would be before the shock of Mandy's attitude change wore off. "It's a nice change, though."

"Yeah," he agreed. "Carly was surprised, too, when Mandy first showed up at her door."

"Your name came up a time or two. Did you really find Carly walking on the road after a date gone bad?"

He grinned and readjusted the Western-style hat that came with the deputy uniform. "She had a knack for choosing the wrong dates."

"But you got her straightened out?" Skylar teased.

Once more, Liam smiled but shook his head. "It was mutual. She and Riley straightened me out, too."

She looked around the sheriff's department. Cluttered desks, stacks of paper and files dominated. "I thought Jonas would have been back by now. He's had the boys all day."

"I saw them coming out of Porter's with ice cream cones as I drove into town. I'm sure they'll be here soon." Liam perched himself on the edge of a desk. "Carly told me the news. Cody doing okay?"

"Not really. Would you be?" Almost as soon as the words exited her mouth, she winced, remembering that Liam had been reunited with his biological father last year during the worst possible time—immediately following the death of his adoptive father, Zane McKenna.

Carly had told Skylar that it had taken Liam quite a while to adjust to the fact that the often-out-of-work and once-heavy-drinking drifter was his father, but the fact that Charlie had spent several summers working at the Circle M as a ranch hand prior to the revelation had helped. Zane had recognized Charlie's interest in Liam and his physical resemblance to the son Zane had adopted, but Charlie had kept his distance and his mouth shut until Zane's final request demanded the father and son come to terms. "I'm sorry. I forgot."

"Not a problem. Actually that's kind of why I brought it up. Discovering you have a father alive and well out of the blue is no small problem to deal with as an adult. I can only imagine what that's like to a kid. He'll come around, but it could take some time."

"Any advice?"

"Let it happen at his own pace. Pushing will only make Cody dig in his heels."

"I guess if I think it's too much for us, it's got to be too much for him, right?" She searched the street in front of the building for any sign of Jonas and the boys.

"Kids are adaptable."

"I know. I just hate the thought of telling Cody the truth, only to find it makes his fantasizing worse."

"I'm no shrink, but even I know kids develop at different rates. Cody's a little more immature than Riley, but his life was hard until he came to us. I'd sacrifice anything to give him back that innocence and immaturity."

She hadn't thought of it that way. She'd been so focused on what Cody's teachers and counselor and the child psychologist had said that she hadn't considered the fact that she might be rushing Cody to develop more quickly than he was ready to.

"Let him have time and space. I can't say Charlie and I will ever win father-son of the year but after Zane passed away it's nice to know I have more family than I did before. One day Cody will appreciate that you did what you had to do. Marcus is a good man, same goes for Ben. They're both men Cody can look up to."

She hoped Liam's words were true. Right now, Cody was too upset to see anything but the fact that his father wasn't the other-worldly hero he'd imagined. But maybe eventually Marcus might be a hero in the making.

"A lot of guys would've tossed in the towel if they'd been in Marcus's place."

"I know." Marcus had made a remarkable comeback, not only finding a new outlet for his athleticism and competitiveness but a new career, as well. And the fact he'd achieved so much drew her to him. The ability to triumph, to succeed despite the odds, was attractive to her.

"Have you seen him in his racer? I clocked him doing forty-six miles an hour one time. Thought I was seeing things."

"He's always been an athlete."

"Damn good one, too. The Cowboys lost a lot when Marcus was injured. Ah, there are our boys," Liam said. "Look at those grins."

Skylar saw Jonas outside the window, leading his grandsons toward the station. While not biologically his, Jonas had accepted both boys without reservation, loving them.

Her mother and Jonas were upset with her because she married Tom even though he wouldn't be around to see Cody's double-digit birthdays. But that kind of thinking implied that life came with a written guarantee. That those decisions meant you'd live to a ripe old age and your children wouldn't have to deal with your death until they had grandchildren of their own. No one knew what the future had in store. What kind of child would Cody be if he hadn't had Tom in his life? There was no guarantee that had she waited around for Marcus to change his mind or raised Cody on her own that he wouldn't have still fantasized about vampire fathers.

"Looks like they've had a good day, eh?" Liam said.

It did. Cody and Riley were so cute, following their grandpa with their ice-cream-covered faces, beautiful smiles and badges pinned to their chests. One glance at her son told her that he was engaged in the conversation, present in the here and now rather than the fantasies in his head.

Coming to Montana *had* been a good strategy on her part. She had to keep reminding herself of that.

"Hi, Mom. You look pretty," Cody said when he saw her waiting for him.

"Thank you. You look like you've had a good day with Grandpa. Yeah?"

"It was awesome. We got to do the siren, and play with the handcuffs."

She and Liam both laughed at that. "Well, I hate to end the fun, but we need to get going. We've got a long drive to the ranch."

After goodbyes were said and hugs given, Skylar made sure Cody was fastened into his seat belt before heading out of town.

"But why do I have to go?" Cody demanded for the dozenth time since they'd left the outskirts of town. "I wanted to stay with Grandpa."

"Grandpa has to get some work done today."

"But I'm tired, too. I don't wanna see Marcus. I wanna watch TV. And you said I could call and talk to Tate," he said, referring to his best friend who lived in the apartment next to theirs.

"You can call Tate later. He's probably at his music lesson right now."

"I need to take a bath," he said finally, his tone cajoling. "I'm dirty."

Clearly he really didn't want to see Marcus. A typical boy, Cody *never* volunteered for baths. "I know this is all really confusing for you, but your dad wants to get to know you."

"No. I don't want him."

Skylar tried to keep her frustration out of her voice. "Cody, I know you're young but you know we don't get to pick who we have for family. That includes mommies and daddies."

"I want you. Just not him. Why can't I have my old daddy? Why do I have to have a new one?"

Okay, so how frank should she be? "Listen—"

"Why did you and Daddy lie? Mrs. Carter says not telling the truth about something is *lying*. Why'd you lie about me?"

How could she possibly get him to understand something so complicated? Something she wasn't even sure she understood entirely herself?

"If I have to have a new dad and he can't be a vampire, I want a cop dad like Uncle Liam and Grandpa."

The headache that had formed ever since Cody had begun his round of questions sharpened as the tension in her shoulders mounted and twisted her muscles into a pretzel. So much for the benefits of her massage. "That's not how things work, Cody. Your father is Marcus." Hesitating briefly, she struggled to spin the conversation in a positive way. "Did you know Marcus played football? He was a quarterback for the Dallas Cowboys. That's pretty cool, isn't it?"

"Yeah. But he can't play now."

No, he couldn't. And while she really didn't want to list Marcus's admirable qualities, she was at a loss for another way to get Cody to see Marcus as the capable man he was. The man who'd lived and lost a dream, only to turn around and build a new life as a metal artist. His workshop was amazing. Maybe taking Cody there to see Marcus work would help show Cody his father's abilities?

"Yeah, well, he also races wheelchairs. Uncle Liam told me how fast Marcus can go." She glanced in the rearview mirror to see Cody staring out the window, his eyes glassy with tears. "Cody, baby, I know this is confusing for you but your dad wants to see you. To get to know you."

"*No.* I don't want to. I won't! He's going to take me away!"

She rolled to a stop outside their cabin. She hurried to get out of the car, shoving the seat forward to give one hundred percent of her attention to him. "Cody, take a deep breath and listen to me. Are you listening? Baby, no one is going to take you away."

Big tears ran down his cheeks, his mouth trembled. "You promise? You won't let him make me live with him the way Jack's dad did?"

"Oh, Cody." So that's what this was about. A nasty custody battle had waged over a little boy in his class. The father had eventually won full custody, and Jack had disappeared after a heartbreaking goodbye party to help the kids cope with his leaving. But to this day, whenever they saw Jack's mom in their neighborhood, she teared up at the sight of Cody.

Skylar helped Cody unbuckle, then held him in her arms and felt the shivers of fear run through him. "Never," she whispered.

. . .

"SO, I WAS WONDERING…" LEXI said five minutes after she'd shown up at Skylar's cabin door with a bag of plastic containers carrying dinner.

Maura was a godsend. Skylar had spent some cuddle time with Cody before filling the tub with bubbles and Cody's action figures and pulling the door mostly closed. With her mother's ear, she heard Cody alternating between different voices for his toys, and songs he'd learned in school.

"Wondering what?" she said, removing her plate from the microwave and placing Cody's inside.

"What do you think about older men?"

She froze, the fork lifted halfway to her mouth.

"I'm only asking because…well." Lexi looked decidedly uncomfortable. "I heard Mom telling Dad that you have a thing for older men, too."

Too? Wasn't family great for always remembering the past? "Oh?"

"Yeah, that guy in New York. And then Tom."

Skylar wondered if she'd ever rid herself of the regret and humiliation she felt at being such a fool when it came to Rick. But at the time, she'd known exactly what she was doing, even if the consequences of her actions had been beyond her comprehension. "Lexi, I'm not proud of what I did. Not at all. If I could change that about myself, I would. In a heartbeat."

"But how can you say that? Tom was older, too, and you married him. Does that mean you wouldn't marry him now?"

Skylar set the fork down and shoved her plate away.

She'd eat later. Maybe. "How old are you talking about exactly?"

Lexi wore a tank top and shorts, which revealed her thermometer-like reaction. A bright red flush crept up her chest, neck and shoulders into her face, all the way to her forehead. "Not as old as that guy you first hooked up with. Or Tom."

"I see," Skylar said, wondering if anything else from her past would come back to haunt her while she was in Montana.

"Skylar, don't be mad. *Please.* Mom didn't mean anything by it. She used you as an example for why I should date guys my age."

I'm an example of what not to do? "Are you dating someone your own age?"

"Yeah. At least, she thinks so."

"Spill it, Lex."

Lexi got off the stool and paced into the living room. She didn't have far to go, but the longer she waited to say whatever was on her mind, the more nervous Skylar became.

"You won't tell anyone, will you?" Lexi asked.

Yeah, *that's* what she was afraid of. "Are you drinking, doing drugs or taking part in anything that might endanger your life? Wait, before you answer that last one, think about all the ways that's possible. You've had sex ed."

More blushes abounded. "It's not like that."

"No?"

"No. Not yet."

Oh, boy.

"A little while ago I went out with this guy who turned twenty-one and Dad flipped because he thought the guy was too old."

"But that's not the guy you're dating now?"

"No. He was a total jerk."

Skylar struggled to follow. "So who are you dating?"

"This boy my age and he's great. He's nice, but we're not exclusive or anything."

"Because?"

"The only reason I'm dating him is to make Dad happy. But I'm seeing someone else."

The picture was becoming clearer. "The older man."

"Yeah. I mean, he's a little older. Not a lot." Lexi rushed to reassure her. "But Dad would freak because he's over twenty-one, you know? Besides, isn't age all relative?"

Wasn't that the catch phrase to use when you were underage and wanted to get something by someone?

The worst thing any adult or parent could do was say something to push a kid deeper into a situation that already tantalized them. And Lexi's body language, her tone, the words she used, said she was way more than tantalized already. "In the scheme of things," Skylar said neutrally. "How old is he, exactly?"

As though suddenly aware of how much she'd already revealed, Lexi hesitated. "Twenty-five."

Twenty-five. To her seventeen? Not a huge difference, but a world of difference between a teenage girl and an adult male. "Oh, Lex."

"You're judging me. I thought you, of all people, wouldn't judge."

"Lexi, I'm not judging. But for me to understand what's going on and what you're struggling to say, I need more information. What are we talking about here?"

"I don't want to go to school in Washington State. It's too far away. So I'm dropping out of the nursing program."

"What? But Maura said you had received a full-ride scholarship. Tuition, books, expenses—everything. She said it's one of the top-ranked schools in the country."

"It is. But I don't want it. And I need you to tell me how to tell my parents I'm not going to college."

Oh, crap. Skylar reached to find a seat because of the sudden weakness in her legs. Didn't she have enough on her plate without this? "You can't give up school, Lex. No man worth having would ask you to do that for him."

"He didn't ask me. But I want to. Skylar, I love him. I want to be with him. If you knew him, you'd understand. He's so sweet, and smart and kind and he loves me, too."

Yeah, she'd just bet. "Lexi, of course he says he loves you but—"

"But it's not true? Is that what you're saying? That he isn't the one?"

The one?

Don't dig a hole. Stay neutral. "I'm saying you are a beautiful, lovable girl. You're old enough to know that when a guy is on the make, he'll say almost anything to get in your pants," she said bluntly.

"It's not like that. He's— Skylar, that's part of why I like him. He's so shy and he's been the perfect gentleman. If anything, I'm the one in danger of jumping him!"

Skylar closed her eyes at the news. "I strongly suggest you don't say that to your father."

"I'm just trying to tell you that there's more to us than that. A lot more. When I'm with him I forget about time and problems and— I only want to be with him."

"Hon, you'll have breaks. You can see him when you come home. Are you really prepared to give up your future? You've *always* wanted to be a nurse."

Lexi shook her head slowly. "I thought I did but now… I don't know."

"But you think he's the one? Lex, you're *seventeen*. You'll meet lots of guys if you give yourself a chance. Do you really think out of a world full of men there's only one for you? That you've met him now, before you've even taken a glance outside North Star?"

"When he's around, I think about the future. I think about having a house and kids, having Christmas together. That means something."

Oh, what could she say to Lexi to convince her not to do this? Not to give up her future?

"I thought for sure you'd understand. I mean, that guy Rick was your *dad's* age and you were *younger* than me. And then Tom— Why do you think I came to you? I need you to help me figure out how to tell my parents so they won't freak out."

Thankfully Cody was still singing in the tub. Good thing, too, because right now Lexi's bombshell took all

Skylar's concentration. "First, I think they're going to freak out over the news no matter what. Second, one of my biggest regrets is meeting Rick. If I could change it, Lex, oh, I would. And I was a senior in college and had already found a job in my chosen career when I married Tom. I wasn't just out of high school."

"But you and Marcus were together."

"We didn't live together."

"Close enough, and you were only a couple of years older than I am."

Maybe so, but she had been a lifetime more mature. She hadn't lived the sheltered, small-town existence Lexi had. As Liam had said today, once the innocence is gone, you can't get it back, no matter how hard you try.

"You think I'm too young to talk about all this, even though I know exactly what I want?"

Yes! "Hear me out, okay? You can talk to me about anything. But before things go further with either one of these guys, I hope you'll really think hard about the consequences. How is the guy your age going to feel when he finds out you're using him as a cover?"

"He'll be hurt."

"That's putting it mildly, don't you think? And what I did when I was fourteen? It's obviously still being talked about today, despite the fact that I really wish it would go away and never come up again. You have to think about the future, not tomorrow or next week or next month, but five *years* from now. Ten. Where is this older guy going to be? You have to be realistic here. If you give up that scholarship now and you break up with this guy next week—what then? Do you see what I'm saying? The things you do now *will* impact your life in the future. Promise me you'll remember that."

"I promise," the girl said softly.

"So who's this man?"

Lexi crossed her arms over her chest, a thoughtful expression on her beautiful face. "He's just a guy. He stopped to help me one day when I had a flat tire, and we started talking. If I were older, no one would say anything."

"But you're not older. Not yet. That's why you're keeping him a secret from your parents. And the fact that you think you can't tell your parents should be a sign. Besides, if he's the great guy you say he is, trust me, he'll wait."

Lexi turned away, but not before Skylar saw her roll her eyes and make a face. She'd lost Lexi's interest. She'd come across too much like a mother and not enough like the teenage confidant Lexi was hoping to find. "Look, Lex—"

"I should be going."

"Sit," she ordered firmly. "I have one more story to tell you."

Lexi performed another eye roll, but did as ordered.

"I know how much you love Marcus, but what if I told you he wanted me to drop out of school and give up my life for his career, back when he played football?"

"I'd say you're crazy for not doing it," Lexi countered. "You could've traveled with him. Been together. Why did you say no?"

"Because where would I have been if I'd given up my schooling and degree to be with him, only to break up later—exactly like we did? Lexi, even then, I knew it was a bad idea to not be self-sufficient. That's what I'm trying to tell you."

"But not everyone is like you. I don't want to live in a big city or have a career. I just want a job and a little house and to be a wife with a family."

Wife? *Wife?* "You're too young to decide that now."

"Says who? So many kids my age don't have a clue what they want, but I do. Young or not, I *know.*"

"Okay, fine. But what about the guy? Sweetie, how many guys have you dated? Having some chemistry doesn't mean you're meant to spend your life together."

"And if I say it's more than chemistry? I remember when you met Marcus. I remember how you acted, but now— You act like you don't even believe in love. Like you're afraid of it."

The ring of her cell phone interrupted them, and being closest to it, Lexi picked it up. "It's Marcus."

Panicking, Skylar accepted the phone, but didn't answer it. "I can call him back."

"No, go ahead. I have to help Mom anyway. Remember, you can't say anything. You promised," Lexi said quickly as she hurried out the door.

Skylar sat in stunned silence, replaying the conversation in her head, steering clear of Lexi's comment about being afraid of love and focusing on the one about how Lexi wanted to be a wife. At seventeen?

The phone rang two more times. And because she needed to talk to Marcus while Cody was still occupied, she pressed the talk button and braced herself. "Hi. I meant to call you, but Lexi stopped by to talk."

"Everything okay?" Marcus asked.

"I don't know. We'll see."

"How's Cody?"

"Fine. He's taking a bath."

"By your tone of voice, I take it he didn't want to see me?" Marcus murmured.

"He just needs time." She was tired of repeating that. While it may be true that they all did need time, it felt as though they were making excuses.

"Yeah. Maybe tomorrow," he said finally.

"Maybe."

Another couple of seconds ticked by. "I need your support with him, Skylar."

She closed her eyes, her fingers clenched around the phone. Of course he did. That was a problem they had faced in the past, too. Marcus expected her to support him no matter what. Blindly, wholeheartedly. Even if it meant going against her deep-seated instincts. "I'm doing the best I can. You can't expect more from me than that."

She pressed the button to end the call and reminded herself that she should feel relieved she didn't have to deal with seeing Marcus again today, especially after the trying conversation with Lexi. Had her threats about no college and wanting to be a wife been sincere? Or said for shock value?

The verbal battles left Skylar's mind racing with long-buried memories and frustrations of how Marcus had always been such a dominating, competitive man, and how those qualities clashed with her own thoughts about independence.

Marcus's about-face with Cody forced her to play mediator between them. Marcus pushed for her to help Cody accept his father, Cody pushed for her to keep Marcus away. For her, it was a no-win deal.

Try as she might, she couldn't decide which was best.

Chapter 12

THEY WERE AVOIDING HIM. MARCUS came to that conclusion around noon the next day after he'd circled their cabin, the dining hall and the riding stable —twice—with no sign of Skylar and Cody.

He'd thought maybe Skylar would bring Cody for the art class, but they didn't show. There was no sign of them anywhere else he could think to look around the main buildings.

"Hey, Marcus," Lexi said. "Heading out for a roll?"

He turned to see Lexi approaching from the ranch garden, a basket of fresh lettuce balanced on her hip. "Yep."

"Need to burn off some steam?"

"Something like that."

"Seems to be a lot of that going around," she murmured.

When he raised an eyebrow, she shrugged. "Skylar took off a while ago for a run. She seemed just as antsy as you to get some distance."

Marcus strapped his gloves over his hands. "Cody around?" he asked, wondering if he could manage some one-on-one time.

"He's in town, playing with Riley."

"Which direction did Skylar go?"

Lexi grinned. "If I tell you, she'll get upset with me."

"Lex, come on. Tell me. I saw your daddy the other day and neglected to mention how you were doing some *reading* in the barn loft."

Lexi's cheeks turned red. "I *was* reading. And she went that way." She pointed toward one of the older ranch roads. "But you might as well wait—a storm's rolling in."

"I can beat it."

Marcus didn't waste any time. He put his arms to work and was about five miles from the main buildings and pondering what his next move with Skylar would be if he caught up with her, when a jagged streak of lightning lit the sky in front of him. Several seconds later, he heard thunder boom and felt the wind pick up. The storm was rolling in over the mountains fast.

His arms ached, but he kept going, knowing there was shelter ahead, past the turnoff toward the McKenna property line. After all, what attracted lightning? Metal—and he was sitting in it.

The air turned heavy and thick. Lightning flashed and thunder rolled again, the ground shaking from the force. He was rolling right into the heart of it. Where was she?

He was still rolling as fast as his arms could pump, determined to reach that line shack. With properties as vast as these ranches, the shacks were built for workers to take emergency shelter when the weather got tough.

Working on the ranch throughout his teen years, he'd used most of them at one time or another. Had Skylar made it that far?

Maneuvering the racer across the field to the shack might end him nose-first in the grass, and there was no doubt he'd get drenched in the process. Head down, he raced the storm, exhilarated by the challenge, squinting against the dust kicked up by the wind.

Almost there. Eight hundred meters. Six hundred. Three. Seconds passed, but he knew he'd made good time. Excellent time considering he'd traveled the last mile so quickly.

He eased down the slope into the field. Rain pelted down, hitting hard enough to actually sting. The lightning and thunder grew closer and the possibility of getting struck increased.

Finally he made it to the line shack and swung the racer around, rolling the modified wheelchair to the edge of the step required to enter the building.

The sky had opened up while he crossed the field, and his arms trembled with fatigue. He wasn't even sure the racer would fit through the shack's narrow door. So much for his cocky response to Lexi about being able to beat the storm.

Water rolled in a sheet over the roof's edge, drenching his head and back and filling the seat of the racer. As he tried to shove the modified wheelchair backward up the step, someone took hold of the chair and pulled hard.

The narrow door frame scraped his knuckles until he got his hands out of the way. Once through, he took control and moved until the edge of his wheels hit the wall behind him and there was enough room to close the door.

"Thanks." He wiped the water from his stinging eyes and tried to focus so he could see who'd helped him.

"You're welcome," Skylar said, her tone wary. "So, who do I need to thank for you following me?"

Wiping his eyes once more, he focused on Skylar, noting in an instant that while not as soaked as he was, she was damp—and cold.

He let his gaze sweep over her, lingering on the front of the sleeveless shirt she wore over a sports bra that was doing a piss-poor job of hiding her nipples. Her running shorts clung like a second skin to thighs he could all too easily remember being wrapped around him.

In an instant, his mind flashed to that long ago time they'd ridden to the lake for a picnic. He'd wanted to give her a pleasant memory of the area to replace the last time she'd been there and had gotten lost in the woods overnight. Before they'd reached their destination, an early snowstorm had come out of nowhere and forced them to take shelter in the closest shack.

Thunder boomed outside and, in that second, Marcus knew he wasn't the only one remembering. The air bristled with electricity that matched the ongoing rumbling and bright flash of light outside the single dirty window.

Reclaiming the blanket she'd apparently shrugged

off when she'd heard him, Skylar turned her back on him to dry off.

"Nevermind. I can guess who told you. I'm sorry about Cody."

"I heard he's playing with Riley."

"Yeah. Someone said they had seen you leave for the day so I told him it was okay."

"He seems eager to spend time with anyone but me."

"Are you surprised?"

The words hurt and he winced in response. Surprised, no. Disappointed? Definitely. "I suppose it's to be expected. But he's never going to get used to me and the way things are going to be if he's allowed to avoid me."

"*The way things are going to be?* You wanna rephrase that?" Skylar gave him a long stare over her shoulder before bending over to dry her long legs.

Marcus grimaced at his blunder, not meaning it the way it had sounded. He removed his right glove and wiped a hand over his face, tracing every line of her body and thinking of the statue he'd made a few years ago—a woman Skylar's size and shape, build. He'd simply titled it *Untouchable*. "You know what I mean."

"No, I don't. Why don't you tell me your version of *how things are going to be?*"

He recognized the signs of when she was spoiling for a fight.

His muscles started to twitch now that the rush of adrenaline was wearing off. The cold seeped in, but he focused on the bite of her tone instead of his rapidly cooling temperature. "What happened?"

"What do you mean?"

"Something happened to put you in this mood. What was it?"

For the first time since his arrival, she looked uncertain. "Cody had a meltdown on the way home from town last night."

"About?"

"He's confused and scared. He's afraid you're going to take him away from me."

Marcus wasn't sure what to say to that. "Is that what you told him? You made me out to be a bad guy who is trying to steal him from you?"

"Of course not. He has friends who have been caught in the middle of custody battles. And even though I've done my best to reassure him, he can probably tell my heart isn't it in it, since I can't forget the fact you *have* mentioned getting attorneys involved."

"To *see* him, Skylar, get to know him. I never said I'd take him away from you. I realize I don't have that right, considering the decision I made before he was born."

He could well imagine the trauma Cody would suffer if he was pulled out of the only home he'd ever known, away from the only stable parent he'd had since birth, to be brought here. As much as Marcus wanted to know his son, he didn't want to traumatize the boy or do something that would make Cody hate him forever.

Pulling up his shirt, he squeezed more water from the material. He was soaked through.

"Yeah, well, it's a little much to take in."

For him, too. But he knew Skylar well enough to know that when she was frightened of something, she got pissed. It was obvious she was fighting her fear of the future, as well. Maybe following her hadn't been such a good idea. At the moment, they were oil and water, stuck in a very small frying pan. "We all need time to adjust, but why don't the two of us use this opportunity to settle some things?"

"Like?"

"Visitation. Terms. Child support. I started a fund for Cody when you had him. It's been sitting there accumulating ever since he was born. What are your financials like?"

Sitting where he was, he saw her hands fist at her sides. "I have a well-paying job and Tom provided for us very well, thank you. I don't want your money, so save it for Cody. As to visitation, you can't expect me to put Cody on a plane and ship him here like some parcel. He's just a little boy."

"I'm very aware of that. But that means you need to plan on visiting often, then."

She muttered under her breath. Something like *here we go again.*

"Marcus, I have a job. A life. I can't hop on a plane and take off every few weeks or months."

He removed his other glove. "You're the one who said it's easier to fly two people here than your family—and mine—to New York," he reminded her.

Dropping the blanket from around her shoulders, she threw it at him, aiming for his face. He caught it with one hand. "Thanks."

Since it was apparent she meant for it to hit him in the face, he wasn't surprised she huffed over to the window, no doubt wondering how long she'd be stuck there before the storm ended. Thankfully there was no break in the cloud bank overhead. They weren't going anywhere. "Anyone know you're here?"

"Lexi. I texted her and told her I'd wait it out."

Even better. He had however long the storm lasted to negotiate amicable terms. "Thunderstorms still make you nervous?"

"No."

Yeah, right. With his study of art and form, he'd learned to read body language and hers reeked of unease. He knew the accident that had killed her father was the reason storms made her nervous. He knew she'd never gotten over it. Who would, considering she'd witnessed her father bleed out at the scene?

Whenever a strong system had blown through, he'd gone out of his way to make her forget about the thunder and lightning. His favorite memory of doing so had taken place at a beach house borrowed from a friend. As the storm rolled in off the ocean, he'd pressed her to the glass door and made love to her until the air inside the home sizzled as hot as the atmosphere outside.

"Stop looking at me like that."

He couldn't stop the flow of memories sliding through his brain any more than he could keep his gaze from sliding over her now. "Nothing like a thunderstorm in big sky country," he mused.

She didn't comment, but he refused to let the time

they would spend there together go by in silence. "Come on, Skylar, let's talk about this. Hash it out once and for all."

"I'm not giving up my life for you."

"I'm not asking you to. But this is home. Your entire family is here. More important, *Cody's* entire family is here. Is it too much to ask that you consider the possibility of moving?"

"Of course you think I should move. Give up my home, my job. My life. You expected it in Dallas and you expect it now. Why am I not surprised?"

It was common sense. Couldn't she see that? "It's the best solution."

"For you, not for me. And not for Cody. Marcus, North Star is great, but Cody is in a private school that is ten times—a hundred times—better academically. Why should he give that up and compromise his future? Why should I leave a job I love? A job that has me excited when I climb out of bed every morning? I work with hundreds of students and a school system that counts on me to be prepared once those doors open. Even if I didn't care about them—which I do—I have a contract I won't blow off. Especially after Travis. We're not moving to Montana. Period."

Why was she putting all of that before her family? And who the hell was Travis? "Who is that?"

"He's—*was*—one of my students. He committed suicide two months ago."

"I'm sorry." Skylar clearly had cared for the kid, and his death had rocked her.

"Me, too. I knew he was under a lot of pressure. I

knew there were issues but I never expected him to hang himself."

"Skylar, whatever the kid was going through, you're not to blame. If someone wants to kill themselves bad enough, they'll find a way."

"I know. But teen suicide often spawns more suicides or attempts. I keep weighing Cody's problems with the idea of another attempt and I'm not convinced I did the right thing by coming here."

"Are you using that as an excuse to get me to back off?" Because it wouldn't work. Yes, he felt for the kids at her school, but Cody was their son. He came first. Yeah, and what kind of hypocrite would he be to say that when he hadn't been involved in Cody's life until now?

"Marcus, my point is that you expected me to follow you like a puppy when you played for the Cowboys, to drop everything for your schedule. How many times do I have to tell you, that's not who I am? Why can't that crack that thick head of yours?"

Yeah, they had fought a lot about whether or not she should travel with him instead of attend classes. But he had hoped she would see that things had changed. He wasn't asking her to follow him on the game circuit, but to move *home*. Maybe after a while, after they settled into a routine, she would be more open to it?

"Fine," he said softly. "I'll fly to New York during school, and you and Cody can stay in Montana every summer—just like you have this year. Same with holidays. Ben doesn't travel much these days, but I know he wants to see his great-grandson."

"Oh, my— So that's it? I mean, I feel for Ben, but don't I get a say on where I spend my holidays? I'm sentenced to spend all my vacation time here?"

Was there no making the woman happy? "It's the beginning of an open discussion," he countered through gritted teeth, his frustration growing by the nanosecond because she refused to budge in her thinking. Concessions. That was the goal, right? Her work was important, he got that, but there were kids in need everywhere. "Both of our families are here. I can't think of another solution that would work as well as what I lined out."

"I don't agree!"

He remembered that Skylar's upset usually indicated fear. Why not call her on it? "Then why are you so angry? It's the best solution short of moving here. You just won't admit it."

She plopped onto the edge of the cot, her knuckles white in the dimness of the shack.

"What if we want to spend Christmas in New York? What about the holidays when I need to work? What then? How do we decide who gets to be with Cody? What about the times I can't travel?"

"Then we'll try to make other arrangements or I'll come to you," he said, cold chills beginning to wrack his body.

"Oh, for the love of— Get out," she ordered, frustration giving her words a bite.

Drying his hair with the blanket, he paused long enough to glare at her. "You're so pissed at me you'd kick me out into a storm?"

Skylar rolled her eyes and stomped over to the racer, shoved it toward the cot.

"You're soaked. Get out of the chair and sit on the bed so you and this thing can dry off."

Her words brought a smile—and more than a twinge of hope. "Care about me, sweetheart?"

Leaning over the racer as she was, Skylar began to pull away but he fastened his hands over her wrists, holding her in position.

When he knew she wouldn't go anywhere, he lifted his hand and palmed her cheek, tugging her lower. The rain pounded against the roof, enveloping them in their own little world. But before he could kiss her, she turned her head away.

"Marcus, no."

Pissed as she was, he backed off before she did something like head-butt him. Without further comment, he unlocked the belt at his waist, then transferred, aware all the while that Skylar watched him, the process. It made him very aware of the conversation he'd had with Seth about intimacy post-injury. She'd known him as an athlete, a football star. Not the way he was now. And he was a little leery about what might be running through her beautiful head.

Settled on the edge of the weatherproof cushion acting as the cot's mattress, he used the blanket to dry off.

"So, um, when's your next race?" she asked.

"Next month."

"What's your best time?"

Marcus recognized an avoidance tactic when he

heard one. He could either ignore her attempts to change the subject and press on with their discussion of visitation or let her have a moment to regroup. Considering seconds ago she'd been bending over his wheelchair and he'd had her breasts in front of him, she wasn't the only one needing to regain the ability to think straight. "One hour, forty-one minutes."

"That's great."

"It's okay. But not the best in the wheelchair division."

"Not all wheelchair athletes can go that fast—but don't let it go to your head," she countered. "Your ego is the size of Texas already."

He grinned at her comment and tried to ignore the way his teeth chattered. The near kiss had definitely warmed his blood but it hadn't taken the chill from his skin.

She twisted her fingers awkwardly as though she wanted to help but knew where it would lead. She poked around the cabin and found a sealed plastic bin in the corner containing another blanket, two ranching magazines, a couple of bottles of water. No food, though, since the scent would attract bears and other animals.

"Jackpot." She waved the folded blanket in the air.

Marcus pulled off his shirt and tossed it over the metal rod on the front of the racer. "Blanket's soaked now. Damn, that was a cold rain."

"It's always a cold rain. You can have this one." She held the blanket out to him. "You were out in it a lot longer than I was."

He scooted backward on the cot, settling against the

wall. He leaned forward to take hold of her wrist, not what she offered.

"You're freezing, too. Sit down. We both need to warm up."

"Is this where you give me some tired old line about needing to take our clothes off and share body heat? Because it's not going to work."

He wished she wasn't so stubborn. "We got naked together for years. If I want to see that again, all I have to do is close my eyes."

"Marcus, stop that."

"I see you," he whispered, grinning as he recalled a few of their more memorable moments. Yeah, that would heat him up.

"Stop it. I mean it. You have no right to be seeing me naked—even if it's in your mind."

He wished they could get along so easily on all fronts, especially the subject of Cody's visitation and future. "Why not? Because I'm thinking if you can't handle sharing a blanket to keep your teeth from chattering, that means there's something you're trying to deny."

"*No.*"

"No?"

"It means nothing," she said, visibly flustered. "Only that I refuse to let a little *chemistry* get in the way of common sense. I will always care about you, Marcus, but we can't undo what's been done. We can't go back in time."

His playful mood disappeared. "I'm very well aware of that." He thought about the football play that had cost him his legs. If he'd veered left instead of right, if he'd hesitated and faked a handoff, maybe things would have been different.

"It's not your injury."

Probably not. So how did he make up for what he had done? Would she ever truly forgive him? "You're giving me a crick in my neck again."

Visibly reluctant, she sat on the edge of the cot, her back to him unless she glanced over her shoulder.

"Comfortable?"

"I'm fine."

"Suit yourself." He spread the blanket over his chest but draped a corner over her shoulders. Her legs were covered with goose bumps. "Tell me about our son," he said. "Besides vampires, what does he like?"

"Boy stuff. He loves video games and his bike, playing with sticks."

"Is he interested in music?"

This time she laughed. "He wants to carry one of the big drums for his band class. It's what Tom did."

The reminder of the man who had acted as Cody's father didn't sit well with Marcus. Tom had lived the life Marcus could have had if he'd acted differently, made different decisions. Fact was, if he hadn't pushed Skylar so hard, maybe… "You loved him?"

"Yes." Her confident whisper rang out like a shot in the room despite the rain still pounding on the roof over their heads.

There was a river of regret between them. So much hurt. So much pain. But no matter how much they might wish it gone, it wouldn't disappear. "Why? I know

I probably shouldn't ask but I've always wanted to know. Why him?"

"Because he never asked more than I could give."

Muttering a soft curse at the way she shivered, Marcus wrapped a thick arm around her shoulders and tugged her down, until her back was pressed to his side, her head pillowed on his biceps, the blanket draped over her and enveloping them both. "Stop," he ordered when she immediately tried to pull away. "Don't fight me or you'll be the one cramping up."

Surprisingly, she didn't argue, which spoke volumes about her physical state. The entire time she'd been standing there, trying to pretend she was dry enough, warm enough, she hadn't been.

Seconds ticked by and gradually her trembling began to slow. "Better?"

She nodded, her cheek soft against his chest.

"Tell me what you mean—that Tom didn't ask more than you could give."

"I knew Tom was dying," Skylar said, her voice emotionless. "You said I'm angry because I married an older man who up and died on me, but that's not true. I knew what I was getting into. Tom was honest with me from the beginning, and he married me because we each had something the other wanted."

The scent of her hair filled his nose. "Cody?"

"Tom wanted a family. He didn't want to die alone."

No man did. And like it or not, Marcus felt a measure of sympathy for Tom. "What about you?"

"I didn't want to be alone, either," she whispered finally.

It was a struggle to control his frustration. If that was the case, why hadn't she stayed with him? Accepted his proposal? "You couldn't be with me, but you wanted him?"

"I don't know if you'll be able to hear this. Marcus, I had dreams—still do. But when we were together, I lost myself in you. To the point I wasn't me—I was only an extension of you. I went from planning my career to becoming an NFL player's girlfriend, who walked in your shadow. *Everything* revolved around you. Your training schedule, your career, you endorsements, what you were doing, what appearances you had to make."

"You didn't seem to mind it at the time," he said, stroking her hair away from her face to better see her.

"I didn't, and that scared me even more. But when you asked me—*expected me*—to drop out of school to travel with you, all I could think about was that I was becoming one of those trophy wives they show during the games."

She wouldn't have been a trophy wife, she would have been *his* wife. When she'd walked away that night, he'd known true fear. After that, his head wasn't in the game, not the way it should have been. Because all he could think about was the fact that she wasn't in the stands.

"That's why I asked for time to think. I had to figure out what I wanted and be strong enough to go after it. But when you fell into bed with that woman, it proved to me that we didn't have a good enough relationship. If I was so easily replaceable when you claimed to love me, what would stop you from replacing me when you didn't love me, or I was still packing baby fat, or I wasn't as beautiful as the other women around you. And if I'd quit school to be with you, and you dumped me for someone else, what would I have? I couldn't do that to myself."

"You weren't replaceable. You aren't," he said, lifting his hand to cradle her shoulder in his palm. He was blown away by her honesty. He'd had no idea that's how she'd seen their relationship. The funny thing was, he loved her independence—it drew him like moth to a flame. At the same time, he could admit that in those days he'd led with his ego—the whole world had been about him. And the more she asserted her independence, the harder he pushed to tie her to him, which only made her want more independence... No wonder she married someone who made no demands on her.

"Did you ever love him the way you loved me?" He called himself every kind of a fool for asking the question, but he had to know.

"Yes, I did. Tom was...safe for me." Skylar stared into his eyes, her expressions changing like the flicker of a candle flame, the burst of lightning illuminating her features, then shadowing them. But the expression she wore told him what he needed to know.

In an instant, he shifted toward her, dipped his head and fastened his lips over hers, kissed her the way he had wanted to when she'd leaned over his wheelchair.

Their tongues brushed and stroked, and the moment he felt her soften against him, he shifted his hands to her shoulders and grasped her arms to tug her up, never once breaking contact. Skylar lay chest to chest with him beneath the blanket, every touch of their mouths lasting longer, getting hotter and more powerful.

He buried a hand in her damp hair and angled her head just so, while his other hand roamed down her body to grasp her behind and squeeze. The move arched her hips into the growing hardness of his and she let out a moan that set him on fire. They had always been hot together, but time and absence had intensified the flame, and he wanted her—wanted what they could have if she let it happen.

He explored her body, palmed her breast, his thumbnail gently, deliberately, scraping over her nipple through the dampness of her shirt and bra. She gasped at the sensation, moaned when he repeated the move again, his mouth on hers. "Do you remember the last time we watched a storm like this roll in? At the beach?" He kissed his way to the sensitive skin of her neck, beneath her ear, knowing exactly what images were flitting through her head. He smoothed his hands over her behind, down the backs of her thighs. He tugged and adjusted her weight until she straddled him, his fingers slipping beneath her running shorts.

"Marcus."

"Shh. Nothing we haven't already done before," he said, before kissing her again. He was drowning in sensation, feeling, lust. How could she deny them? This? She needed to get over her fear and let things go, let them be together. "Skylar," he breathed, his breath tickling her ear and drawing even more gooseflesh to the surface of her skin. He smiled at the feel of them against his mouth.

Shifting against her, his thumb slipped between her legs and stroked. She tensed to push herself away, but he found her softness, slipping, sliding, back and forth until she gasped for breath and clutched at his shoulders with strangled whimpers, until she slipped over the edge, her head buried in his neck and body trembling hard as it found release. "You are so beautiful," he whispered against her throat. "Ah, honey. We can work everything out so long as we have this."

His words seemed to jerk Skylar from the fog of pleasure. She froze, huddled against his chest, her eyes wide.

The rain pelting the roof had dwindled down to a mild shower. The storm was almost over and he hoped their past had washed away with it.

Marcus rubbed her back, kissed her forehead, his body throbbing for release. "It's okay." He palmed the back of her head and brushed his lips over her forehead again. "Given our history, I know we need to wait until we can be protected."

Gasping, she shoved herself up, a flush rising into her neck and cheeks when she had to *un*straddle him to get off the bed.

Damn, why hadn't he kept his mouth shut? He took a deep breath and forced himself to stay calm. "You're still going to fight me on working things out, given what we just did?"

"*That's* why you just—"

"No!" he said, grimacing. "Damn it, Skylar, you know better than that."

"I know you want your son and, even though I told

you I wouldn't give up my life for you, you tried to seduce me."

"I did seduce you," he corrected softly. "But it wasn't because of Cody. Skylar, we're good together, sweetheart. We have something worth pursuing, *especially* considering we now have Cody to think of."

She retreated, her expression pinched and uneasy. "Cody will be eight years old. He didn't just appear."

He winced at his blunder. "I know. I meant——"

"I have to go."

"Skylar, it's still raining."

"Not hard," she said, trying to right her clothes. "Lexi knows I'm here, so she'll send someone. I'll meet them along the way. Goodbye, Marcus."

Curses flew from his lips as he reached for the racer, but she grabbed it and moved it out of his reach. "What the hell are you doing?"

She swallowed audibly.

"Giving myself a head start."

"Why? Are you going to stand there and try to tell me that meant nothing to you?"

"It was a climax, Marcus. Single moms don't have a lot of time for dating."

Of all the— So that was it? She wanted to get off and now that she had, she was leaving? "I'm not buying it, sweetheart."

"Well, you'd better start buying it. I just told you I loved Tom."

"Yes, you did." And he knew her words were meant to drive a wedge between them. But she wouldn't be throwing them in his face if she wasn't panicked, and that told him more than she wanted him to know.

He leaned against the wall once more, lacing his hands behind his head as he stared at her. "You weren't thinking about your dead husband. That's why you're in such a hurry to get out of here."

Skylar stalked toward the door. "Good*bye*, Marcus."

Anticipation filled him. The first time she'd broken up with him, he hadn't realized what he was losing. Now he did—and he refused to go down without one hell of a fight.

"Not for long," he called out, grinning as she stumbled over the threshold and hightailed it out the door.

Chapter 13

DESPITE THE RAIN STILL COMING down in light sprinkles, Skylar ran toward the ranch. Once Marcus cleared the field and made it to the road leading to the ranch, he could catch up with her in a matter of minutes if he wanted to.

And given the look on his face when he'd realized she was going to leave him in the shack with his racer out of reach?

"What did you do?" she whispered, looking over her shoulder repeatedly because she imagined Marcus breathing down her neck, ready to extract revenge for such a low, sneaky trick.

But he wasn't there. The shack's door was still open, a dark hole in the center of the weathered wood structure.

No, she made it all the way to the bend in the road before she paused again, long enough to take another look.

The air left her lungs. She was too far away to see

his expression, but she easily made out his dark hair and broad shoulders filling the frame.

He watched her. She felt his gaze on her almost as strongly and tangibly as she'd felt his touch just minutes ago when he'd made her bite her lips to keep from screaming in pleasure.

Would he come after her?

A shiver raced through her, but it wasn't one of fear. She wasn't afraid of Marcus. The shiver was...anticipation?

No. No, no, no.

The cheery beep of a horn drew her attention. One of the ranch trucks was headed toward her, a blond head behind the wheel. It wasn't until the truck got closer that Skylar was able to make out the driver as Maura.

Moving to the side of the road, Skylar forced a smile. She grabbed the door handle before the truck came to a full stop.

"Why didn't you stay in the line shack?" Maura asked, handing over a towel and a jacket from the bench seat.

"I'm fine. Nothing a hot shower won't fix."

Maura headed to the very edge of the road and swung the truck wide to turn it around. She had to stop and back up a time or two in order to keep from going off into the rain-soaked field, and when Maura stopped a third time, Skylar had to lock her jaw to keep from screaming at Maura to hurry.

"You okay? You seem really tense. Oh, I forgot," Maura said, sending Skylar a sympathetic glance. "Do you still think of the accident whenever it storms like it did earlier?"

"No. Not always." Now she thought of other things. *Like Marcus and beach houses.*

Maybe that memory was why she'd succumbed to his touch? Because it was there in her head and he was there in the shack and—

"I hated leaving you stuck out there, but Lexi said you were safe and sound."

"I was fine. Really."

Maura ground the gears shoving the older Ford truck into First, and Skylar winced, her hands clenched beneath the towel now lying over her lap.

"Ahh. I see you weren't alone."

The response prompted a glance at Maura, and Skylar saw that the other woman's gaze had shifted to the rearview mirror.

Skylar stifled a groan, looking into the passenger-side mirror in time to confirm her suspicions. Marcus had left the porch and was now out in the open, crossing the field.

"Are we really going to leave him out here?" Maura asked gently.

Though her stomach hurt from holding her muscles so tight, Skylar never took her gaze from the mirror. She watched as Marcus maneuvered the racer up the incline to the road. The sheer brute strength behind such a move was beyond her comprehension, especially when she thought of the tenderness he'd displayed when they were making out on the cot.

Once Marcus made it onto the road, she released

the breath she didn't know she held. "He's fine. Keep going."

"Oh, Skylar. Are you sure?"

Marcus began rolling, the distance between him and the truck disappearing much too quickly. And just like that, her panic returned. "Yes. *Go.*"

MARCUS MADE IT HOME HALF an hour later. He was in his workshop, washing the mud and muck off the racer and in need of a shower himself when his grandfather ambled out of the house with his stiff-legged, hand-crutch wobble. He sat in the recliner with a telling grunt. "Weather got you hurting today?"

"Some. Looks like you got a bit wet."

"Some," he said, grinning. It was worth it, though. Getting stuck with Skylar had spun things in a new direction. Maybe he'd seduced her, but she'd kissed him back. Responded. If he could just continue whittling away at her, maybe…

"Where'd the mud come from?"

"Took shelter in one of the Rowlands' line shacks," he said, washing off the last of the soap and grabbing a towel to wipe down the wheels. He paid close attention to the task, trying to formulate a plan of action where Skylar was concerned. Her response today had confirmed the stirrings of hope inside him that they could build on the past they shared. She was leery, and with good reason, but it was a start, right?

His biggest problem was bringing Cody around. If he could do that, show Skylar that he and his son should be together, maybe combined with the pressure he figured her family was placing on her, he might be able to sway her to rethink moving.

"This mean I don't get to meet my grandson today?"

His mood soured. Getting Cody on his side wasn't going to be easy. "Not today. The boy isn't thrilled to have me as his father. He...wants a superhero."

"What's that?"

Marcus shook his head and tossed the towel aside, wheeling himself away from the racer before turning around. "He wants his father to be able to run and jump."

Ben's expression didn't change. "Those are the words of a child who hasn't been shown all his daddy can do."

"Yeah, well, it's kind of hard to show him when he doesn't want anything to do with me. You have any suggestions on how to change that?"

Ben pondered the question, pursing his lips and smoothing a wrinkled hand back and forth over the arm of the chair.

Marcus rolled over to one of the worktables to see how the pieces he'd left soaking were doing.

"Big Billy," Ben said abruptly.

Marcus lifted his head, his mind shooting toward the memories of Big Billy and the fun he'd had that day so long ago. "I had forgotten about that old turtle. You think he's still around?"

Ben smiled, a sight that cracked Marcus up and made him laugh. Ben had left his dentures in the house and, with his wizened skin and sharp nose, he looked a bit like Big Billy himself.

"Hard to tell. But I'll bet you anything that boy of yours would like to find out."

THAT SAME EVENING, SKYLAR rolled over in bed—it wasn't as if she was actually sleeping—and grabbed her cell phone off the nightstand.

After Maura had dropped her off at the cabin, she'd quickly showered and relieved Lexi of her babysitting duties. Then she closed the blinds, locked the door and turned out the lights while she and Cody watched a Disney movie she'd downloaded onto her computer.

She and Cody could've gone to Game Night, because Lexi and Maura had both invited them, but Skylar had begged off and chosen a quiet evening in instead. She'd hoped to figure out a plan of action tonight, since the movie was one they'd seen before, but rather than figuring out how to handle Cody's custodial issues, holidays and the like, she'd spent much of the two hours staring dazedly at nothing, replaying the scene in the cabin over and over again.

Thankfully Cody was so exhausted from his day of play, he went to bed early and without protest, but when she'd gone to tuck him in she'd noticed he had once again chosen the top bunk. He'd stared up at the moon and the mountains it shone on, a heartbreaking expression on his face. *I want you, not him.*

It was almost ten, but was it any wonder sleep was elusive?

After unplugging the cell from the charge cord, she scrolled through her contacts list until she found the name she was looking for and pressed the call button. The phone rang twice, three times.

"Jill Bronwitz," her attorney neighbor said.

"Were you asleep?"

"I wish. Actually, I just grabbed a cab to head home. Big dinner with clients tonight."

"How'd it go?"

"Excellent. I won the case, so we went to celebrate. But that's not why you're calling me so late. What's up? Is Cody okay? Is the trip helping him?"

She smiled at the rapid-fire questions, well aware that for Jill they were the norm. "He's fine and it's still too soon to tell," she said, not wanting to get into the details of her and Marcus's relationship unless she absolutely had to. If the time came that she needed an attorney, Jill was the woman to call, but maybe there wouldn't be a need? "Jill, I need a favor."

"Okay. What's up?"

"Do you remember when we took the boys skiing in New Hampshire last winter and Pierce knew that guy who had gone to the Paralympics?" Jill's husband seemed to know everyone and Skylar hoped he wouldn't mind her taking advantage of that. As it was, she felt a twinge of guilt going behind Marcus's back. But if her idea worked out, she would be doing something nice for him. Something that would better allow him to be the athlete and competitor he'd always been. That he was still.

Something that would take Marcus's attention away from Cody and the issue of custody and visitation?

Maybe making the call wasn't an entirely selfless act but...

"Booker, yeah. He's a great guy, isn't he? Actually, he retired a few months ago and took a job as a coach at the Olympic training center in Atlanta."

A coach? Wasn't that a sign that it was meant to be? "Perfect," she breathed, shoving the guilt away. All she was doing was setting up an opportunity. Whatever happened afterward was up to them.

"Oh? Why perfect?"

"Do you think he'd be receptive to taking a trip to Montana? Like, now?" You think this will make up for abandoning Marcus at the line shack? That it's not totally obvious you're running from what happened between you?

Maybe it was obvious. But sometimes a girl's survival instinct had to be obeyed. Marcus wouldn't stop until he got his way, and he had made a valid point about her family and his being located in North Star. But if Marcus wasn't here...

"It would depend on his schedule, I suppose, but— Are you kidding me? He'd love it. He's an adventure hound and totally into you."

"That's not why I'm asking."

Jill's sigh carried over the miles separating them. "I figured as much but a girl can hope. I take it you're hoping to do a good deed for some unsuspecting soul? I thought you were taking a vacation, Miss Counselor."

Her fingers tightened over the phone. "I am. This just...came up."

"So what do I tell Booker?"

"Tell him there's a guy here wheelchair racing at over forty miles an hour. Forty-six if he wants specifics, and…I looked his marathon times up and he's finishing just under the international champion."

"Wow."

"Yeah. And tell him…tell him it's Marcus White-feather."

"The *quarterback?*"

Skylar had forgotten Jill and her husband, Pierce, were such football fans. "Yeah."

"I'll call him right now."

Skylar laughed. "It's late."

"I don't think Booker will care. Seriously? You're talking about Marcus Whitefeather? You *know* Marcus Whitefeather? Is this a new acquaintance or old?"

"Um…old."

"And *why* haven't you mentioned knowing him before? Can you get me an autograph for Pierce?"

Inhaling because she knew she'd have to explain sooner or later, Skylar snuggled down in the bed and prepared herself for a long conversation. "Jill…"

"Uh-oh. What's wrong?"

"Everything." She sighed and ran a hand over her gritty eyes. "Truth is, I've known Marcus since I was a teenager. It's a long story but…I might need your legal advice later."

"Don't you dare leave me hanging. Why would you need legal advice? What's going on?"

"Marcus is Cody's father."

Jill's silence was deafening.

"Hello? Jill, are you still there?"

"Skylar, I'm going to call Booker right now before it gets any later but as soon as I get home I'm calling you back so you and I can have a long talk about the things friends are required to share with each other. Understood?"

Skylar wanted to protest but knew better. Maybe it was best to get it all out in the open while she was still freaked out by what had happened in the line shack earlier. Otherwise…she might actually find herself tempted—which wouldn't do at all. "I can't wait."

"MORNIN'," MARCUS SAID THE MOMENT he saw Skylar step out of the cabin behind Cody. He paid close attention to Skylar's reaction, watched as surprise and unease changed her expression from coaxing mother into guarded protectiveness. He pulled his gaze from her beautiful features long enough to include Cody in the greeting before shifting his attention back to Skylar.

Today she wore khaki shorts that ended midthigh and a dark purple T-shirt that revealed the curve of her breasts. The material strained a bit across her front but showcased the narrowness of her waist and flare of her hips. Unlike the boyish figures of the models on magazines and television, Skylar had the curvy shape of a woman, and he appreciated every hill and valley.

"What are you doing here?" she asked, looking more than a bit nervous.

After leaving him in the line shack, she had reason to feel nervous. Because even though he should be furious after her little stunt, he found himself ready for the challenge. Yesterday—he'd definitely gotten close and he meant to stay that way.

He wanted to give her another reason to come to Montana—or invite him to New York—that had nothing to do with Cody and everything to do with the two of them as a couple. Truth be told, there had never been another woman for him. No one could ever measure up to Skylar.

The spark was still there, the tension. Now he had to get her to trust him again, because when she'd needed him most, he'd proved himself as unreliable and untrustworthy as the other men in her life. Her father, her first "boyfriend." Even Tom had left her in the end, and while Skylar had known the man was dying, it wasn't like you could ever prepare yourself for such a thing.

"I'm waiting for you two," he said simply. "I was beginning to wonder if you were ever going to drag yourselves out of bed."

She blinked at him as if she was having a hard time following the conversation.

"Why?" she asked.

Focusing entirely on Cody now, Marcus smiled, trying to gentle his expression, because the boy looked scared to death. Given their first meeting in the barn and the way he'd yelled at Cody, Marcus had only himself to blame. One art class wasn't going to change Cody's perception of him, especially when any progress had been undone by the disappointing news of having a crippled man for a father.

"Maura packed us a picnic basket," he said, tilting

his head toward the basket waiting for them by the ramp. "She said she put all your favorites in there, Cody. Oh, and I got you this," he said, snagging a kid-size fishing pole from where he'd leaned it against the porch rail. "You probably don't fish much in downtown New York, so I ran into town this morning to get it for you. I hope you like it. I thought we could go see if we could spot Big Billy. Have you ever heard of him?"

Marcus held the pole out for Cody to take, but Cody didn't move a muscle. The moment stretched out for several seconds, longer than it should take most anyone, especially a kid, to accept a gift.

Marcus managed another smile. Barely. "This is called a Big Green Fishin' Machine. Riley has one just like this. Caught an eight pounder not that long ago."

Cody accepted the fishing pole with its matching tackle box, but he continued to look as if he was holding a rattlesnake rather than the source of a lot of fun.

"Thank you."

"You're welcome."

"But you can take it back if you want," Cody said. "I don't know how to fish."

Marcus struggled to hold on to his smile, wondering if everything with Cody was going to be a battle of wills. If Cody was anything like his mother... "That's all right. I'll teach you."

"You?"

Cody's query was instilled with doubt and it didn't take a genius to figure out why. Like the comment Cody had made in the barn and again when he'd been told the truth of who Marcus was, Cody saw only the wheelchair. His son didn't think him capable of fishing. *Or anything else.*

Marcus fastened his hands on the push-rims of his wheelchair and reminded himself that trust took time, patience and a whole lot of getting to know each other. Sitting side by side on the creek bank was a good place to start the process, considering the best way of proving something was by example. It was time to show Cody what his father was capable of, no matter how long it took.

The same was true for Skylar. "Yeah, me. There's a great spot to fish not far from here. It's close to where Riley caught that fish, and it used to be a favorite spot of Big Billy's. Stretch your arms out to your sides, real wide. Yeah, like that. Have you ever seen a turtle so big his shell is as wide as your arms?"

"No."

"Then why don't we try to spot him? If we get hungry, we can have a picnic and try out that pole, too. Maybe catch some fish. Sound fun?"

"I guess." Cody turned the pole over in his hands as though testing the weight of it. "Can my mom come?"

The question was innocent enough, but in an instant Marcus's mind flashed back to yesterday and what had happened in the line shack. Skylar on the cot, her head tilted back, eyes closed. "She sure can."

His tone gave him away, because Skylar's face turned hot pink and he knew without a doubt she was remembering what had taken place, as well.

"I've never been fishing." Cody glanced up at his mother. "Can we, Mom?"

Skylar didn't want to say yes, that much was obvious, but Marcus could tell the moment she capitulated and put Cody's request above her own hesitations.

"I suppose we can. For a little while."

Despite the agreement, Skylar shot him a warning stare and Marcus winked at her, causing her to huff as she opened the door to the cabin long enough to leave her purse inside for safekeeping.

Marcus held the picnic basket on his lap as he eased down the ramp after his son. At the bottom, he waited for Skylar, noticing the way her long bare legs moved with such ease as she joined him.

"Ready," she said.

"Not yet. I have something for you, too. Hold out your hand." Marcus dug into the basket.

"What is it?" she said, looking more than a little leery but curious, as well.

Skylar liked surprises. She always had.

He placed the bag of M&M's in her hand and waited for her response.

Football games were won one yard at a time. Skylar's response at the line shack was again of twenty. Cody's acceptance of the fishing pole, even though it meant spending time with the father he didn't want…another first down.

"M&M's," she whispered.

Her teeth clamped down on her lip as her expression softened, and nothing could stop the grin curling his lips as he turned and led the way to the creek.

Touchdown.

Chapter 14

SKYLAR WAS TORN BETWEEN watching Marcus and Cody at the edge of the creek, and staring down at the bag of M&M's on the sun-warmed rock beside her.

In the time since their arrival at the wheelchair-accessible spot, Cody had slowly opened up to Marcus, thanks to Marcus instructing Cody on how to bait his hook and cast his line, and explaining that patience was required to slowly reel the line in to entice the fish.

"Where's Batman and Robin today?" Marcus asked.

Cody sent Skylar a look over his bony shoulder.

"They're in time-out because I hit that girl."

"Ah. Will they be there long?"

"A whole week," Cody said, the words mumbled and filled with disdain.

"Well, I suppose that's all right. Even superheroes need a vacation, don't you think? They would get too hot out here fishing. Maybe even melt sitting out in the sun."

"I s'pose. This is fun. And I don't want to lose 'em or for them to melt."

As she watched, Cody went back to casting his line, repeating the process several times. Memories of her past with Marcus flitted through her head like the hummingbirds zipping from flower to flower along the bank. The breeze and sun and gentle roll of the water did nothing to soothe the anxiety Marcus's surprise had created.

The very first time Marcus had compared her to an M&M sprang from the shadows of her mind. She'd bought herself a pack of M&M's as a treat one day after high school. The day had been long and filled with tests, people and situations that had a way of getting under her skin.

She'd aced the quizzes, because her mother and Jonas had said she couldn't go out with Marcus if she didn't bring her grades up. Then she'd kicked Mandy's butt at volleyball in gym class and managed to escape a tardy bell by the squeak of her sneakers as she slid into her chair in English lit.

Marcus had had football practice after school as always, but she'd hung out until he could drive her home afterward, just so they could spend some time together.

"Heard you lucked out today in the hall on your way to lit class. Cutting it close, weren't you?"

She popped an M&M's into her mouth and grinned at him. "I made it. Besides, Coach was on duty and he wouldn't dare give me a tardy. It might upset his star player and distract you from the game."

"You try to be such a badass."

"I *am* a badass," she said. "I can turn you into a shaking puddle of goo in no time," she'd teased, lowering her voice to a throaty pitch guaranteed to make him pull over someplace private before he took her home.

Marcus wrapped his arm around her shoulders and pulled her closer to him on the bench seat of his grand-dad's old truck. He lowered his head and kissed her without taking his eyes off the road.

Five minutes later, they were parked on one of the many isolated ranch roads, the windows steaming up at a fast rate.

"See?" she teased. "Goo. You like my bad side."

"I won't deny that. But you just think you're badass," he said, his hand on her breast, thumb teasing her nipple through her cami. "You're really one of those M&M's you like so much. You try to be all hard and crunchy on the outside, but inside you're soft and sweet."

"I am not sweet," she growled into his neck.

Marcus's hand slipped under her shirt. "Liar. I've cracked your shell, sweetheart. I know who you really are," he said, shifting her so that she was the one groaning when his mouth followed his hand. "Don't you ever forget it."

"I THOUGHT YOU'D HAVE DUG into dessert by now," Marcus said, rolling toward her.

Her gaze immediately shifted to Cody, checking on him, before meeting Marcus's gaze again. The packet of M&M's remained unopened on the rock between them.

"What? No badass comment? Are you slipping?"

Was she? That scared her more than she cared to admit. Way more. She couldn't afford softness where Marcus was concerned, because she knew what happened when she softened toward him. She wasn't herself. She became dependent, lost.

And if she wasn't careful, she would be right back to that pathetic girl, sobbing because of Marcus. Except, this time Tom wasn't there to help her get back on her feet.

In the past twenty-four hours, Marcus had proved he still had what it took to get to her and, if she knew one thing, it was that she had to fortify the barriers crumbling beneath her. Fast.

While Marcus watched Cody practice his casting, she took the moment to observe the man disrupting her life. Marcus wore a blue T-shirt that intensified the color of his eyes to knee-weakening levels, and darkened his Native American skin. Atop his head, were the dark sunglasses he'd shoved up and out of his way once they'd reached the shade.

There were some women in the world who would dismiss Marcus due to his injury and lifelong condition. But knowing Marcus before... She couldn't help but think the issues he'd faced had given him character, because to her mind he was better looking now than he'd been while they had dated.

No, her reasons for avoiding him had nothing to do with Marcus's injury and everything to do with the power he held. Marcus had no clue what a basket case she'd become after their breakup or how deeply his betrayal had scarred her. And so long as she could help it, he would never know. She wouldn't—couldn't—become that girl again. Cody depended on her to be strong and, when it came to Marcus, she…wasn't.

No matter how much she might desire Marcus, the fear of becoming that dark, bitter, depressed person again was stronger. Everyone got hurt at some time in their life, but not everyone recovered.

"Instead of studying me so hard, why don't you ask me whatever it is going on in that head of yours," he murmured.

The gush of air she released from her lungs did nothing to ease the tension within her. "Being in Cody's life doesn't mean being in mine, Marcus. I want to make it clear that what happened yesterday won't happen again."

"Why's that?"

Because it couldn't. Not only for Cody's sake but her own. Decadent desserts were good, but they weren't good for you. And to her, Marcus was the most decadent dessert of all. "Marcus, stop. We're too old to play games."

The panic she'd felt the moment she'd laid eyes on him had continued to grow during the past week. And when he looked at her the way he did right now, that panic bloomed to monstrous proportions because she felt the stirrings of temptation, felt herself teetering with indecision, when she *knew better*. Wasn't having her heart decimated once enough? How many times after their breakup had she thought that the world wouldn't...*miss* her if she wasn't in it?

That was why her student's suicide was so hard to absorb. Why her feelings of guilt surrounding Travis's death were so strong. Because she knew what it was like to feel that way, to want everything to *end*. Why put herself through that again?

Maybe it wouldn't be like that. The doctors said it was pregnancy hormones and the timing of the breakup but...

Maybe not. Could she afford to take the risk?

After her breakup with Marcus, she had drowned in a well of depression so deep and mind-numbingly strong there were times when Tom wouldn't leave her alone in a room. Toss in postpartum depression and Cody had been two years old before she had managed to feel somewhat normal again. By helping those kids, she helped herself.

"I'm not playing a game, sweetheart," Marcus murmured. "I'm just looking at all the potential possibilities available to us due to the fact there's a lot of heat still between us."

Her heart skidded even more out of control at his words, thumping against her ribs until a light sheen of sweat beaded on her face and she felt sick to her stomach. Who knew fear left a bitter taste in a person's mouth? That bitterness was all she tasted now. "What happened yesterday changed nothing. It was a *slip* that won't happen again. Marcus, I won't let you push me into doing something I don't want to do, into giving up everything for you."

"I'm not belittling your job or your abilities, but there are other jobs and other teens and schools you can help. If you tried, I'll bet you could find something here."

"I don't want to find something here!" Skylar thought of her co-counselor Nina and the kids at her New York school and shook her head firmly back and forth. She had a life, a job, friends. A support system that didn't judge her based on the past. Small towns had long memories and she had no desire to stay. She hadn't liked living in North Star. Visiting was okay, sure, but living day-to-day? She was a New York girl. But there he was, asking her to change for him. Again. Like a broken record. "No."

"Why? What could I do to change your mind? Why do you get so bent out of shape about moving back?" he asked, his gaze zeroing in on her face to the point she wanted to squirm. But she knew it would reveal her weakness.

She knew to keep her mouth shut after being in the counseling world for so long. One whiff of the phrase *emotional dysfunction* or *instability* could bring about disaster. To reveal her true reasons would hand Marcus the ammunition he needed in court should he ever decide visitation wasn't enough.

She *was* afraid. Not only of Marcus, but her family. Look at how they had responded to the news of Cody's paternity. She'd screwed up so often, and so bad, as a teenager, she knew that all her family and the town saw when they looked at her was an emotionally messed-up girl. That constant pressure, the feelings of insecurity and unworthiness… She'd fought hard to put them behind her, to build up her self-confidence, and she couldn't let them—or a moment of brutal honesty—change that.

"Marcus, will you show me how to bait the hook again?" Cody asked.

She had been so focused on Marcus that she hadn't even noticed Cody's approach. And the fact Cody approached Marcus instead of her? "I can do it," she said, straightening her legs to get off the rock and put some distance between them.

"That's okay, he can," Cody said, holding out a wriggling worm toward Marcus.

Another, harder, shaft of fear shot through her like a rocket. Cody had been in Marcus's company all of thirty minutes and already her son's defenses were lowering. Not a good thing.

She glanced from Cody to his father and back to Cody again as Marcus accepted the worm and the hook, near-identical expressions on both their faces as Marcus showed Cody the best way of making sure the worm stayed put.

But with Cody's statement, Skylar knew the transformation had begun… Marcus had always had a way with people. On the field, on the sports-news screens being interviewed live, behind the scenes… All it had taken was a fishing pole and some one-on-one time for Marcus to break through Cody's shell to the soft, sweet center inside.

What would happen to Cody's emotions if the

novelty of being a parent wore off and Marcus's demands for visitation faded?

She watched as Marcus finished the task and followed Cody to the creek, his dark hair such a contrast to Cody's white-blond. But side by side, she saw their similarities, too. The cant of their heads, the way they both pursed their lips, so like Ben, as they concentrated on making the perfect cast. The smiles they shared when Cody sent the line into the water with all the skill any almost-eight-year-old first-time fisherman could possibly possess.

"Good job, son. That was perfect."

Yeah, it was. But once again her heart stuttered and pinched. The praise, the look on Cody's face when he glanced up at Marcus, and she knew talking to Marcus about her "fears" would never be a good idea.

What if, after all this time, she lost Cody to the father he wanted so bad? What if, when their time in Montana was up, Cody wanted to stay? She loved her son, would do anything for him—but she couldn't stay here. Not even for Cody. "Marcus, I forgot to tell you…" she said, drawing his attention. "I know someone you might be interested in who could help with your racing. I was talking to a friend last night and mentioned your name. Jill is a major football fan, and a fan of yours. Anyway, Jill said she would name drop."

Marcus turned his head to face her, his gaze narrowing on hers with a look way too similar to her son's when Marcus had asked where Batman and Robin were.

"Name drop to who?"

"Booker Phipps. Have you heard of him?" she asked, forcing a casualness into her tone she didn't feel.

"I know the name."

Good. Very, very good. Because that meant Marcus had done his research into the sport. Which also meant he was more interested than he was letting on. Marcus was a busy man. He wouldn't have known the name of a medal-winning trainer without reason. "Well, I doubt anything will come of it, but I thought I'd mention it to you. Jill says Booker has gone to the Olympics three times to race in the Paralympic Games and won quite a few medals."

Skylar felt a little guilty for letting Marcus think the phone call was entirely innocent, but if Booker Phipps *was* interested in Marcus, that would go a long way in removing some of the pressure she felt where Marcus was concerned.

"I've got one! I've got one!" Cody cried, nearly dropping the pole in excitement.

Skylar stood to watch Cody reel the fish in with his father's help. The two high-fived and Marcus pulled out his cell phone to take a picture of Cody holding his prize—with Cody hamming it up, grinning like a loon. With a few presses of his thumb, Marcus set the picture to pop up whenever his cell phone was active.

The gesture wasn't lost on her and another prickle of unease skittered over her, serving to confirm her fears.

Booker had to come to Montana, had to show an interest in Marcus.

Because Marcus's response would tell her exactly

how serious he was about being Cody's father.

"THEY LOOK LIKE THEY'RE having fun."

Skylar turned to find her mother approaching her inside the dining hall. Lunch wouldn't start for another hour, but Maura and her crew were busy in the back of the building, preparing for the crowd. "Yeah."

"Have fun fishing?"

Really? Was her mom actually going to do the small-talk routine? "Cody had fun."

"He's loosening up around Marcus. That's good."

"Is it?" she said, before she could stop herself.

"Skylar."

Rissa's tone was scolding, her disapproval evident.

"I just don't want Cody to get hurt. Parenting isn't all fun and games. It's the hard stuff, too."

"Yes, it is."

Skylar felt her mother's hand on her shoulder an instant before Rissa nudged her to turn around and face her instead of the window.

"What did I do to make you feel you couldn't come to me?"

"Mom—"

"I want to know. Help me understand, because it kills me to think I've hurt you that way."

"It wasn't entirely you. It was me and how, no matter how hard I tried, I kept screwing up. I couldn't face you *again* and tell you… I couldn't tell you." And what did it say about their relationship that she couldn't tell her mother something as important as that? It made

Skylar realize she wanted a different relationship between her and Cody.

"How many times do I have to say you are not to blame for your father's accident?"

"Rationally, I know that," she said, staring into eyes so similar to her own, before having to look away. "But I also know, as well as you, that had I not done the things I'd done, we wouldn't have been in the car racing down the highway to Rick's house. I know I wasn't driving the car, or speeding or the cause of the thunderstorm. But I am partially to blame and I always will be."

Rissa shook her head in denial. "What does that have to do with you and Marcus? How is it related?"

That's where things really got sticky.

"Sky, Marcus is a good man. He isn't perfect, and I'd say, like most men, he can be a jerk sometimes. But he's a good man, and you two have…something. Something everyone can see. If you're truly not interested in him, fine. But if you're pushing him away because of some other reason… Oh, baby, happiness doesn't come along every day. Be careful about denying things you really want but are too stubborn to accept."

Skylar looked away, out the window. "He wants Cody."

"And you. We can all see that. Why can't you believe in him? In love?"

Because…sometimes love wasn't enough. "You're taking his side. Again. But after everything that has happened between me and Marcus, how could I ever believe Marcus isn't pursuing me because of Cody? Because he wants to do the right thing, now that all of you know the truth? Mom, I'm not a consolation prize and I refuse to be guilted into being one."

"Skylar, I would never do that and if you think I am —you're wrong. Do you hear me? *Wrong.* I have never, ever wanted you to feel guilty about anything."

"Yeah, right," she said, tilting her head back, a bitter smile curling her lips.

"What? What do you mean by that?"

"I mean, the way you look at me. No matter how old I get, anytime my past is brought up—which seems to be pretty often, considering I'm being used as a teaching tool for Lexi—you get the exact expression on your face that you did when you found out about me and Rick. And you know what? Each time I see it, I feel even *dirtier* than I did then."

"No. Oh, Sky, no, that's not—" Rissa sounded horrified. "That's not true. That look? It's because, when I think about what he did to you, I see Rick's face and I want to rip his throat out because he hurt you. It's not directed toward you at all. You're a mother now. What if someone took advantage of Cody that way? How would you feel? Wouldn't you want to do them bodily harm?"

She would. And then some. All this time, she had thought her mother's look was one of disgust, censure, for her.

"Skylar, I know you're not perfect, and I do not expect you to be. We are who we are," she said, brushing a tendril of hair away from Skylar's face. "I love you. And I love Cody, and I want what's best for you. That's all."

"I want that, too." Skylar straightened from the

window, the move distancing her from her mother's touch. "But it's not staying here. And it's not Marcus."

"Are you sure about that?" her mother asked, her gaze narrowed on Skylar's face. "Or are you afraid of trying again because it didn't work in the past?"

"Does it matter? Either way, I can't be with a man who wants me to give up everything I am for him."

"YOU LIKE THAT, EH?" MARCUS asked Cody, laughing because of his son's reaction to the racer's speed. They'd barely topped five miles an hour, but Cody's excitement soothed Marcus's soul. His son sat in his lap, secure in the restraint Marcus had rigged up for Cody's safety, so there was no chance of him slipping off and falling to the ground. "Wanna go faster?"

"Yeah!" Cody held his hands up as if he was on a roller-coaster ride.

"Lean forward a bit," Marcus ordered, his gloved hands gripping the rims and propelling them to a quicker pace.

Cody's excited yells drew attention from the ranch's guests and workers, who smiled at the fun they were having. Marcus kept the racer under careful control, knowing full well Skylar watched from inside the building, where Maura worked to prepare lunch.

When he'd asked Cody if he wanted to go for a ride, Skylar had sat on the porch to wait them out. Then Cody repeatedly asked to go again, Skylar had said she was going inside to get herself something to drink and would be back in a minute.

"Go faster, go faster!"

Marcus picked up speed, though they barely reached ten miles per hour, if that. Turning to head back, he matched the pace, relishing the sound of Cody's laughter.

He had a lot of work waiting for him at his studio. A deadline to meet for the commissioned piece for the state capital. But nothing was going to ruin this moment. He might not have had his priorities in line when Cody was conceived, but he did now.

"Can we do it again?"

Marcus laughed, wondering how many times he was going to hear that, grateful for each and every one. "You bet ya."

They made another lap, but when Marcus slowed to approach the turn in the center of the main buildings, Cody's laughter died and his hands lowered.

"Cody?" Marcus slowed the racer even more and shifted so he could better see Cody's expression. The boy stared off to the right—at the kids watching them in the racer. "Something wrong?"

Cody looked down, and was fiddling with the excess strap of the cinch Marcus had used as a seat belt for the boy.

"They don't like me."

"Oh, I'm sure that's not true."

"It is. None of them will play with me now."

Marcus shifted his attention back to the group of kids huddled together in the shade of one of the buildings. They were a mix of able-bodied and wheelchair users, but Marcus didn't doubt they were the same kids who had teased Cody about his fantasy father. "Well, don't worry about them. You'll probably never see those kids again in your life."

"But what about now? Sometimes I wanna play, too."

The sadness in Cody's tone touched a place in Marcus he didn't know he possessed. Maybe he had a father's heart after all? "Give them some time. You just had a disagreement, but it will blow over soon. You'll see."

He'd been so focused on Cody that Marcus didn't see the children approach until they were only a few feet away.

"That's a cool wheelchair," a girl said shyly.

She wore her hair in pigtails along the side of her neck and sported a cowgirl hat with a zebra-striped bandana tied around the arm of her wheelchair.

"Thanks. That's a mighty fine hat you have there," he said, winking at her.

Her blushing smile revealed a mouthful of braces.

"Would you give us rides? I've never gone that fast."

"Yeah, why's he so special? He's mean," a second girl added, sending Cody a glare.

"I'm sorry I hit you," Cody said, the words barely having sound.

Marcus could tell the apology was sincere, though. Cody regretted the fight, especially now that the kids were giving him the cold shoulder.

"So will you?" the first girl asked again.

"No, honey, I'd better not. I'm sorry but one of you might get hurt."

"But you took him," the fight-girl said. "Why does he get to ride and not my sister?"

"Because Cody's my son."

The statement silenced the group and it took Marcus a second or two to catch on as to why.

"I thought your dad was a *vampire*," one of the girls said loud enough for all to hear.

And to get a laugh.

Cody stiffened on Marcus's lap, but Marcus squeezed his shoulder in an attempt to soften the blow of the kids' responses.

"Marcus?" Ben said, his shuffling, double-caned walk carrying him closer. "Heard you two got a mighty fine catch this morning. Maura says she's got it all cooked up for our lunch. You ready to eat?"

Marcus glanced down at Cody and found the boy still staring at the kids, silent. Ben probably hoped Marcus would introduce him to his great-grandson, but now wasn't the time. "Yeah, I think we're done. See you later, kids."

Marcus rolled slowly toward the van, where he'd left his wheelchair. "Cody, unbuckle the belt and hop off, okay?"

It took Cody a couple of tries to get the cinch undone, because he kept getting distracted by the kids. The group had resumed a game, but they whispered and talked and stared at Cody as much as Cody stared at them.

"Don't worry about them. If they say anything else about me not taking them for a ride, just tell them it's against the ranch rules." Cody didn't answer, so Marcus tried again. "It was good rolling with you, Cody. I've got an extra racer at my house if you'd like to come over and try it yourself. Your mom is welcome to come, too. Maybe tomorrow?"

"Maybe," Cody said.

"Marcus, you going to introduce me?" Ben prodded.

Marcus smiled up at his grandfather and tried to shrug off the feelings of disappointment he felt at Cody's lackluster response to the invitation. Cody's good-humored mood had evaporated with the kids' comments. "Absolutely. Ben, this is Cody," he said. "Cody, this is your great-grandfather, Ben Whitefeather. He used to fly helicopters just like your Grandma."

On his feet now, Cody looked up at Ben, back to Marcus and at Ben again. Marcus couldn't blame the boy for his curiosity. Marcus had the dark skin and dark hair passed down from his ancestral heritage, but Ben looked more like the Native Americans from the old black-and-white movies that still played on television.

"Hi," Cody said, looking shy.

Balancing carefully on one crutch, Ben held out his hand. Seconds passed, but Cody reached up and shook it.

"Nice to meet you, Cody. I understand you caught quite a few fish today. Did you have fun?" Ben asked.

"Yeah. We saw a turtle named Big Billy."

"You did? Let's go get some grub. I want to hear the story from my great-grandson."

Chapter 15

MARCUS HAD A HEISMAN IN HIS display case at home, and a Super Bowl ring he kept locked in a safe-deposit box in town. But entering the theater that next evening with Skylar and Cody at his side, he felt a satisfaction he'd never felt before.

This was what he had always wanted with Skylar. To be a family, to do things together. And here they were.

Heads turned, a few people whispered and weren't shy about it, but he didn't care. Nor did he care that Skylar didn't want him tagging along. After a strained lunch yesterday, in which everyone talked but Skylar, Cody had mentioned going to the movies. Marcus had quickly said he'd like to go, too, and before his mother could stop him, Cody had invited him along. Sitting at the table surrounded by both their families as they had been, Skylar hadn't exactly been in a position to argue.

He and Ben had left soon after, and Marcus had worked on the statehouse project, rolled and waited for a phone call from Skylar with an excuse as to why he couldn't go with them.

Even more surprising was that the call never came. So, like a nervous teenager on his first date, he had picked them up at the appointed time, driven them to town and wondered what the evening would bring.

Cody had kept up a steady stream of chatter on the drive, but conversation with Skylar consisted of bland yes and no responses, because she seemed more interested in checking her cell for messages and email. They hadn't made it halfway to town before he'd had to fight the urge to fling the device out the window.

Waiting in line at the concession stand for popcorn proved entertaining, as well. Cody had a sweet tooth like his mother and by the time they made it to the counter, the boy had changed his mind five times over on what he wanted to get, foregoing popcorn for one of those little bottles of miniature M&M's.

As Cody made his choice, Marcus didn't bother hiding his amusement, but he grinned outright when Skylar nearly burst into flames her face got so red. She looked as though she had a mouth full of Sugar Daddy candy and no drink in sight.

Waiting for their order to be filled, Marcus spotted Lexi two rows over. The theater lobby was crowded with young and old alike, but the girl said hello, lifting the hand holding a large drink in greeting and hugging her popcorn to her chest, before she turned away and headed toward her theater. Given her haste, she either had a guy waiting on her or her movie was about to start.

If Marcus had to guess, given the somewhat anxious glance Lexi slid over her shoulder toward them before she disappeared into the crowd, it was that she was with whoever had been in the hayloft that day in the barn.

He frowned, wondering if he should try to make some excuse to follow Lexi just to catch a glimpse of the person the girl was seeing, but then reminded himself it was none of his business. Lexi was heading off to college and when he and Skylar were that age… Well, he had no room to judge.

"Let's go, let's go!" Cody said, tugging on his mother's hand and following the crowd toward the theaters.

In theater number three of three, Marcus made a point of getting ahead of Cody and Skylar so he could lead the way to the wheelchair rows. He didn't want Cody running down the aisle, Skylar following and then realizing they were limited to the back of the theater.

Thankfully, Cody was too busy turning his plastic container of M&M's into a maraca and shaking it. Once Skylar seated herself, Cody simply hopped into the middle seat between them.

He tried to think of something witty and entertaining, but nothing came to mind. The room darkened a bit and the screen filled with the recorded voice asking everyone to turn off cell phones and pagers and to not text during the movie. After that, trivia questions were posted.

"I know that one—Robert Redford," Skylar said, shooting him a superior glance over the top of Cody's head. Giving into his competitive spirit, they spent the next fifteen minutes playing movie trivia. Cody got all the Disney-movie questions correct, and Marcus held up his hand for a high-five—which Cody delivered with a chocolate-coated smile.

Animated, colorful and loud, the movie did a great job at holding Cody's seven-year-old attention. The theater wasn't very crowded for the second showing, and he attributed it to most of the target audience being home in bed.

Sitting in the low-profile wheelchair he preferred, Marcus was able to stretch his arm across the back of Cody's chair and get comfortable, but he spent the entire movie watching his son's face reflect his delight at the goings-on onscreen. Once when Cody burst out laughing at something, Skylar laughed because Cody found it so amusing. From then on, Marcus watched her, his fingers able to reach her silky soft hair draped over the back of the seat.

Her skin was warm, the nape of her neck sensitive to his touch. More than once, he saw her attempt to suppress a shiver and fail. Seeing her response was such a turn-on. And the looks she shot his way?

Those were supposed to be glares, but every time she zeroed in on him like that, he ran his finger and thumb along the soft lobe of her ear and that was the end of that. She was too busy shifting and turning and trying to escape his reach, unable to go far because toward the end of the movie Cody kept pulling Skylar's arm over the seat divider to use as a pillow. She was well and truly stuck. And he had no problem taking advantage of it.

The credits rolled and the majority of the moviegoers exited the theater. Marcus nodded and said hello to a few of the people he knew, but when Skylar tried to rouse Cody enough for the walk to the car, Marcus stopped her. "Let me get him."

He scooped Cody into his arms and Skylar stood to help get Cody settled. In his sleepiness, Cody wrapped his arms around Marcus's neck, his head lolling on Marcus's shoulder.

Skylar bent over them and tried to loosen Cody's stranglehold, but once more Marcus stopped her. "Don't," he said, gently brushing her hand away. "I've missed too many of these. When you leave, I'll miss it even more," he said, unable to resign himself to the fact that Skylar would indeed fly home at the end of her vacation unless he stepped up his game.

He rubbed Cody's narrow back and stared at his son's mother, wondering how he'd ever thought anything was more important, or more devastating, than losing the two of them. Every day that passed brought them closer to their return to New York, and he'd be lying if he said he wasn't feeling the pressure, with seconds on the clock and only one shot at making his play count.

Skylar began gathering their trash and her purse, but when she tried to push his chair, Marcus stopped her again. He might not be able to walk, but he could take care of his family.

He adjusted Cody's position on his lap and grabbed the push-rims, then slowly rolled his sleeping son out the theater doors.

The drive home was mostly performed in silence but

it gave Marcus time to think. Or rather, rethink some of the things Skylar had said to him about their relationship, both past and present. The real sticking point had been his request—more of a demand—that she give up the things she loved to stay with him in North Star.

Maybe it was easier for her to do so, but he wouldn't want her to move there and be unhappy, either. Which left only one choice. "Tell me about your kids at school," he said, shooting her a glance across the darkened interior of the van.

"What do you want to know?"

Her voice was husky from the night air blowing in the window.

"Tell me about the kid who killed himself. What was going on?"

"Same thing that happens everywhere. Lots of pressure to succeed, to get into the right schools with the right grades, the right fellowships. Travis modeled, played sports, kept a 4.0, but it was never enough."

"Did he…talk to you about what he was thinking?"

"Not in so many words, no. I had a feeling he was reaching the breaking point."

"Why is that? What tipped you off?"

"Sometimes you just know the signs."

He frowned, hearing something in her tone he'd only ever heard once before, when she'd said she had lost herself in him. "It may surprise you to hear me say this but—I've been selfish."

Marcus smiled. Not even the dim light of the cab kept him from seeing the shock on her face. "I've been thinking of my convenience and the families' when I said it would be easier for you to move here, but I wasn't taking into account the importance of your job or what it means to you."

He glanced at her again and found her staring at him, her mouth open in surprise. Speechless? That was a first.

"Marcus…what are you saying?"

"I'm saying I'm still open to talking about our options here, that's all. Lots of people have two residences. Maybe I could look into getting a time-share or something and stay in New York a few weeks at a time during the school year. God knows racing there might be a lot easier than on these backroads."

"You'd do that?"

When would she get it? Understand that Cody wasn't the only one he wanted to see? Be with?

Time, he promised himself. If she knew he was open to a compromise on New York, maybe that would also change how she viewed their relationship. "Skylar, I made a huge mistake when I let you go. I won't make it again."

MARCUS'S WORDS STAYED WITH her as they drove down the ranch road toward her cabin. They had fallen into silence after his comment, and Marcus seemed as lost in thought as she was, trying to decipher the next step in their very unusual relationship.

Marcus had made a major concession, but she had to remember his desire to know his son was at the core.

Every now and again, she'd brave a glance in

Marcus's direction, and she noted his capability in driving the specially equipped van, his comfort behind the wheel.

How many times had they gone to the movies together when they had dated and lived in North Star? Tonight was different, though. Used to be, when they had sat in the back of the theater it wasn't because of Marcus's wheelchair. And on top of that, Cody's presence acted as a huge reminder of all they'd been through to get to this point in their separate lives, only to find themselves back together again.

No, not together. Wasn't once enough for you?

She saw all too well how easy it would be to fall right back into a relationship with Marcus. The desire was there. His willingness. And she knew no matter how many years passed, whether she was twenty-nine or seventy-nine, she would know the moment Marcus entered a room. The emotions were there, good feelings and bad ones. The screwed-up ones, too. What would she do if Marcus *did* come to New York? How would she handle his presence there? Seeing him on a regular basis?

"I'm not going to be around much the next two days," Marcus said abruptly. "I have to put the finishing touches on the sculpture for the statehouse and it's going to take some time. The movers are coming to pick it up on Thursday for the ceremony on Friday afternoon."

"You must be very excited. It's a beautiful piece."

Marcus took his gaze off the road for a second to look at her. "Thank you. That means a lot."

She lifted a hand to her hair to brush it away from

her face, but the wind blew it right back again. "You're welcome," she said softly, feeling inanely awkward having a normal conversation, considering the abundance of physical and decidedly sensual things she'd done with him in the past. Not to mention the arguments they'd had, too. Or the statement he'd just made. She was so confused. What would be best for them all?

"Actually, the ceremony is something I wanted to talk to you about. I was hoping you and Cody would come with me. The dedication is kind of a big deal, and I'd like Cody to see it."

"I'm sure he'd like that."

"So you'll come?"

Her, too? "Um…yeah, sure. I don't see why we couldn't drive to Helena for the day."

"You could…or you could just ride with me. It's a whole event. The dedication is that afternoon, with a dinner reception that evening. I was hoping you would go as my date. Jake and Maura will be there," he added. "Jake's rented a room at one of the hotels and Lexi will be watching the kids. If you're willing to stay, I'd rent us a room—two rooms—and Cody could stay with the kids for a few hours while we go out that evening."

She blinked a few times, unable to comprehend the man's thinking. First he said he'd consider *moving* to New York. Now this? *Be afraid. Be very afraid.* "You're asking me out?"

Marcus released a low chuckle that reminded her of old times. "I'm a little out of practice, but yeah. So will you go? Both of you?"

The event was obviously a big deal and she could see

it meant a lot to Marcus, but to go as his *date?* She struggled to find a suitable response other than "no-freaking-way." "Why is Jake going? Did I hear someone say Jake is thinking about getting into politics?" she asked, her thoughts whirling.

"I think that's Ben's wishful thinking. Jake would do well, though, if he did. The ranchers and people like him. But I don't think Jake intends to do more than try to be elected Judge." Marcus sent her another glance. "Will you go with me?"

"Marcus…"

"Two rooms, Skylar. If you insist," he added, a sexy, oh-so-gorgeous curl to his lips.

The things that man could do with his lips…

"I suppose I could bring Cody, but I didn't come prepared for dinner. I'll have to pass."

Even in the dark, she felt the impact of Marcus's smile. He'd dazzled the media and sports crews, his fans, with that grin. "You're turning down a crippled man?" he asked, one hand shooting up to cover his heart.

"Marcus, even if I wanted to go—which I don't—I don't think it's a good idea."

"I do. And, besides, if we're over, what's it going to hurt? It's dinner. Are you saying you can't sit at the same table with me? Because if you are…"

It would mean she still had feelings for him that went beyond the old boyfriend stage and into the realm of —*more.* "I am perfectly capable of eating dinner with you, so long as you know it's just dinner."

"I'm sure you'll keep reminding me," he said, a smile in his tone.

What had she just agreed to? Nothing could be that easy. Especially not where Marcus was concerned. Why was she putting herself through this? Just say no! "Oh, I forgot. I didn't pack anything fancy and it's too late to make a trip to shop." She hadn't exactly packed a little black dress in her bag of boots and sneakers and shorts.

"Already coming up with excuses, huh?"

"It's a legitimate reason. I doubt dinner at the state-house is summer-vacation casual."

"I'm sure you'll look gorgeous, no matter what you wear. You always do. And I'm holding you to your agreement."

Skylar frowned at the thrill she received at the compliment and promise in his words, and turned her attention back to her window. Going with Marcus to such an event would probably be more trouble and effort than it was worth, but it was obviously important to him. After she'd seen him cradle Cody so close in the theater, the truth was she didn't have the heart to say no. Like he said, it was dinner—and it certainly wouldn't go further. She *would* keep reminding him of that if necessary.

She had to think long term when it came to Marcus. As in how her relationship with him would affect Cody's emotional growth. Cody had experienced so many changes in such a short amount of time, she couldn't allow her fears and biases of the past interfere with the future now that Marcus had inserted himself into Cody's life. Dinner a few times a year, a few outings together, didn't make a couple or family. Not in today's world.

One of her favorite songs came on the radio and she leaned forward to turn up the volume, hoping that once the song was over Marcus would leave the volume where it was and they wouldn't have to talk.

Ten minutes later, Marcus rolled to a stop outside the cabin.

"Thanks for the movie. I'll get Cody."

Marcus unbuckled his seat belt and unlocked his wheelchair from its position in front of the wheel.

"I'll get Cody. You get the door," he ordered, pressing the button that opened the side door of the van and prepared the hydraulic lift.

She gathered up her purse and dug out her key card. She wished she could wake Cody up long enough so he could brush his teeth considering all the sugar he ate, but before she could debate the matter further, Marcus was there, gently wheeling their son up the ramp and into the house.

In Cody's bedroom, Skylar hurried to turn down the lower bunk. Cody hadn't slept there recently, only played, but a quick swipe across the surface rid the mattress of toys.

"Thanks," Marcus said, the tone of his voice making her wonder if he'd realized Cody had been sleeping in the top bunk.

Shoes off, and snoring lightly, Cody snuggled beneath the sheet without waking.

Marcus sat there for a while and watched, not even blinking.

"Are you okay?" she whispered.

"No." Abruptly, he turned and wheeled himself out

of the room as if it was on fire. And because she did care, damn it, she rolled her eyes, called herself a fool, and went after him, catching up with him at his van. He was in his chair, on the lift about a foot or so off the ground. At eye level. Spying the button on the door, she pressed it for the lift to stop. "What are you doing? You take us out, buy us dinner and a movie, ask us out again on Friday and make a huge deal out of being able to hold Cody, and then you just leave without a word?"

"Guess I figured a kiss was off-limits, since you keep telling me how you're leaving soon."

"It is. And I *am* leaving, but that doesn't mean you shouldn't have the decency to say good-night," she countered. "Marcus, what happened in there?"

He stared off toward the left, into the night.

"If I had been a better man, things could've been different. Sometimes it's hard to stomach all the mistakes I've made."

That was definitely a feeling she could identify with. "We make certain choices because they're the best for us. Regretting them doesn't change the reason why we made those choices in the first place. You...sent us away because you couldn't handle what had happened in your life. I know that now. Good night, Marcus."

His gaze fastened on hers, before lowering to the general vicinity of her mouth. Her lips tingled in response—until she reached out and pressed the button to raise the lift higher so he could enter the van.

She turned away to head back to the cabin when she heard him call her name.

"You're still going to that reception with me," he said.

Biting back an unwelcome smile and keeping her back to him, she shrugged. "And you're still booking two rooms."

Chapter 16

THE AFTERNOON OF THE STATEHOUSE dedication, Skylar barely managed to restrain her own nervousness when she saw Marcus shift in his wheelchair for the fifth time in five minutes.

Careful to keep hold of Cody's hand so she didn't lose him in the crowd, she leaned over Marcus's shoulder and whispered, "It's phenomenal and they'll love it. Stop worrying."

In response, Marcus reached up and snagged her hand, giving her a look that heated her insides to volcanic levels. He brought her hand to his mouth, brushed a kiss over her knuckles. He still held her hand against his lips when a member of the governor's team said it was time for him to join the others in front of the assembled crowd.

She was thankful for the interruption. Her hand tingled in response to the caress and, given their very public surroundings, she couldn't exactly take Marcus to task on the gesture.

Nearly an hour later after a lot of clapping, introductions and typical political speeches, Marcus's creation was unveiled and her words were proved correct by the awed gasps and cheering of the crowd. The governor, mayor and city officials made a show of walking around the sculpture of the grizzly bear, inspecting all of the details. They called it amazing. A masterpiece. A talent that was meant to be seen by everyone.

Was it true everything happened for a reason? It was a common concept a lot of people shared, but one she'd never really focused on until now. But how could it not be true in Marcus's case? Had he continued to play football, the odds were he never would have discovered his artistic side. That he wouldn't be doing this now.

Marcus was introduced and the crowd's cheers drew Skylar out of her thoughts. She picked Cody up and held him so he could see.

"Everybody's cheering for him," Cody said, visibly awed. "That's cool. Mom! Look at the sign," he said, pointing.

Someone had made a sign in the shape of a football jersey with Marcus's last name and number on it. The sign bobbed as the person cheered.

Once the crowd quieted down, the governor shook Marcus's hand before handing him the microphone. Marcus flashed his gorgeous grin and caused yet another ruckus as some of the women in the crowd screamed, earning more laughs from the crowd of officials surrounding him.

"Thank you," Marcus said, his gaze scanning the

visitors lining the statehouse lawn. "It was an honor being asked to create a piece to represent our wonderful state and to have my name go down in history as something other than a bad tackle."

Marcus paused when the crowd alternated between laughing awkwardly at his joke and cheering him again. When that died down, he continued, his voice ringing with sincerity and humbleness. Throughout his short speech, he continued to make eye contact with Skylar. The official photographer who'd seen her with Marcus earlier began snapping pictures of her with Cody in her arms.

The ceremony over, Marcus remained on stage, chatting with the governor and city officials while the crowd thinned. When he rolled down the short ramp erected for his appearance, those lingering rushed Marcus to get jerseys and photographs autographed, and have their picture taken with him.

"There you are," Maura said. "Jake spotted you once things began, but there were too many people to get to you. Hope you didn't mind braving that crowd alone."

"No, Cody and I were fine."

"Kids," Jake said abruptly. "Best behavior."

Glancing around, Skylar quickly spotted the reason for Jake's warning. Marcus rolled toward them with the governor at his side. After introductions, they were thanked for attending and the governor tousled Cody's hair.

"You know, you are a very special young man to have Marcus Whitefeather as your father. He's one of the bravest people I've had the pleasure of meeting," the man said. "A real hero."

"Really?" Cody asked, looking visibly surprised by the news.

"Without a doubt," the governor confirmed with a nod. "Your dad proved to a lot of people just how strong we Montanans can be."

The governor said his goodbyes, shook Marcus's hand again and then pulled Jake aside for a few quiet words. Maura tried hard not to stare, but Skylar noticed she couldn't help herself. "Is that about those rumors I've been hearing?" she asked softly.

"Oh, I hope not."

"You don't want to sleep with a politician?" Skylar teased, careful to keep her voice low. "It's all the rage."

Maura laughed and smacked Skylar gently on the arm.

Finally the group was together and discussing what to do next.

"We're heading to the hotel now," Maura said. "Do you want us to take Cody with us?"

"Actually," Marcus said, "I remember how long it takes Skylar to get ready—" His gaze gleamed with amusement when it met hers. "—And the dinner isn't until late tonight. Cody and I need to be fed, so I thought I'd drop Skylar off at the hotel and we could go pick up some food. What do you say, Cody? Shouldn't take more than few a minutes to pick it up and drive back to the hotel to your mom. You want to come with me?"

"Can I, Mom?"

Seeing as how Cody was still getting to know Marcus and had been leery of going somewhere totally alone with him, she knew this was a huge step. One she couldn't negate. Cody was making great strides in his relationship with Marcus. And while a little wary and sad and upset because she knew it was only the beginning, she was happy, too.

The vampire fascination hadn't disappeared. Cody had played with his newly returned Batman and Robin dolls the entire way to Helena. Marcus had distracted Cody from wanting to bring the dolls along to the ceremony by offering to let him ride on the back of the wheelchair. With his feet braced on the support bars on either side, Cody had to have his hands free to hold on.

Her son had asked if she could put the dolls in her purse, but Skylar's handbag was too little, so he'd reluctantly left them behind to "guard" the van for safekeeping. But to want to go with Marcus? "Sounds good to me. But only if you grab me some ribs from Ray's," she said, referring to a favorite spot. It was where Marcus had given her his class ring and asked her to the prom. Where he'd taken her to celebrate when he'd decided on a college.

Marcus grinned. "Already on the menu. I preordered them yesterday, just for you."

"Aw, how romantic," Lexi said.

Maura quickly shushed her, but it was too late because Skylar felt the same way. It *was* romantic. And sweet. Kind. Marcus knew how much she loved Ray's food, and the fact that he had been thoughtful enough to think that far ahead…

The group split up to head toward their vehicles and, on the way to the van, Skylar placed her hand on Marcus's shoulder as they lagged behind the others. "Thank you. For the food."

Hands on his wheels, Marcus leaned his head low, the gentle rasp of his chin and jaw against the back of her hand sending a sharp pang of longing through her.

"My pleasure."

She bit her lip and kept walking, focusing on putting one foot in front of the other, because it took every ounce of brainpower she had to remind herself she had less than two weeks left in North Star.

MARCUS TOOK ONE LAST LOOK in the mirror before he grabbed his hotel key card and wallet and headed out the door. He'd hoped to get their hotel rooms side by side, but instead Skylar and Cody had wound up down the hall by Jake and Maura, and the room they'd booked for Lexi and the kids.

He heard the television blaring in the room next door to Skylar's as he lifted his hand to knock.

A door opened, but not the one he expected.

"Wow. You look hot, Marcus," Lexi said with a grin, leaning against the jamb. Almost immediately, the twins poked their heads out, and before he had time to respond, Cody's appeared below them.

He chuckled at the stacked image until Skylar's door opened—and then he couldn't make a sound.

"Surprised I'm ready on time?" she asked, a definite spark in her tone. "What do you think?"

He took his time formulating an opinion. He checked out the blond hair she'd pulled back into an elegant-looking twist, the dangling earrings that sparkled even in the dim light and hung halfway down her neck, and the body-molding grayish-blue dress that left one shoulder bare and was split up the side to midthigh. Sparkling high heels completed the outfit, and showed off the mouthwatering shape of her long legs. "You're…"

"He's *speechless.*" Lexi laughed. "Mom, get out here. You have to see this. Look at Marcus."

Aware of the flush rising up his neck into his face, he shook his head and tried not to look like an ass. "It wouldn't be so embarrassing if it wasn't true," he said finally. "I *am* speechless. You look amazing."

"So do you. You've always looked nice in a tux."

He grinned again. Today had been a good day. The ceremony, Cody going with him for a drive. Skylar.

"Three proms together. We ought to have this down pat by now," he said. "Nice dress."

"This old thing?" She made a face. "Let's just say you owe me for the last-minute notice."

"Because…?"

"When I mentioned to Carly that I needed a dress for this evening, she insisted she knew the perfect place —then proceeded to take me to Mandy's house to shop her closet."

That bit of news brought out a whistle he couldn't hold back. "I would've liked to be a fly on the wall." He let his gaze sweep over her again. "But I can't say I'm not glad you went."

"You look pretty, Mom."

Skylar winked at their son. "Thank you, Cody. Be good and listen to Lexi, okay? Pay attention and do what she says."

"Okay."

Maura and Jake ordered the kids back inside the connecting room, only to fill the doorway themselves. Jake was still in his shirtsleeves, Maura fastening an earring.

Marcus nodded in greeting and informed the other couple that they were getting ready to leave. "Cody all set for the night?"

"Lexi's taking them down to the pool," Maura said.

"All three of them?" Wouldn't that be too much? She couldn't watch all three of them in the water, could she?

Jake worked to button his shirtsleeves. "She's a certified lifeguard and trained in CPR. They'll be fine, and she has her phone to call us if needed. Get going and drive safe. We'll see you there," Jake said, tugging Maura back into the room.

Marcus glanced at Skylar and found her watching him with a peculiar expression. "What?"

"Nothing. You looked like a concerned dad just then. It was…unexpected—but nice," she added, as if she didn't want to spoil the mood.

Skylar stepped out of her hotel room with her purse and wrap in hand, pausing long enough to double-check that the door shut properly behind her. When she turned toward the elevators, Marcus began wheeling himself along behind her. "You like anything else?" he asked casually.

"Your humility," she quipped, pressing the elevator button.

"I can list some things I like about you," he said, tilting his head to see her face, but just as quickly glancing right back down, because on this level he had the perfect view of where that slit in her dress ended.

"Marcus!"

"What?" he asked, pretending innocence as the elevator chimed and the doors slid open. "You know blue is my favorite color." The color of her eyes. One of the Cowboy's team colors. The Montana sky he loved so much.

Staring at Skylar, with her cool blond hair and creamy skin, the blue dress, he found himself digging out his cell phone. "Come here. We need to document this occasion."

"Are you serious?" she said when she saw him tap the camera app.

"For Ben," he said, hoping she didn't call him on the lie.

Shifting until she stood behind him, he framed them in the screen and took their picture.

The elevator stopped and chimed again, and Skylar moved into the hotel lobby. The moment she did, every head turned, but when he followed behind her in his tux and wheelchair, he noticed a few of the men narrow their gazes in contemplation, as if they didn't get why someone as beautiful as Skylar was with a guy like him.

Hands gripping the wheels, he kept going, pacing

himself to roll beside her. But it wasn't until Skylar placed her hand on his shoulder and left it there as they crossed to the entrance that he knew she'd seen the looks they had garnered. Despite the issues between them, Skylar was letting people think they were together, a couple. At least for tonight.

Which meant he had to make tonight last as long as possible.

THROUGHOUT DINNER, SKYLAR found herself in constant conflict with herself. Marcus was being very sweet. He'd not only bought her favorite ribs today, but he and Cody had also picked up a bouquet of flowers for her—from Cody, of course.

But sitting beside him at the elegant table during the long boring speeches that came with an evening such as this, she couldn't concentrate, her mind choosing instead to focus on the memories of her past with Marcus. Everything that had gone wrong—and everything that had been right.

All the long looks and touches seemed natural after what they'd shared, and she wasn't blind. She had seen the way people had looked at them in the hotel lobby and the looks on some of the men's faces... The surge of protectiveness had come automatically. So many men would look at Marcus with pity, but she saw all that he'd accomplished and she admired it. He wasn't the boy she'd known. He'd become a man, and she wished she had been around to watch it happen. But would she be the same person had she stayed?

Finally the events of the evening were over. Marcus was once again honored on stage and she found herself on her feet, clapping along with everyone else. Better still, a text from Nina read:

So far so good, still. No other problems. The kids are handling things really well all things considered. Hope you're having fun!

She smiled at the message, surprised because she really was having fun. Marcus was funny, good-looking, able to carry on a well-educated conversation about a multitude of subjects with the others at the table. It was a nice way to spend the evening.

Maura and Jake waved as they left the ballroom, but Marcus was waylaid by people wanting to talk to him, both about his art and his football days. Then finally they were able to make their escape.

"You're awfully quiet," Marcus murmured as they exited the hotel elevator on their floor.

Rolling along, he pulled his key card from his jacket pocket and tucked it beneath his leg. "Tired?"

It was late, well after midnight. Lexi had also sent a text at 10:30 p.m. saying Cody had fallen asleep in the kids' room and they would see her in the morning. "Just thinking."

"Skylar, I'm…sorry I couldn't dance with you tonight." She stopped in the hallway, unable to take another step. Her room was at the end of the hall but she didn't want their voices to wake the children.

When Marcus realized she'd stopped walking, he swung himself around to face her. "I really wish you'd stop doing that."

"Yeah? Well, I wish you wouldn't apologize for stupid stuff like dancing."

"I saw you tapping your foot. You enjoyed the music. You wanted to dance."

She pulled the sheer wrap tighter around her shoulders and fought the voice inside her head. "Is that right? Because I don't remember wanting to dance. What I remember—" She slipped off her shoes one at a time. "—Is tapping my foot, trying to get feeling back in my toes because these shoes are *killing* me."

She tossed the killer heels at Marcus and like the "man with the magic hands" quarterback he'd been, he caught them, one in each hand.

Head down, he studied the shoes for several seconds before dropping them in his lap. Then he looked just about everywhere but at her.

"Marcus?"

This wasn't the Marcus she knew. This man was vulnerable and on edge. Because he'd thought she wanted to dance? "Marcus, I had a really nice time tonight. I'm…glad you asked me to go."

Her words brought a huff of air from his chest and a curl to his lips. He stared at her, his expression so full of frustration and raw with his thoughts her heart beat out of rhythm.

"I am, too. But now that the evening is over, I want to kiss you good-night," he said, his voice husky. "But short of grabbing you and tugging you down, there's no way to…even things up."

Skylar's body warmed like it always did whenever

Marcus looked at her a certain way. But the way he looked at her now?

Even though she knew she walked a very narrow ledge when it came to him, she closed the distance between them, dropped her clutch and the wrap in his lap on top of the shoes and placed both hands on the low arms of his wheelchair, well aware that when she did so the dress borrowed from Mandy's closet dipped *really* low. "Why didn't you just ask me?" she breathed, taking his ability to ask anything away by lowering her head and planting her lips on his in a light, chaste kiss.

It sounded clichéd but with that one heady brush of their lips, she felt her body hum. Which led to another, slower, meeting of their mouths that stroked tongue against tongue, mingled breath with breath and created a furnace-blast of need in an instant.

Marcus's hands cupped her face, his thumbs at her jawline, just beneath each ear in that sensitive spot that made her shiver.

When she managed to pry her eyes back open, the first thing she saw was the way Marcus's gaze had darkened. Yeah, *that* was the look that made her want to rip her clothes off. Like, now.

"If I ask you to stay with me, will you? One night. The way we ended things before... We should've at least had a proper goodbye."

The humming got worse, setting every nerve ending in her body on fire. Do or don't. Stay or go. Love or... leave? "Are you asking?"

Her heart pounded so hard she felt dizzy, but while her mind screamed for her to say no, her heart was racing toward the finish line. She would leave. Go back to New York. Keep her life, no matter what.

"Sweetheart, I'm begging," he said, his voice husky —rich with need.

Glancing down, she spied his key card and reached out to slip it from beneath his leg. "Which door?"

IT WAS RIDICULOUS TO FEEL this nervous. It wasn't as though they hadn't made love before. Many, many times. In many, many ways. But as Marcus followed Skylar into his hotel room and locked the door behind him, he shook like an untried boy.

"This is a nice hotel," she said softly. "Very spacious compared to some."

He'd left the entry light on and now it was the only light in the room, but as he peered into the dimly lit interior he couldn't help but think all hotel rooms looked the same. Bed, dresser, television, bath. There was only one thing—one person—in this room that made it special. "Do you want anything? A drink?"

"No."

Skylar walked deeper into the wheelchair-accessible room, looking around.

"You are still as neat as ever, huh?"

The words were said with dry humor meant to bring out a smile. "Yeah, I guess. I could turn on some music?"

Skylar stared at him with a look he was afraid to try to interpret. She sat on the edge of his king-size bed, her hands at her sides.

"If you like."

Yeah, this wasn't awkward. Of all the times to do this, he really should've picked a day when they were both wearing less-complicated clothing. When there weren't doors to navigate, transfers to make. Something more…natural. "Marcus, why are you so nervous?" she asked, her voice soft but direct. "If you've changed your mind…"

"I haven't. I just…" He was blowing it. He needed to stop thinking and start doing, go back to kissing her. Why had he stopped in the first place?

Skylar crossed her long legs and the act left the slit of her dress open to her upper thigh. He almost swallowed his tongue and apparently she noticed because she tilted her head to the side and smiled at him the way she had back in high school. Ah, the things that girl could do to him.

"Marcus, it's just me. And I know I'm not the first woman you've been with since your accident."

Wheeling himself to the bed, he locked the wheels and transferred over to sit beside her, the awkwardness of the moment leaving him unable to look at her. "No," he admitted, feeling guilty because the few women he'd been with had all had blond hair. Blue eyes.

"So what's the problem?" she asked, reaching over to loosen his tie.

The scent of her surrounded him and for a moment he closed his eyes and brushed his lips against her hair, breathing her in.

When her fingers began undoing the buttons of his

tuxedo shirt, he forced himself to respond. "None of them knew me before the accident."

Her fingers paused in their work for the briefest of seconds, then continued on, seemingly with renewed purpose, yanking his shirt from his pants and unbuttoning buttons until it hung open and loose.

Skylar leaned back a bit to survey her work, and he couldn't help but tense when her fingers found his chest, slid over his pec and then down his belly.

"Do you know what I'd give to have a stomach as hard as this?" she said.

Her fingertips traced the muscle, every stroke driving him closer to the edge of no return.

She leaned toward him, her hands caressing his chest to wrap around his neck, her mouth inches from his.

"You're not the only one who's changed. Pregnancy and childbirth does a number on a woman's body."

"You look fantastic."

She wove her fingers through his hair, slid her palms down and pushed his jacket off his shoulders. "You haven't seen my battle scars yet."

"It doesn't matter."

When her lips curved into a slow smile and she met his gaze once more, he realized the trap she'd set. Knew the changes in his body didn't matter to her, either. And because knowing that was such a turn-on, he closed the distance between them and kissed her, not the slow, sweet kisses they'd exchanged outside in the hall but a deep, hard, desperate melding of their mouths that held nearly eight years of missing her. Wanting her.

He finally had her in his arms again. But for how long? What would it take for her to realize there was no one else for him?

SKYLAR WAS ALL TOO AWARE OF MARCUS'S touch, every breath, every kiss, every stroke of his hands over her body as they sat on the bed.

His hesitation had ripped open a place deep inside her. The one she'd buried and protected and sheltered for too many years. There were so many questions she should ask, at least know the answers to. But she wouldn't and she didn't and right now—this was the only thing that was important. This moment, these feelings.

Marcus was the father of her child, and right or wrong or screwed up or not, she wouldn't turn him away.

She felt his hands roaming her body, searching for the fastener of her dress. She stopped the blazing kisses to pull away, shoving herself up off the bed. Before Marcus could think the worst, however, she turned her back to him and curled her arms behind her, fingertips finding and pulling the zipper low.

The air was cool on her supersensitive skin, the strap of her gown falling down her arm because of the lack of tension. Keeping her back turned to him, she stepped out of the dress and draped it over the arm of a nearby chair.

"Turn around."

Only now did she hesitate. A depressed pregnant

woman knew no bounds when it came to eating. Her body had grown too fast, the skin on her stomach unable to keep up. And despite dieting and running and too many damn crunches to count, she still couldn't lose the flab around her belly button. Or the ugly stretch marks.

A lot of people looked at her blond hair and blue eyes and saw a pretty image but they had no clue—and most didn't care—about the person inside. They saw breasts and legs and clothes and formed an opinion, judged, not knowing what it was like to be on the receiving end of things.

And if she hadn't seen the looks Marcus had garnered while exiting the hotel lobby, if she didn't know for a fact that he understood what it was like being on the receiving end of those judgments, she might not have had the courage to do as he said.

She turned slowly, stomach sucked in as tight as she could make it. Marcus sat straighter on the bed and she didn't dare breathe as his gaze swept over her, lingering on her generous chest anchored by a strapless bra, down to her mostly taut long legs. She'd always been curvy, but all the running kept things in as good condition as she could make them—and acted as stress relief and meditation.

Her hands fluttered over her stomach. "Battle scars," she said softly.

"Beautiful," he countered.

Marcus shrugged off his shirt, his cuff links sparkling in the dim light of the entry. But when he moved to unfasten his shoes, she retraced the steps to the bed, placed her hand on his shoulder and shoved him back, trailing her fingertips down his mouthwatering torso, over the growing hardness of him and lower still. In seconds, his feet were bare, pants stripped off, condom located. Marcus was hard at work on her bra, which came undone with very little effort, despite the difficulty she'd had getting herself stuffed into it.

He pulled her onto the bed and she fell forward with a muffled laugh that turned into a gasp when his mouth found her nipple, his hand sliding with unmistakable purpose down over her belly to that spot between her thighs.

"Say my name," he ordered, the words growled into her ear.

"What?" She couldn't think when he touched her, especially considering where he touched her.

"Say my name."

She grasped his head in her hands to stop the kissing, held him back far enough that she could focus.

The naked pain on his face told her what Marcus wasn't saying. He knew her relationship to Tom had started off as a mutual agreement born of shattered souls, but Marcus had never asked if it had also been physical. He was asking this of her instead.

She'd be lying if she said she and Tom hadn't sought comfort from each other in the years of their marriage after Cody was born, both of them desperate to have as normal a relationship as possible. Seven years was a long time to be married to a man who wanted to live every moment he had left. They had been friends. Good friends.

But here and now, there was no one else in this bed. Not the girl she'd discovered Marcus with that night. And definitely not Tom.

She pushed against his shoulders, shifting so that he was on his back. Skylar swung her leg over him, straddling him, her hands roaming over his gloriously muscled chest. Marcus was…unbelievable. Hard and honed.

She squeezed her thighs tight around his hips and drew a groan from him before she leaned over him and brushed her lips over his to absorb the sound. *"Marcus."*

Some of the tension in his expression eased. His eyes smiled at her when she lowered her head again, gave him a blazing kiss so hot she rubbed against the heat of him, inching herself down, pressing kisses against every lickable ab, tonguing his belly button, kissing her way south until she pulled his shorts low.

"Skylar."

"I knew I'd get you to say my name. I didn't even *have* to ask," she teased.

In an instant, Marcus lifted her up—he was so strong!—and placed her beside him on the bed while he ripped open the condom. But she wasn't going to make it that easy for him. His breathing was already ragged and harsh, his hands all thumbs. But because she was bent on making this a night neither one of them would ever forget, she curled around him once more, gave him one last, long, very intimate kiss that had Marcus sucking in a sharp breath and forgetting the condom long enough to hold her hair back so he could watch.

When he could take no more, she helped cover him

and moaned low when he took control, rolling her onto her back, holding her hands to the mattress, his weight balanced on his hands and knees. "Don't," she bit out, not sure of what to say, but not wanting to hurt him. "I can…"

"So can I," he muttered.

Marcus slid inside her, not hard, not fast. Slow. So slow she closed her eyes and arched her back because her body wanted more.

He began to pump his hips, grinding into her with precise movements meant to drive her crazy. Skylar lifted her knees, drawing a moan from them both when it sent him deeper.

The hotel room was filled with the sounds they made. Marcus kissed her until she clutched his shoulders, her grip urging him on. The friction built the tension inside her to a feverish peak until it spread, expanded. Shattered through her until all she could do was hold on to Marcus until he buried his head in her neck and groaned.

"I love you… Ah, sweetheart, I love you."

Chapter 17

WITH HER SHOES, CLUTCH AND wrap in hand, Skylar eased out of Marcus's hotel room and breathed a sigh of relief when the door closed with a soft click. Now to get into her room with the same result, that of not waking anyone up.

She covered her yawn with her hand. If ever there was a good reason to lose sleep, last night had been it. Now if only she knew how she would handle facing him in the light of day, given what he'd said to her. Breakup goodbyes didn't usually end with those three little words.

She opened her small clutch and dug around inside for her key. Lipstick, compact, ID, tissue—but no key card? "No," she whispered. "Nooo." She had left the key card out on the dresser to put in her clutch but forgot to put it in because Marcus had knocked.

Groaning, she looked around the empty hallway. She was locked out of her room, locked out of Marcus's room unless she wanted to wake him up and explain why she'd snuck out because she couldn't face the whole

I love you mess. And she couldn't wake Maura or Jake without them figuring out where she had been in the hours since she and Marcus had left the statehouse.

Head down, she walked toward the seating area tucked beneath a window overlooking the city and dropped down onto the sofa. Was she really going to have to do the walk of shame through the lobby to registration to get a new key?

Better that than the alternative.

She retraced her steps down the hall, past Marcus's room, trying to juggle her things and smooth her sex-hair at the same time.

The elevator door dinged before she had a chance to push the button, and considering she was still dressed for her evening out, she stepped back to let the current passengers off, hoping to get on unnoticed. Instead she heard a laugh that was quickly shushed by the sound of a man's groan.

Skylar looked up in shock to find Lexi in the process of French kissing some guy who had to stoop a good foot to reach her. Apparently in an effort to ease the strain, he'd lifted Lex up by her behind and held her at kissing level with his hands planted firmly on her bottom. Lexi's hair hung wet down her back, her two-piece bathing suit barely there.

Just when Skylar was about ready to break the glass over the floor's fire-safety equipment and unleash the water hose, the two came up for air.

Neither of them had spotted her standing there off to the side, and she was torn between wanting to confront them and wanting to hide.

Anger won out in the end. "Have fun swimming?"

Lexi faced her, both hands flying to her mouth to cover her gasp.

Skylar realized her mistake in confronting them now when Lexi's gaze ran over her crinkled dress and mussed hair.

"Yeah, we did. Where were you?" the girl countered.

Skylar stalked forward on her bare feet, the carpet absorbing the sound. "I'm of age. You, on the other hand, are barely past jailbait and you're supposed to be in that room, babysitting. How long have you been gone?" When Lexi paled and didn't answer, Skylar raised her eyebrows. "Answer me or we go bang on your parents' door right now."

"J-Jailbait?" the guy asked.

"I'm sorry. I'm so sorry I lied, but I'll be eighteen soon."

"You s-said nineteen."

Skylar pinned the guy—who for the most part looked truly contrite and horrified—with a glare. "She's *seventeen*, and you look like you're old enough to know the difference."

Bright red color rushed into the guy's face and he took a step back, his gaze fastening on Lexi. Shaking his head slowly, he opened his mouth to say something, but words apparently failed him. He punched the elevator button, but just as quickly swore and took off down the hall toward the stairs.

"Wait! Justin, please! Let me explain."

The guy didn't so much as pause but shoved the door to the stairs open with a loud bang.

"Skylar, how could you? He'll never speak to me again."

"Sounds as though maybe he shouldn't," she said. "Lex, I get wanting to be older. I even pretended to be older a time or two myself when I was your age, but you are being paid to stay with those kids and make sure they're okay. What were you doing with Justin that you couldn't do at a reasonable hour—and don't think for a second it doesn't *tick me off* that you're making me sound like our mothers."

"Nothing. We were just swimming."

"Lexi."

"All right, we messed around some, but not…that."

"But I'm right in thinking he is the older guy?"

Skylar crossed her arms over her chest, her skin chilled. The air-conditioned hallway was definitely drafty but she wasn't about to let Lexi off the hook yet.

"Yes. I told him I was going to be here, so he came to meet me."

"And the fact that you are supposed to be supervising the kids? What if one of them had woken up? Gotten sick? What if a fire had broken out? I entrusted my child to you and you're not even in there!"

"I'm sorry."

"No, you're not. Maybe if you were, I wouldn't be so angry right now. Lexi, we talked about this. And if that guy can't meet with you at a time and place with your parents' approval… How dare you leave those kids in there alone and not tell anyone."

Lexi's eyes filled with tears but Skylar hardened her heart at the sight.

"I am sorry. I know it seems wrong——"

"It *is* wrong," Skylar corrected.

"But I waited until Mom and Dad were back. I figured if they did wake up, they'd go through the door into the other room."

"And when they said they couldn't find you? What then? Let your parents worry and freak out not knowing where you were?"

Lexi swallowed audibly. "I hoped they wouldn't."

"No, what you're saying is you gambled on the fact that they wouldn't wake up and you'd get away with sneaking out."

"You're not in your room, either."

"Again, Lexi, I'm an adult."

"And Marcus is nice but you're not going to stay with him, are you? How's it right to sleep with him and leave? Everyone's talking about how great he is with Cody."

Moving forward with such purpose that Lexi backed away—smart girl—Skylar waited until Lexi's eyes widened in fear before she sidestepped at the last minute and walked on by her. "You want to tell your Mom and Dad I slept with Marcus? Let's go," she said, praying Lexi wouldn't let her take more than a few steps down the long hallway toward their rooms.

"Skylar, no. Please!" Lexi called, her voice low and ragged. "Please, please, don't tell them about Justin. Dad will freak out because Justin's older, but Justin isn't like that. Please," she begged, catching up with Skylar and grabbing her arm. "I'm sorry. I'm really, really sorry. It won't happen again."

"Don't lie to me, Lex."

"I'm not. I knew it was stupid and I should've been more responsible, but I *love* him. I want to see him, be with him." Lexi exhaled, tears streaming down her cheeks. "I lied to him, okay? He thinks I'm older—nineteen, like he said. And I told him I was here for the dedication, not because I was babysitting."

"Oh, Lexi. Why? If you can't be honest with him *or* your parents, how would it ever work?"

"I'm almost eighteen. And he just turned twenty-five. It's only seven years."

"That's a lot when you're that age, though. Honey, he's a man and you're still—"

"A little girl? No, I'm not. I've had boyfriends, but that's just it—they were boys. Justin isn't like them. He's quiet and shy, and, yeah, he's older but he's… It's not what you and my parents make the whole age thing out to be."

"Lex, the truth is most guys his age want one thing. Are you ready for that kind of relationship? Isn't going away to college enough to deal with right now?"

"I told you, I don't want to go. I—I turned down the scholarship."

"Lexi, nooo."

"It's too late. I did it. And whatever happens, happens."

Skylar gave her cousin a hard stare. "Justin didn't look too thrilled at the fact you've been lying to him. Especially that you're underage."

"I know. I'll talk to him."

"Lexi, do you think this guy cares for you? You think

you mean something to him? If that's true, have him prove it to you. Make him wait. If he's still around in two years after you've gotten to know each other really well? I guarantee your parents will have a different opinion of him."

"And if he isn't?" Lexi asked. "Do you know what some of the girls in my school did with their boyfriends? With guys that *aren't* even their boyfriends?"

Oh, she remembered that pressure. That horrible expectation all guys seem to have. Why didn't it ever get any easier? "Yeah, honey, I do. But I promise you, if Justin cares for you, he'll know you're worth the wait. Don't sell yourself short and give yourself to a guy who wouldn't care if it's you he's screwing or someone else."

"He's not like that."

"Are you sure? Really sure? Because guys talk a good game but too often girls are just replaceable bodies and you have to be strong enough and smart enough to recognize the difference."

Lexi cried now, silent tears trickling down her cheeks. And because Skylar knew a lecture could do only so much, she tilted her head toward the door, knowing without a doubt Lexi wouldn't be going anywhere else tonight. "I have to go get my key card replaced. Go to bed."

"Are you going to tell my parents?"

She had to think long and hard about that one but considering Lexi *was* on her way to college in the fall, the girl had to start dealing with sexual responsibility, otherwise her college days might very well be a feeding frenzy. "I don't know yet," she said honestly. "If it was

Cody sneaking out...I'd want to know. I'd want someone to tell me, because like it or not, you *are* only seventeen."

"*Please* don't. You know they have this thing about age and who I can date."

Because of Skylar and all her mistakes with older men. She was a teaching tool of what not to do. Yeah, she got that. "You need to talk to them, Lex. I'm sure your mom and dad can remember what it was like to be young."

Lexi wiped her face and shivered, her hair still wet from her swim.

"Go to bed, Lexi. And no more sneaking out. Not now, not later. Let things settle down with Justin before you talk to him."

"Okay."

Skylar waited while Lexi oh-so-carefully opened the door to the room where the twins and Cody slept, listening as the door shut just as quietly and the lock slid into place.

Turning to finally go get that key, she caught a hint of sound before the door next to Lexi's swung open without a sound. Skylar jumped in surprise, immediately backing up because New Yorkers didn't like surprises that came out of the dark—until Jake stepped into the light, dressed in jeans and an untucked shirt.

With a whoosh, the air left Skylar's lungs. *Busted.* "You were listening the whole time?"

"Most of it. Do I want to know what they were doing when they got off that elevator?"

Picturing the scene, Skylar winced. Most dads

wouldn't want to see their daughters in an embrace like that.

"I thought so. Thanks for talking to her. I don't think I could've held my temper long enough. I barely made it as it was. You did a better job than I could manage right now. I want to rip the guy's head off."

"Well, for what it's worth, I think he was just as surprised and disappointed. He looked…hurt. Like he really does care."

Jake inhaled and sighed at the news. "Good to know. Maybe in the morning I'll be calm enough to talk to her about it. And the scholarship mess. Damn it, that was a full ride."

"Maybe you can talk to the school officials."

"Maybe. Lex is right about one thing, though," Jake whispered. "Marcus doesn't deserve to have you mess around and then take off again. Not when he's finally gotten his life back together. You need to remember that."

"I know." Lexi wasn't the only one who'd made a mistake tonight. Marcus's *I love you* had proven that.

SKYLAR GLANCED OVER HER shoulder to where Cody sat in the backseat of Marcus's van and smiled. He'd asked if he could listen to music on her phone. He looked so grown up with the white earbuds dangling out of his ears, head nodding in time with the song. A while back, she'd made a selection of Cody's favorites but soon she was going to have to break down and buy him his own iPod to keep him from constantly taking her phone. Maybe for his birthday? It wasn't until September, but since they were here…maybe she should have a little surprise party for him at the ranch so all the family could be there. Marcus, too.

Turning back around, she watched as Helena began to fade from view.

"You okay?" Marcus asked softly.

She smiled, probably a little too much. "Yeah. I'm good. You?"

"Yeah," he said, his hands gripping the wheel.

Oh, this was awkward. It's not like she didn't know why he was asking. "Look, Marcus…about last night."

"Don't say anything."

"But that's why you're so tense, isn't it?" By the time she'd retrieved her key and fallen asleep in her room, it had been time to get up and meet Cody and the others for breakfast. Lexi was present, looking just as bleary-eyed as Skylar felt, but it didn't appear as if her parents had said anything to her about her nocturnal adventures.

Watching him now, she saw Marcus glance in the rearview mirror as though to check on Cody.

"I'm tense because I promised myself if we—if what happened last night was a possibility, I wouldn't screw it up again."

His words slid home, more revealing and heartfelt than all of the apologies he'd voiced since she'd discovered him with that girl. "You didn't screw anything up, Marcus."

"No? I shouldn't have said what I did. I'm sure it was a surprise and it puts you under a lot of pressure."

"Not at all," she said, managing to get the words out. "Don't worry about it. I know it was an accident. A heat-of-the-moment type of thing. Like old times, right?"

Marcus muttered something she couldn't hear and probably didn't want to.

"No, that's not right." He shot her a long glance before turning his attention back to the wheel. "Skylar, I *meant* what I said to you. What I'm trying to explain is that I told myself if we ever...got together again, I wouldn't rush you. I wouldn't pressure you the way I did before. I know you didn't plan on what happened. I didn't, either."

No, definitely not. But— "You were prepared for it," she reminded him.

"Because I'd hoped." He flashed her his insanely gorgeous grin. "I definitely hoped it would happen."

"Me, too," she said, surprising herself with her honesty. But really, when she'd seen that dress and thought about spending the evening with him, she couldn't lie and say a few fantasies hadn't popped into her own head. Marcus had always liked the color blue on her....

"We'll take this a day at a time. An hour at a time. We can do that, right?"

Maybe. Possibly. Some long-distance relationships worked and so long as Marcus knew she would never give up her life in New York... If he accepted and respected that... She knew plenty of couples who were married but not having sex. Couples who were divorced but having sex. Couples that lived separately for most of the year but got together whenever they could. It wasn't like she was interested in seeing anyone else. She would have Cody the majority of the time, her job, her friends, her life, her home—and Marcus, too.

Maybe…it could work?

MARCUS WASN'T SURE WHAT to expect when they got back to the ranch that Sunday afternoon. On the trip back to North Star, all he could think about was being without Skylar and Cody now that he'd known what it was like to be with them. And seeing as how Skylar was dead-set against moving to Montana, that meant he had to follow up on his idea of finding a place in New York. Damn, but that wasn't going to be cheap. He'd brought it up, though, and had to keep his word.

Skylar had been able to forgive him enough to stay with him last night, but he didn't want only a night. He wanted more. He wanted his family.

The passion and chemistry was as strong as ever. Surely they could build on that, on the mistakes of their past they knew better than to repeat, and start fresh?

Seeing them drive up, the Rowland twins ran to the cabin to see if Cody could play at Jake and Maura's house before everyone went to the fire pit for the evening social.

Skylar said yes.

Lexi slowly joined them for the walk back to their house tucked deeper into the woods, away from the cabins dotting the valley floor, but when the girl got close, Marcus was surprised to see her eyes all puffy.

"Something wrong, Lexi?"

Lexi immediately glanced at Skylar before shaking her head.

"No. Just tired. We'd better go. I have to get back and help Mom. She said to tell you that we'll bring Cody to the campfire and keep an eye on him so you can come whenever you want to."

Skylar looked so anxious at actually being left alone with him that Marcus almost smiled. Maybe one day it would be funny but it wasn't yet. "Tell Maura we said thanks," he said, wheeling himself to the door with Skylar's overnight bag on his lap.

"I can take that," Skylar said, propping it open with her body.

"I've got it," he said, wheeling himself inside. "Do you know why Lexi was upset?" he asked casually.

"Yeah. It's a long story. Um, shouldn't you go check on Ben?"

"He's fine. I called this morning before I left the hotel and told him I wouldn't be home until later."

"Oh." She turned toward the kitchenette, dropping her purse on the counter.

Marcus followed her, and didn't stop rolling until he was right behind her, close enough to snag her hips and pull her into his lap.

"Marcus…"

He kissed her shoulder, licked her skin. She tasted like salt and vanilla.

Shifting her into the right position wasn't easy, but when you want something bad enough, you make any and every situation work for you. "You're saying my name again," he said, tugging her low until he nuzzled her lips. "How about we see if we can get you to scream it?"

The moment her eyes darkened, he knew he had her.

They barely made it to her bedroom. Marcus took his time stripping her down. Today was easy. Shorts, T-shirt, bra and panties. Her flip-flops were lost along the way, one in the kitchen, one while riding down the hall with her sprawled on his lap. Maybe he couldn't carry her, but he easily rolled them to bed.

Within seconds, she was naked and out of breath, lying on the bed like a feast. Just for him.

Knees against the mattress, he drew her to the very edge of the bed.

"Marcus, you're not going to— *Ohhh.*"

He smiled at her surprise, at the heady, intoxicating sound of her voice going from normal to very, very seductive.

No other woman existed in his mind. In his heart. No one else looked like her, all creamy soft skin, beautiful eyes. No one else smelled like her, rich and sweet. No other woman tasted like her or made his blood pulse through his veins.

Last night, they'd made love in a rush of excitement and need. Now he drew out every caress, every stroke, until her fingers clenched the covers and she bit her lips to muffle the sounds she made. But he didn't want her to deny him anything. "Let me hear you."

He pressed a kiss to her inner thigh. Another to the jut of her hip. Her ragged breathing filled the air, and with every soft, nibbling kiss, her breathing grew more and more labored.

"Marcus," she whispered.

"Louder," he urged, gripping her legs in his hands when she tried to shift and change position.

Finally he gave into the unbearable urge to taste her again and her moans filled his ears. He built the tension higher, never giving her enough until—

"Marcus."

The desperate plea satisfied his desire to dominate this moment, to dominate her, because in this she couldn't deny him, wouldn't. He gave into the passion fueling his need for her and Skylar's entire body went taut, her back arched and she moaned her pleasure.

While she lay gasping on the bed, he pulled his shirt over his head, transferred to the bed and stripped down. He'd barely gotten his pants off when Skylar grabbed the condom out of his hand, rolled it on and settled herself in his lap.

Her expression was soft, flushed and sated, but her eyes glinted with such fire he found himself smiling.

"You look mighty pleased with yourself," she murmured in a throaty voice.

"I must say, I am."

Her gaze scanned his chest, her hands followed and he loved the fact she was so visibly turned on by what she saw. Loved her. Period.

Her thumb slid into his navel and he sucked in a sharp breath.

"Oh. So sensitive," she teased, a sensual grin curling the corners of her mouth.

She skimmed her palms back up, over his abs, up his pecs and down his arms, leaning over him, her beautiful breasts jiggling, distracting him.

"How long can you last, speed racer?"

He closed his eyes and breathed her in, his mouth finding her breast for a brief moment while she positioned him and slid down, hard. "Not...long."

Her pleased laugh drew him and he opened his eyes to see her, watch her. Head thrown back, body moving.

She was beautiful. His.

He just had to figure out a way to make her realize she no longer had to be afraid of loving him.

Chapter 18

"SKYLAR, HEY."

Three days later, Skylar turned at the sound of her name and immediately recognized Booker Phipps, the Olympic trainer she'd asked her neighbor and attorney-friend, Jill, to mention Marcus's name to.

Booker was dressed in sneakers, jeans and a loose T-shirt, and his sun-streaked hair and dark tan told of the many hours he spent outdoors. "Hey, yourself. You're here," she said dazedly. "Last I heard from Jill, she said your schedule was full. I thought you weren't coming."

"It took some doing to rearrange a few things." He looked around the main buildings. "This is a great place."

"Yeah, it is. I'll introduce you to Seth and Grace, the owners."

"Already met them. And as much as I'd like to stay and hang out, I've got today and tonight before I go back to the airport tomorrow morning."

"Quick trip, huh?"

"Yeah, but hopefully I'll be able to make a trip back and enjoy it."

"So what happens now?"

"Any way I can see Marcus in action? Get an idea of his form? I can usually tell with one glance if someone has what it takes and needs a little work or if it's a lost cause."

She glanced at her watch and knew Marcus was usually rolling this time of morning so he could get his miles in before the heat of the day. "I think that can be arranged."

"You're awfully nice to do this. Most exes wouldn't be trying to help like this."

His words brought a wave of unease and guilt— and more than a little fear. When she'd made the call, she had wanted Booker to provide an opportunity to get Marcus *out* of her life and Cody's. Now… Cody knew the truth, and she and Marcus had… But if Marcus had the potential to train for the Olympics, that was good, right? "Yeah, well, I suppose we're not…typical."

Thirty minutes later, Skylar, Cody and Booker were parked on high ground along the highway—at Seth Rowland's recommendation—waiting for Marcus to come into view. A few minutes later, Liam rolled to a stop behind them in an SUV with a sheriff's decal on the side.

"Hey, you having car trouble?"

"No," she said, explaining the situation and introducing Liam to Booker. "Actually, Liam is the one who told me how fast Marcus can go."

Booker's gaze narrowed. "You wouldn't want to put the radar gun to him again, would you?"

"You bet."

"Now," Booker said as Liam walked away. "Any suggestions as to how we get him to top speed?"

"Mom, can I get out? I wanna see."

"Sure, Cody, come on," she said, opening the door. Cody left his toys behind in the car and had one foot on the plastic tread of the car to jump when his other foot caught on something and sent him tumbling out of the vehicle, headfirst. "Cody!"

Skylar couldn't catch him in time and Cody landed on the hot asphalt on his hands.

"Owww."

She helped get Cody out and onto his feet, turning his palms over and brushing away the tiny rocks sticking to them. His palms were a little pink. "No blood."

"Good," he said, surprising her.

Just a few weeks ago that statement would've brought out a sigh of sadness because the blood might attract vampires, which meant his vampire "father" would come see him. "Can you call Marcus and tell him to hurry?"

She laughed. "I'm sure he'll get here soon."

"Actually that's not a bad idea," Liam said as he rejoined them. "I know if I were Marcus, I'd hurry if you called me and said Cody was waiting. You know, given the circumstances."

Skylar straightened. Because she knew Marcus *would* hurry for Cody. She pulled out her cell phone.

Cody wants to see how fast you can go. We're

parked along the highway on the hill before the Second Chance turnoff. You close?

Hesitating briefly, she pressed the send button and hoped she hadn't made a huge mistake in inviting Booker to the ranch. She'd mentioned it to Marcus earlier, but they hadn't discussed the matter since.

"Is he coming?" Cody asked, hopping up and down, the fall from the car obviously forgotten.

"Yup," Liam said with a wink. "All we have to do now is wait."

They did—but not for long.

6 miles from ranch. B right there.

"See?" Liam said after Skylar read Marcus's message aloud.

Booker chuckled and nodded his approval.

So they waited some more, Liam holding the radar gun at the ready.

And then they saw him. Marcus topped the low rise across the valley from where they'd parked. His head was down, body bent forward over his knees. Arms working, pumping the wheels.

He was…flying.

"Wow, he's going fast!" Cody said, jumping up and down. "Do you see him, Mom? Do you see him?"

"I see him."

Booker whistled.

"Thirty-five," Liam said. "Thirty-seven."

The gun made beeping noises as Liam clocked Marcus's speed.

"Forty. Forty-three."

"He's building up quite a punch." Booker straightened and leaned forward. "Question is can he keep it?"

"Forty-five."

"Come on," Booker whispered excitedly. "Show me what you've got."

Skylar held Cody's hand—and her breath. She'd known Marcus could go fast, but that fast? In a modified wheelchair?

"Forty-six. Forty-seven."

Even Liam was getting excited now.

"Forty-seven… Forty-*eight.*"

Booker was nearly beside himself with delight, never taking his gaze off Marcus, but shaking his head, pumping his fist. "*Yes.* Dude, that is awesome."

Skylar was almost afraid to ask, but she had to know. "So what do you think? Do you think Marcus has what it takes?" she asked, unsure of what to wish for—that Marcus had the potential to succeed, or that he didn't.

Her question brought out a chuckle from Booker.

"Honey, if Marcus could bring that to the table consistently in the upcoming heats? He could bring home the gold."

She smiled at the response, knowing without a doubt Marcus would be thrilled at the prospect of competing. So thrilled he'd choose it over them?

MARCUS HAD SEEN THE GROUP waiting up ahead and since Cody had wanted to see how fast the racer could go, Marcus had given it all he had.

Now he passed the group and wondered who the man was with Skylar. The guy was smiling up at her as

Marcus rolled by, and a sharp bolt of jealousy spiked through him as he let the racer slow on its own so he could catch his breath.

Wheeling the racer around, he approached the group slowly. He felt like he was missing something important. "Hey. Am I late to the party?" he asked.

"You went really fast," Cody said, his expression filled with awe. "Just like a vampire would."

"Cody," Skylar warned with a slight shake of her head.

"I fell down," Cody continued, holding up his hands. "But I'm okay. No blood. See?"

Marcus motioned for Cody to come closer. "Let me take a look."

Cody approached and Marcus took a few seconds to inspect his son's hands. Other than some redness, dirt and something sticky, they looked fine. "Looks good to me. You wanted to see me race, huh?"

Cody nodded. "And I wanted to see the number on the gun."

"The gun?" he asked, lifting his head.

For the first time, Marcus noticed Liam held a radar gun in his hand.

"That's some mighty impressive speed you had back there," the other man in a wheelchair said.

Marcus didn't recognize the other man but he did know the guy was interested in Skylar. Instinct, his gut, whatever, told him that loud and clear. "Thanks."

Skylar performed the introductions. It took Marcus a moment or two to catch on. Booker Phipps. The guy from the Olympic training center?

He removed his sunglasses and pulled the bandana tied around his head low to wipe the sweat from his face. "I didn't know you were coming to Montana."

"I didn't know he was, either," Skylar said. "Booker surprised me, too, but he says you might have a shot at the gold."

"You'd still have to go through all the qualifiers and make the team," Booker inserted, "but I definitely see potential if you're interested in training for the trials."

For the Olympics? Seriously? It was a lot to take in, but just the thought of it made his heart pump faster.

"Ahh, I know that expression. That's the look of a competitor," the man said with a grin. "I take it you're interested in hearing some more about the program? Getting some details?"

Of course he was interested. Majorly interested. But he also couldn't help but wonder why Skylar was being so accommodating with this turn of events, seeing as how the last time they were together, she'd resented the time he'd spent training....

Or was that why she'd asked the man to come in the first place?

Marcus was still pondering the answer to his many questions later that evening in Skylar's cabin.

"Cody's asleep," she said, shutting the bedroom door behind her and padding down the short hall to the living room, where he waited. "He said to tell you that you could have a sleepover. You get the bottom," she said, flashing him a grin. "And while I know it's a good offer, I have a counteroffer."

Watching her approach, he played along. "What's

that?"

"Hmm…"

She lowered herself onto his lap, her legs hanging over the low arm of his wheelchair.

"Well, we'll probably have to negotiate top or bottom, but you could stay in my bed until around six, and his bunk until seven? The kid has a built-in clock. Even in summer he's up at seven, on the dot, unless he's sick or just really exhausted."

"He got that from me. You would sleep all day if you could."

After leaving the highway today, Skylar had driven Booker back to the Second Chance, while Liam had taken Marcus and his racer to his house long enough for Marcus to swap them out for his wheelchair and his van so he could drive over himself. While he and Booker had talked, Skylar had spent the afternoon with Cody, Carly and Riley at the ranch's small pool.

"Sleep is good for you," she said. "I'll have to remember how swimming wears Cody out. He's never gone to bed so easily. Did you hear any of what he was telling the other kids? About how fast you could go? He compared you to a superhero."

Marcus glanced away, his arm around her back tensing involuntarily. Yeah, he'd heard. And while it should have made him happy that Cody was finally claiming him as his father, all he could do was focus on the decision that had to be made and the consequences of it. "Yeah, I heard."

"Thanks for watching him while I showered off the chlorine."

His frustration boiled hotter at her words. "You don't have to thank me. He's my son, Skylar."

"You're angry. I thought you'd be happy."

Staring into her beautiful face, he frowned. "You think I don't know why you asked Booker to come?"

"Marcus, it's an amazing opportunity. The moment the Olympics were mentioned, you lit up like a rocket."

He couldn't bite back the string of curses that raced from his lips.

Skylar straightened and sat up. "Marcus, you have a calendar listing races circled in red marker. You put in thousands of miles a year rolling every day like you do. This is what you wanted."

Reaching out, he brushed her hair over her shoulder before sliding his palm beneath the thick silk. The chance to compete, to represent his country— Yeah, he wanted it. But he wanted them, too. And if he accepted? "You want me to do this."

Skylar removed herself from his lap and crossed the room. "You sent me away after your accident and one of the reasons you gave was that you didn't know who you were anymore. Marcus, this is your chance to be an athlete. I thought you'd relish it."

"I am. I do. But I'm not supposed to question the timing of it? Yeah, I like competing, Skylar. We are both aware of that. But training for the Paralymics means setting everything else aside and focusing almost entirely on that. Between training and working, when would I see Cody? How would I see him? Or you? Isn't that the real reason you gave my name to Booker? Because you hoped I was good enough and you knew I'd be interested—but more than anything, it meant it would take the pressure off you to share Cody?"

Skylar folded her arms across her chest and he tried to ignore the way the move plumped up her boobs in the cami she'd put on for pjs.

"Booker came to Montana because he heard the ex-quarterback for the Dallas Cowboys is in even better shape now than he used to be *and* he's interested in racing."

"And that's it? You had no other reason for telling him about me?" he asked, watching her closely. "You blamed me, my career, time constraints, whatever excuse you could find to keep from having to own up to your own problem."

"What problem?"

"The *problem* that I love you. But because of stupid things that happened with you in the past when I wasn't even around, you can't accept that people care for you, love you, so you throw up barriers when they get too close. You did it then and you're doing it now."

She shook her head, mute.

"It's true, sweetheart. You hated it when I was away playing football and training. And if I say yes to taking this on, I'm giving you another reason to believe I want it more than I want you, even though you're the one who made that call. At least be woman enough to admit it."

She flicked her tongue over her dry lips, not ready to have this talk. "Fine. At the time...yes. I talked to Jill because I thought if you chose to do that it meant you would back off. But the fact remains this *is* a good opportunity. A once-in-a-lifetime opportunity. The initial reason I called Jill doesn't matter now."

"Because you care for me?" he asked. "Want me to be happy?"

"Of course."

"The training center is in Atlanta."

"I know," she whispered, uneasy with the way he was staring at her.

Because they both knew Atlanta was a long way from New York.

"But that's okay. I mean, we agreed you would come to New York when you could, and Cody and I would visit in summer. It's just geography."

He muttered a raw curse and shook his head. "So you set this up hoping I'd disappear again? I'm damned if I do, and damned if I don't?"

Skylar followed him when he rolled toward the door. "Marcus, what do you want from me? We weren't together at the time and I thought it would be easy. *Easier,*" she whispered, "if you had something else to focus on. I made the call so you could have something you *want.*"

Marcus shoved his way outside. "You don't know what I want. You're still that frightened little girl who's afraid to believe in love, who's so afraid to share the best thing that ever happened to both of us, you're trying to make damned sure I keep my distance."

"Marcus…"

He paused long enough to glare at her. "Tell Cody I'll call him."

• • •

THREE DAYS LATER, SKYLAR sat around the campfire and tried to pretend she and Marcus weren't fighting. The impromptu birthday-party guests consisted of their small and extended family, complete with cake and presents and a few balloons.

But as brief as Booker's visit had been, the effect of his presence had taken a toll on what friendship she and Marcus had managed to rebuild.

In the days since, Marcus had claimed he had artwork he needed to complete, so whenever he took time to call it was to talk to Cody, not her. And if she asked about his decision, Marcus's only response was that he was still thinking it over.

Wasn't that all she needed to know? Maybe it wasn't fair, maybe she *had* brought Booker to Montana to see Marcus, and had placed them right back into the same scenario as the past, but the fact that Marcus had to *think about it* spoke volumes. So, yeah, fair or not, he was damned if he took the opportunity. And, yeah, she felt like the ultimate bitch because she had engineered the whole thing.

"Is this where the outcasts sit?" Lexi asked as she walked into the circle of light cast by the flame.

Skylar noted the girl's wan appearance and, even though she was still aggravated by Lexi's behavior at the hotel, she didn't have the heart to send her away. After all, a person could be alone with their thoughts for only so long. "Apparently so. Bad day?"

"Um…yeah. You could say that."

"What's going on with Justin and your parents?"

"Do you really want to know?"

"Sure. We can compare sob stories. You go first. Sit."

Lexi plopped down beside Skylar on the bale of straw. "Dad's pissed because I let the scholarship go. It's gone for good, too, because the school already gave it to someone else."

"Ouch."

"Yeah," the girl said, ripping a piece of straw from the bale and wrapping the length around her finger. "He's really ticked, even though I told him I don't want the stupid scholarship anymore, because I don't want to be a nurse. Now Mom's trying to play referee between me and Dad, and they're fighting because she took up for me. Our house is a war zone. Even the twins are laying low."

Skylar glanced toward Lexi and leaned sideways to nudge the girl's shoulder. "Sounds like your mom is standing up for you already," she said, Maura's actions reminding her a lot of Rissa's when Rissa had taken on Jonas on Skylar's behalf. "That's one in your corner. And Jake will come around soon."

"I know you don't think I should give up the scholarship—"

"Hey, that's ultimately up to you, but no guy is worth giving up your dreams."

"I'm *not*. It's just the dream has changed. And Mom agreed with me that if I didn't want to go away to college, I shouldn't be forced to. I mean, I'm still going, but now... It will cost them," she said, wincing. "But then—Mom blew it."

Surprised, Skylar frowned. "How?"

"Mom reminded Dad that she was only four years older than I am now when they got married, *and* that they had dated for several years before that, which made her not much older than me, and Dad was about Jake's age, so…"

Holy crap. "I take it your Dad wasn't amused?"

"Not quite. Especially when Mom said not all men could be lumped into the sex-fiend group that Dad considers all boys to be in. She also said that if he can't give Justin the benefit of the doubt based on the whole 'innocent until proven guilty' thing Dad lives by," Lexi said, referring to Jake being an attorney, "and considering how Justin didn't know I was younger, then Dad had to put himself in that category, too—which is just gross."

Struggling hard not to laugh, Skylar nodded several times. "And that ended with?"

"Dad going off the rails and locking himself in his office for the evening," Lexi finished simply.

Well able to see that happening, Skylar couldn't help but grimace. "Youch. Okay, I see Maura's point, but Dads can't look at their little girls and see them as grown-ups. It's impossible. The men in their daughter's lives will always be sex fiends. Things will get better, though. You'll see. What about you and Justin?"

Lexi prodded a rock with the toe of her boot, her expression sad. "He's still not answering my calls, but he did text me once."

"Yeah? And?"

"He said… He said he meant what he said about

loving me, but that he didn't want me giving up school for him."

Wow. Maybe this Justin was more likeable than most guys his age. "That was awfully grown-up of him."

Tears sparkled in Lexi's eyes. "But then he said he won't see me anymore because I lied to him."

She could see that the girl's heart had been broken, but in Skylar's mind it was for the best. Lexi had a lot of years ahead of her for boys and dating.

"I still invited him to come tonight but I know he won't. He's too mad at me, and when he's mad, his stutter gets worse. And with everything that happened…"

"Wait— He stutters for real?" She remembered the guy stumbling over his words a bit in the hotel hallway that night, but she had chalked it up to either nerves or alcohol.

"Yeah. And then he gets embarrassed. And he's so shy. But even if he could forgive me for lying, now that everyone knows what happened he's embarrassed. I feel so bad. I never meant to hurt him. I was going to tell him the truth. I just didn't want to right away, because I *knew* he'd think I was too young. He's kinda old-fashioned like Dad in that way. Crap, I can't believe I just said that."

The girl's horror had Skylar laughing again. Marcus was nothing like her father… But maybe a little like Jonas? "Justin will come around. You never know. In the meantime, what are you going to do about school? You have to make a decision."

"I did. I enrolled at Montana State today."

Not quite the elite school Lexi had first chosen, but Skylar could see that the girl was happy with her decision. "Nursing?"

"Nope. Speech therapy. I had a lot of fun working with Justin on the exercises I found online. I know I'll enjoy doing that more than nursing."

Skylar wrapped her arms around her front to ward off the chill of the breeze blowing through the valley. "You know, Lex, I have to admit, I had my doubts about your decision, but it sounds as though you really do know what you want. Good for you."

The girl smiled with pride and a self-confidence Skylar wished she had possessed at that age.

"So what about you and Marcus? I was only kidding about the outcast thing earlier. How come you're not sitting with him?"

"It's complicated."

"You broke up?"

"No. You can't break up when you're not a couple," she said, hoping the words got through to the girl.

"But Marcus loves you. And I know you love him."

"Yeah, well, sometimes, that's not enough. Sometimes the most important thing is to be true to yourself, to who you are. Loving someone shouldn't mean sacrifice."

"YOU'RE SURE MOM'S COMING?" Cody asked after his birthday party had ended.

"As soon as she's done cleaning up." Marcus kept the

smile nailed to his lips and kept rolling toward the cabin assigned to Skylar and Cody.

Cody had fallen asleep on Marcus's lap sometime during Skylar's conversation with Lexi and while he had sat there and stared into the flames, he'd also listened to every word the two women shared.

After her comment about how loving shouldn't mean sacrificing who a person is, the conversation had ended, but Skylar's point had lingered in his head right up until Skylar had asked him to take Cody back to the cabin. He didn't doubt it was an attempt to avoid even more of the tension that had plagued their responses to each other since Booker had made his appearance, but he'd jumped at the chance to spend some alone-time with his son.

Along the bumpy ride to his bed, Cody had woken up, but for once Marcus wished his son had stayed asleep. Because in exactly seven days Skylar would take Cody home to New York. His time with Cody was coming to an end and he wasn't sure how to deal with it —or whether or not he should accept Booker's offer. Racing in the Olympics was a dream come true for any athlete.

But was he going to sacrifice his time with Cody to do so? Was he going to sacrifice his dream of racing because it *might* make Skylar happy, or would she simply find another excuse to push him away? Of all the women to fall in love with, why did he have to choose *the* most stubborn one?

Inside the cabin, Cody brushed his teeth and

changed into dinosaur pajamas before emerging from the bathroom.

"That was quite a birthday party tonight, huh? Did you have fun riding the horses?"

"Yeah."

Cody's tone said he thought otherwise. But was it because he was nervous about being there without his mom, or something else? "What about the other kids? Did you have fun playing with them?"

"I guess."

Marcus rolled himself closer to his son. "What happened?"

Cody dropped to his knees beside the couch and grabbed the Batman and Robin dolls, which he'd left behind so he wouldn't lose them.

Marcus had noticed that Cody was doing better about the whole vampire thing but it hadn't gone away entirely. Like now. Cody was feeling uncomfortable about something, so out came the dolls.

"Nothing… Everybody was just talking about the campout."

Ahh… Every two weeks during the summer months Seth Rowland and a few of the ranch employees took those interested on an overnight campout at the lake.

"What about it? Are they all going?"

"Yeah. But their dads are taking them."

Okay. "Do you want to go?"

Cody's gaze shifted toward Marcus's wheelchair.

"No. It's okay."

"Cody, the campout is for everyone, abled and disabled. I've gone on them plenty of times in the past."

"Really?"

Damn, did the kid have to look so surprised whenever he said he could do stuff? What happened to thinking he was cool because he could go so fast in the racer? "Yeah. Really. Would you like to go? I'd be happy to take you."

Cody's gaze shifted back to the wheelchair. He knew it would take time for Cody to come to terms with things, but the boy had to get used to the reality of wheelchairs. Especially considering there was nothing he could do about it.

"I don't know. I've never been camping. Mom might not like it."

Was that kid code? Was Cody afraid he wouldn't like it? "It's not that far to the lake. We could go, and if you didn't want to spend the night and camp out, I could bring you back to the cabin."

"Yeah?"

"Yeah. I'll clear it with your mom as soon as she gets home. Until then, why don't we crack open one of those brand-new art sets I bought you?"

A half hour later, Skylar entered the house, carrying the last of the cake, a bunch of balloons and more of Cody's presents.

"Sorry it took so long. How did it go?" she asked.

"Fine. We need to talk about the campout this Friday. Cody wants to go and I said we would."

"Oh, Marcus, I wish you wouldn't have told him that. You know I hate camping."

"I said I'd take him," he said, his voice sharper than he'd intended. Wincing, he shook his head. "You don't have to go. In fact, I'd like to do this with Cody on my own. Just the two of us," he said, wheeling himself toward the door.

"Marcus... Don't go. Stay. We need to talk about what is going on."

Tired and frustrated and more than a little pissed—because just when he thought things were going well he ran into another wall—he shook his head. "If I stay, it won't be to talk."

"Marcus..."

Skylar stepped in front of his chair. Holding his gaze, she placed both hands on the low arms of his chair, dropping her head for a slow, heady kiss.

"Don't go. Not talking works for me, too."

Because the sex was good. Because single mothers didn't have time for dating. Because she couldn't wait to get back to New York, especially now that Cody was spending more time in reality.

He palmed her face, kissed her hard, pouring every ounce of frustration and anger and pain into the kiss until the air sizzled.

By the time Skylar broke away, they were both breathing heavily.

"Stay," she whispered, her lips rosy and wet. "We'll be gone soon enough."

Hating himself, hating her words, he still found himself following her to her bedroom. Willing to take what he could get because he knew it wasn't going to last.

Chapter 19

"SO YOU CAN WALK?" Cody asked Friday morning when the path widened enough that Marcus shortened the lead rope and drew Cody's mount up beside him.

In the past couple of days, he and Skylar had fallen into a frighteningly familiar routine, that of using sex—a lot of it, whenever and wherever they could get together —to make up for the lack of decision-making taking place.

Maybe the campout would be good for other things, too, like helping him clear his head where Skylar was concerned.

Their first stop at the river was up ahead and it would be nice to get some lunch. "Yes, with my braces on. But only for a while. Too much and my legs hurt."

"Can you run?"

He shook his head. "Nope. Why do you think I like the racer so much?"

How ironic was it that Skylar could run like a demon when she wanted to, both physically and emotionally, whereas he couldn't do anything to escape reality. Sitting in a wheelchair had a way of giving a person perspective. Staring at people's asses all day did that.

He'd deliberately shown up in the last few minutes before the group had taken off, so his contact with Skylar would be limited. Not that she seemed to mind.

"Why are you wearing them now?"

Marcus grinned at Cody's ongoing questions. The entire way up the trail, Cody had asked a multitude of *whys*. "Because they help keep my feet on straight."

His comment proved that several of the other adults were listening. They laughed because the statement sounded like a joke, but he meant it. With the braces fastened above his knees and over his boots, they gave him the support needed to walk with the aid of canes.

But wearing them allowed him to use his thighs to better control the horse, and tap his heels against the horse's flanks, thus making riding a lot easier.

Up ahead, Seth gave the signal to stop. The workers from the ranch immediately set out to help those with disabilities, while the able-bodied members dismounted and were instructed on how to take care of their horses.

Marcus dismounted and grabbed his canes from where they were strapped, going over to help Cody down next. "You ride pretty well for being new at it."

"Thank you."

"Why don't you go over and play with the kids while I help Seth set up for lunch. Sound good?"

Cody's nose scrunched up beneath the cowboy hat Marcus had purchased for him as he eyed the kids gathering into a small pack.

"That's okay."

"Come on. You know you're going to be bored with all of us grown-ups. Go play. Look, there are the twins," he said, seeing Jake and his boys bringing up the rear of the group. Since the twins were also out of school, Jake had taken the day off to spend some time with his family and help out with the ranch's visitors, as well. "You've gotten to know them pretty well."

"Okay."

Marcus was glad to note Cody had at least made friends with the Rowland boys. "Be sure you don't wander off. And stay away from the river," Marcus added, knowing he was beginning to sound like Skylar but unable to help himself. "It's running pretty fast because of all the rain yesterday, and it's no fun riding wet and cold."

Watching Cody go over to the twins, Marcus staked both their horses. The ranch hands helping with this part of the ride would take care of the animals, with a little help from those guests wanting to pitch in, so he focused on finding lunch as soon as possible. Along the way, he passed one of the Rowlands' old herding dogs that had found a shady spot beneath the tree nearby and plopped down, tongue out and panting.

Marcus helped Seth, Jake and some of the others unpack their lunch, careful to keep an eye on Cody. More than once, he saw the boy talking to the other kids on the ride but he also saw some of them laughing, like maybe Cody was taking some teasing.

"Heard you got some news," Seth said. "Am I looking at a future Olympian?"

Marcus smiled and shook his head. "Don't know yet. I'm thinking it over. There is a lot to consider."

"But—you have to do it."

Marcus turned to find Cody standing behind him. Man, the kid could run. That was no small distance to cover in that short amount of time.

Marcus glanced at the other men and excused himself, ordering Cody to follow him. He led the way to a downed log placed for a seating area. "Why do I have to do it?"

"Because I told them you were. If you don't, they'll make fun even more."

"Why are they teasing you?" Marcus asked, not taking his eyes off Cody to bother looking at the other kids.

Cody's head lowered. "One of 'em is from before," he whispered. "When I talked about my dad being a vampire and stuff. He told the other kids. I told 'em I was just playing," he said, scratching his face, "but if you don't do it now, they're going to think I lied again."

"I wouldn't worry too much about them. You're not going to see them again once they leave, anyway."

"But you're really fast. You have to go to the Olympics. You have to try."

"You think I should?"

"Yeah!" Cody said, jumping up and down. "You'd be a cool dad, and you'd be famous again."

"It's not about being famous." *Especially when you're alone.* "Truth is, I'd choose you and your mama over fame any day."

"But you like racing."

"That I do. Because it's about testing myself, and challenging myself to do things I'm not even sure I'm strong enough to do."

"But you're strong. I know you can do it."

Marcus stared into the deep blue eyes of his son and smiled. The way Cody looked at him, he believed he could do it, too. "Thanks, buddy. That means a lot to me that you think so. Look, I'm going to think about the whole Olympic thing, but don't be telling more people until I make up my mind, okay? I might not go to Atlanta."

"How come?"

Marcus stared into Cody's innocent face and tried to ignore the disappointment he saw there. "Because some things are more important."

A HALF HOUR LATER, MARCUS looked up and stared at the girl in a wheelchair heading toward him. "Hey, sweetheart. Can I help you?"

She turned her pigtailed head and pointed. "Look."

Marcus followed her outstretched arm and finger to see Cody—lying belly down and inching his way across a downed tree hanging over the rushing river to retrieve his cowboy hat. "Shit— Sorry," he said, tossing the phone aside and grabbing his canes. Just as quickly, he pulled the girl from her chair and gently set her aside. "I'll bring it back," he told the girl.

In seconds, he was pushing the chair over the uneven terrain, hurrying toward the river's edge, every shove of his hands harder, propelling him faster.

He still didn't make it in time. Cody stretched his hand out to retrieve his hat, which was caught on the tip of a branch, and lost his balance, falling into the river.

"Cody!" Marcus rolled the wheelchair into the water's edge, before lunging forward and slinging himself into the current after his son. Cody hadn't come up for air yet.

Marcus swam with the current, the cold shock stealing his breath. The river flowed from Canada through northern Montana and still held the chill of winter. He had to get to Cody fast.

Reaching out, he snagged Cody's shirt and pulled the boy to his chest, flipping him over until his face was out of the water. "I got you, I got you. Cody?"

If Cody answered, Marcus couldn't hear him, but he felt Cody clutching his arm to hold on. The current continued to carry them downstream. Along the way, they were close enough to the bank that Marcus tried to grab hold of a limb dangling overhead. Both times, the branch ripped through his hands and slipped away.

Finally he was able to grab on to a downed tree, and he boosted Cody on top of it.

Cody was shaking, crying silently, his mouth blue with cold. "Get me out," he said, teeth chattering.

Marcus looked around, but there was no one there capable of doing what Cody wanted. Not even himself. He tried to hoist himself onto the log beside Cody, but the current was too strong. He couldn't get a good enough grip and it felt like one of his braces was caught on something, because the current had carried his legs beneath the log Cody now clung to. Water rolled over his neck and head, pushing hard.

"Daddy, get me out!"

The sound of Cody calling him Daddy caused a lump in his throat. "I can't. I'm sorry, Cody… I can't. Just hold on. Okay? Just hold on." Marcus's hand slipped and it was everything he could do to keep his head above water while they waited for help.

"Marcus!"

On the river's edge, Seth had a rope swinging.

"Don't leave me!" Cody screamed, sobbing.

Marcus spit more water. "I won't leave you. You'll go first."

Seth's years in the rodeo and ranching paid off when the rope slipped over Cody's head and shoulders without fail.

"Put it around you, under your arms," Marcus ordered, his hands numb.

The moment the rope was secure, Seth and the others pulled Cody back into the water to get him to shore.

"Daddy! Daddy, you come, too!"

Marcus put his forehead on the log, Cody's screams in his ears.

"Marcus! Grab it!"

Losing more and more feeling in his hands and arms, Marcus took a breath, knowing when he held up his arm, he was going to go under....

And then he did—and the water sucked him beneath the fallen tree.

Chapter 20

"MARCUS WANTS TO see you."

That evening, Skylar looked up from where she lay snuggled in Cody's hospital bed. She'd been in the dining hall with Maura when the emergency call had come in. Before she'd even had time to rush outside, she heard the *whomp-whomp-whomp* of her mother's helicopter flying overhead to perform an emergency transport.

"Skylar? Did you hear me?" Carly said. "Marcus wants to see you. I'll stay with Cody. The doctor is signing the release papers now. He said you can take him home in a little bit."

She had to clear her throat twice before she could speak. "What about Marcus?"

Carly grimaced. "He has to stay overnight, but he wants to see you before you go."

Shifting away from the warmth of Cody's body, she kissed his cheek, never so thankful for her mother's piloting skills as when she'd arrived and whisked Cody and Marcus off to the hospital. "How is he?"

"Quiet," Carly said. "Skylar, whatever you decide about the two of you? You and Marcus? Don't do it now. You'll understand when you see him."

Nodding, Skylar left the bed and hugged her arms around her waist for warmth. Hospitals were always too cold. The sterile smell was overwhelming.

Outside the curtained room, she saw her mother and Jonas talking to the doctor.

"He's in room two-eighteen," Jonas said.

The elevator ride up was too slow, the hallway too long. But then it seemed neither journey had taken long enough, because suddenly she was there.

Ben stood by Marcus's bed, his body stooped, his expression thankful. The moment he looked up and spotted her, he inched toward the door in his shuffling walk.

"I need some coffee. Be back in a while, Marcus."

"Hey," she said to Marcus once Ben was gone. "How do you feel?"

He looked horrible. His mouth still had a bluish tinge, there were dark shadows beneath his eyes and his bed was mounded with blankets and topped with several heating pads.

"Warmer."

"I bet." She moved to the bed and sat beside him, leaning forward to brush his mouth with a kiss.

He didn't make an attempt to return the caress. "Marcus?" She tilted her head, seeing the questions in his gaze. "Marcus, Cody is fine. They're releasing him right now. You saved him."

He squeezed his eyes shut tight. "Barely. But if I could've made it there a few seconds faster, he might not have fallen in."

"You can't blame yourself for what happened." But he did. She could see it in his eyes, his expression. And even though she had been scared out of her mind today, she couldn't let Marcus think he was at fault. "Once, when Cody was two, he was sitting in his high chair, eating. I was in the room, not *two feet* from him, but I was cooking and I didn't notice anything was wrong until I turned around and his face was purple. He was choking and I was just standing there."

She put her hand against Marcus's cheek so that he'd look at her. "What happened today was not your fault. Don't try to take the blame for something you didn't do."

Marcus wrapped her hand in his and pulled it away from his face.

"I'm taking Booker up on his offer."

So he could go a few seconds faster? "Marcus, not now. Please. Just get warm, rest. We can talk about this later."

Marcus stared at her, his expression grim. "There's nothing more to talk about. I've made my decision. I'm going to Atlanta. The question is whether or not you and Cody will come with me. I want you there. I need my family. I need *you*."

Fear slammed through her. Memories. "Marcus…"

Marcus's mouth flattened into a hard, unwavering line at her tone, and she knew then that she had answered his question. It was football all over again, just like she'd feared. If she agreed, it would mean working around his schedule, traveling, meals alone while he practiced. Focusing her life around his.

"Love will never be enough, will it?" Marcus muttered.

"What do you mean?"

"You will always have an excuse for why we shouldn't be together."

He was blaming her? He knew how she felt about things. It took two people to keep a relationship going. "Marcus, please. You've had a horrible day. Just *rest*."

Marcus looked down and plucked her hand from his chest, held it against his lips.

"I can't rest until I know. Do you love me?"

"Yes," she whispered, meaning it with all her heart. She *loved* him. She had loved him since she was fifteen and even though their lives had gone separate ways, she'd never stopped, but he wanted *everything*.

"You told Lexi that love shouldn't be a sacrifice, that we need to be true to who we are." He kissed her fingers, squeezed them, as his gaze met hers. "That goes for me, too. I have to be true to who *I* am. You can't be angry with me for accepting an opportunity you put into play."

"I know." It hurt to breathe. Her chest felt tight, the room too hot.

"And you know what it would mean to me if you and Cody would—"

She squeezed her eyes shut, fighting the burn. "I know."

"I won't be able to take off and fly to New York while I'm training. I'll come when I can, but it won't be often."

"I know." *Smarter, wiser, stronger.* She wouldn't repeat the past. "You need to rest. I—I should go."

She stepped away from the bed, every muscle in her body protesting as though she was the one who'd been dipped in the cold water and dragged to shore. "I'll bring Cody to see you tomorrow. We'll get together as much as we can before we leave for New York, okay?"

Unlike the last time she had stood in Marcus's hospital room, Marcus wasn't screaming at her to leave, but asking her to stay. To be with him, support him.

But like that day eight years ago, she forced herself to walk out the door.

SKYLAR STUMBLED HER WAY BACK to Cody's room, trying to gather her frazzled nerves and composure. Every step away from Marcus's room was like walking in drying concrete, heavier, harder to manage.

Carly was standing outside Cody's room, talking on her cell phone, one hand pressed to her other ear to block out the voice paging a doctor over the speaker.

Not wanting to talk and knowing Carly would ask too many questions, Skylar ducked her head and slipped into Cody's room to find her son not only dressed but sitting on the edge of his bed, feet dangling toward the floor and swinging back and forth. "Hey, you look raring to go. Where's Grandma?"

"She went to get coffee with Grandpa Ben. Aunt Carly is outside. Uncle Liam called to check on me."

"I saw her." Putting on a brave face wasn't easy but staring at Cody sitting there, well and whole and unharmed, gave her the strength she needed. Somehow, someway, she had to hold herself together until she was able to get Cody to the cabin and she could have some time alone to— What? Fall apart?

Again?

She couldn't let that happen. Falling apart over Marcus was exactly what she had tried so hard to avoid. But knowing she and Cody were going to leave soon, that she wasn't going to see him every day. Be with him every day…

"You want some?" Cody asked, holding up his hand. "They're really good. The doctor gave them to me. Carly said it was okay."

A short laugh escaped her when she realized what he held. Of course. M&M's. The candy most any kid loved and one that probably made the doctor a favorite. "It's…fine."

"Here—take 'em."

Cody opened his soft, little-boy hand and she stared down at the candy, instantly transported back in time. Heart pumping out of sync, she knew her response to the candy was ridiculous. Silly. But one of the pieces was cracked, the shell broken, revealing the soft candy center inside.

Shaking, breathless, she found herself on her knees on the floor in front of Cody's hospital bed, staring at the brown bag with happy M&M's on the front, the words she'd said to Lexi bouncing through her head once more.

Love shouldn't be a sacrifice but what was she doing? She was sacrificing *love* and for what?

Marcus loved her. Loved Cody. The kind of love that lasted, meant something. Was worth *everything.* How many times had she dreamed of being with Marcus? How many times had she wished things were different?

And that comment to Lexi about being true to yourself?

"What's wrong, Mom?" Cody said. "Don't you want some?"

Yes. She wanted some. She wanted Marcus's softness, his sincerity. His love and strength and that tough outer shell that didn't disguise the man beneath. She didn't have to lose herself in him. All this time, she'd thought that kind of love made a person weak but—she felt stronger now. *That's* why Marcus wanted them with him in Atlanta, because they made him stronger.

And Marcus was right. Atlanta was a far cry from a town the size of North Star. It had a rich history, museums, art, culture. Starbucks! Was that really a sacrifice?

And your students?

Oh… Her students…

She would *miss* her students but they would be well-cared for in Nina's capable hands. And she could find another school, one in need of someone who knew what it was like to be abused and hurt and uncomfortable in her own skin.

Was she *really* going to stand by and let the past repeat itself for another eight years? Or was she going to stand up for herself and for Cody? For love? For their family? *Believe* in it?

Marcus was right about her pushing him away, pushing everyone away, because even though she said the right words, she hadn't believed them. Hadn't admitted her own flaws and insecurities. It was way past time for her to grow up and realize life wasn't all about her. "Cody, I need to ask you something and I need you to pay close attention, okay? Would you like to see your dad all the time?"

"Yeah. He's cool. He saved me."

"I know. But he's going to train for the Olympics and it's in Atlanta, so to see him means moving, and going to a new school."

Cody plopped an M&M's in his mouth and chewed. "You and Dad will be there?"

"Yes. We would all be together."

He nodded, his expression very grown-up for such a little boy. "I can do it. I might be a little scared but if you and Dad are there, I'll be okay," he said, his tone decisive. "Can we live *with* Dad?"

Skylar smiled, happier than she had been in a long, long time. Call her crazy for letting M&M's be her deciding factor but… "Let's go find out," she said, holding out her hand.

Cody jumped off the bed and, without a word to Carly, they took off down the hall toward the elevator. Giggling and shushing each other as if they were spies on a secret mission, they raced to Marcus's room. Ben hadn't returned from his coffee run, so Marcus was alone.

"Dad?"

Marcus opened his eyes, his gaze dull but sharpening quickly when he saw them.

"Hey, Cody. Come to say goodbye?"

Cody glanced at Skylar and she smiled, urging him to complete the plan so quickly formulated in the elevator.

"I brought you something. They're from me and Mom both."

She watched as Marcus focused on Cody's hand.

When he realized what they were, Marcus's gaze shot back to hers.

"What can I say?" she whispered, sitting on the edge of Marcus's bed so she could be close to him. "I'm goo."

"Skylar...what's going on?"

What could she possibly say to make Marcus understand that she was finally ready? She used to be afraid because she loved Marcus so much, afraid of how it made her feel. But scarier than that? She was afraid of being without him. They had lost too much time already. *Smarter, wiser. Stronger.*

"I've changed my mind. But don't worry, I won't change it again."

Marcus shifted in the bed, shoving the blankets off his bare chest. And darn it if she didn't notice. She'd bet every nurse on the floor was vying to take care of him.

"And that means?"

"I love you," she said simply. "We both do," she said with a glance at Cody. "And we're moving to Atlanta," she told him without a smidge of doubt or hesitation. "Hopefully, to live with you."

"Yes," Marcus confirmed. "You're sure?"

"Without a doubt. I'm not a kid anymore. I don't expect the world to revolve around me. There are kids needing counseling everywhere. Maybe I can even talk a few Olympic trainees into putting in some time with them."

"I'd be honored."

Marcus slid his fingers into her hair, his gaze holding hers as they sealed their lips with a kiss. Her heart tugged because she could feel Marcus trembling with the force of his emotions, and wasn't that the way to a girl's heart?

"Are you gonna kiss all the time? Because that's gross."

Cody's observation left them both laughing. Marcus leaned sideways and grabbed Cody, pulling him onto the bed to snuggle the boy between them, the M&M's bag clutched in Cody's hand.

Marcus stared into her eyes over Cody's head.

"So you'll go for the gold with me? Fifty years of marriage?"

Fifty years? Yeah, that might be long enough. Or maybe they could shoot for more. "I should probably warn you I have watched that show about Atlanta housewives. I think I have potential."

Marcus couldn't stop laughing as he kissed her. "Lord help us all. Goth-girl turned Southern belle. You'll have your own reality show before the year is out."

Epilogue

Three years later…

"IS HE THERE YET?" Cody asked, hopping up and down, trying to see over the fence in front of him.

"Go!" Skylar said, aware that Justin, Lexi's guest at the final qualifying race and steady date for the last year, hefted Cody into his arms and onto his shoulders so Cody would have a better view. "*Goooooo!* Go, go, go!" she screamed, never taking her eyes off the track.

The noise level in the crowd rose as the racers approached the finish line. Marcus and the current world champion were wheel-to-wheel.

"He can do it," Lexi said, holding Skylar close as the race rushed to an end.

Tears stung her eyes but she didn't dare blink, afraid she'd miss the finish. They were so close, flying toward the line—past it.

The air froze in her lungs because it looked like Marcus's wheel hit the finish line just a hair ahead of the other racer. But *did* it?

The crowd exploded, cheering, stomping their feet. Screaming. But now that it was over, Skylar couldn't say a word.

"Did he win? Did he, Mom?"

"We don't know yet, Cody," Lexi said. "Listen to the announcer and see if they say your daddy's name."

Skylar prayed hard as the officials reviewed the results.

Her first year with Marcus had been spent packing, moving, interviewing for a new job. It had taken months of traveling to Atlanta or Marcus flying to New York to be together, but it had all been worth it. The condo in New York had sold, and they had found a house with a yard for Cody and Marcus's dog, Cassie.

They'd flown home to Montana for Christmas and had a surprise wedding ceremony so everyone could be there, most especially Ben. Marcus's grandfather had decided to split his time between the home state he loved to summer in, and the warmer winter state that didn't leave him aching quite so bad.

Atlanta wasn't the same as New York City and it never would be. But the city had a beauty all its own, one she'd grown to appreciate. There were times when the streets were filled with the scent of magnolias, every store rich with the smell of peaches. She'd learned to love sweet, sweet tea and Southern fried chicken. She loved the accent, even though her new friends and colleagues at the outreach counseling program teased Skylar about hers.

It wasn't long before they had settled into a routine, traveling to competitions, going to Cody's school plays and band recitals. Spending a lot of time watching Marcus race.

Marcus's smile was huge as he rolled toward them. People patted her while her cell phone buzzed in her pocket, no doubt the ranch calling because they were watching the races and awaited news, but she didn't take her eyes off Marcus.

The moment she was able, she wrapped her arms around Marcus while Cody jumped up and down and screamed in his excitement. Lexi and Justin looked just as nervous as they waited for word.

Turned out, Lexi wasn't kidding when she'd said she knew what she wanted. Once Justin had gotten over his anger—and Lexi had turned eighteen—they'd started dating again. Skylar had to give them credit, she had never seen a couple so in love.

A buzzer sounded and the official results announced.

"Daddy won! Mom, Daddy won! They said his name! He won! *He won!*"

Marcus let out a whoop and dragged her down onto his lap for a kiss that left her laughing and gasping, the noise of the crowd quickly fading to a dull roar.

The final trial race was over. Marcus was going for the gold—and she looked forward to being right there by his side.

I HOPE YOU ENJOYED READING SECOND CHANCE HERO. KEEP READING FOR A SNIPPET OF BLIND MAN'S BLUFF**, THE FIRST FULL-LENGTH NOVEL IN THE STONE GAP MOUNTAIN SERIES.**

Ian's nerve endings itched with the awareness of the

late hour, the sensation interrupted by the sound of something going on outside in the direction of the stable.

Owen's SUV had arrived twenty minutes ago with its low thrumming engine, Duncan's bike following close behind. Doors opened and closed then...barking?

The itching got worse, pushing him out of the chair. Quinn could cook when he wanted to and often used wine or beer in his concoctions to enhance the flavors.

The thought made Ian pause before he took another step forward, this one more purposeful than the last despite the self-disgust filling his head.

Pathetic. He knew the signs of alcoholism, and he walked a very narrow line these days. But if it took the edge off and made his claustrophobia disappear for a while...

He shoved the guilt away to focus on remembering the twists and turns of the large house. It had been years since he'd stepped foot in it, and he'd barely left his room since his arrival four weeks ago.

The house was big and old, with many additions to the main section forming an angled U around the pool and what used to be the gardens in back.

Maybe coming here wasn't such a good idea, but he couldn't hack another moment in Duncan's Atlanta townhouse, listening to the world go by him like nothing had ever happened.

He wanted to be left alone, and even if it meant putting up with Duncan and all the workmen readying the house for a blind occupant, once the updates were completed, Duncan and the others would leave. And when they did... What then? Crawl around the house waiting on the years to pass? How would he survive? Eat? What would he do?

Slowly, inching his way along his room because of the broken glass and the shambles he'd created earlier, he finally made it to the door, out into the hallway.

"Hey," Duncan said from the left. "Where are you going?"

The slight breeze blowing through the house thanks to the powerful A/C unit carried a not-so-pleasant scent with it. "What's that smell?"

Wildfires weren't only a danger in the west. The house sat atop a mountain surrounded by woods.

Still want to live here alone?

"The smell is me."

His grip on the door trim tightened as he recognized Emma Wyatt's voice. It was late, too late for her to be traveling the mountain roads alone. "What are you doing here?"

"Emma's moving in," Duncan stated matter-of-factly. "She'll be staying in the room beside yours."

"No. Dammit, Duncan, I don't want or need a tutor." Ian held out a hand and inched forward, toward the sound of their voices.

Ian didn't stop until Duncan's hand pressed into his shoulder, warning him he was in danger of bumping into something. Most likely *her*. Up close, the burnt smell made his nose twitch with the threat of a sneeze. "That's not wood smoke."

"Very good," Emma said dryly. "You're right, it's not."

"What happened?" he demanded.

"Ian," Duncan warned. "I'll fill you in later."

"Fill me in now," he ordered.

"My house burned to the ground this evening."

Duncan squeezed Ian's shoulder to the point of pain but Ian didn't know if it was a subconscious move or a warning. Either way, it was a reminder of the blow Duncan had landed earlier and the fact that if Ian smarted off, Duncan would likely hit him again. Tempted, he asked, "How did it start?"

"In the kitchen," Duncan said, his tone sharp.

The vague response added to the intrigue teasing Ian's brain. He almost smiled. Finally there was something to focus on instead of the phobia kicking his ass. "How?"

"Oh, for pity's sake, it was *my* fault, okay? That's what he's not saying. What you want to hear, right? I accidentally started the fire while I was cooking. There, story over."

She was angry and upset, tired, from the sound of it. Possibly in shock. But it was the hint of vulnerability Ian heard in her voice that cut through his irritation that she had returned. "Somehow I get the impression there is more to the story."

"What do you want me to say?" she asked softly. "I'm human. I make mistakes, and this time," her voice cracked with emotion but she quickly cleared her throat, "my father lost his home as a result. Happy?"

Duncan was right. This wasn't the time. And since she was there because she no longer had a home to go to, well, kicking her out wasn't an option.

Annoyed as he was at his brother's insistence about the tutoring thing, he wasn't heartless. "You're welcome to stay as long as you need to."

"Thank you."

"No problem. Just be sure that while you're here, you stay the hell away from me," Ian ordered, carefully backing into his room so he could shut the door before Duncan saw the damage to the bedroom and commented on it in front of their guest.

FIND OUT WHAT HAPPENS WHEN IAN LEARNS EMMA ISN'T A GUEST BUT A TUTOR HIRED TO HELP HIM COPE WITH BEING BLIND. KEEP READING BLIND MAN'S BLUFF!

THE STONE GAP MOUNTAIN SERIES
THAT SOUTHERN SUMMER NIGHT
BLIND MAN'S BLUFF
HER UNWANTED PROTECTOR
REDEMPTION ROAD
THEIR SECRET SNOWBOUND CHRISTMAS
OWEN'S RETURN

THE REDEEMING LOVE SERIES
HER REDEEMING LOVE
HIS REDEEMING LOVE
REDEEMING US

MONTANA SKIES SERIES
HER MONTANA COWBOY
HER COWBOY SHERIFF
PROTECTING THE SHERIFF'S DAUGHTER

IVY JAMES

COWBOY MEETS HIS MATCH
MONTANA CHRISTMAS
SECOND CHANCE HERO

OTHER BOOKS:
The Crash Before Christmas
Return to Eden

Coming soon:

TENNESSEE TULANES SERIES
HER SNOWBOUND HERO
THE REBEL'S SECRET BARGAIN
HIS BABY PROPOSAL
THE DOCTOR'S NANNY
A HERO IN HIDING

Ivy James Books
CONTEMPORARY ROMANCE NOVELS

THE STONE GAP MOUNTAIN SERIES

THAT SOUTHERN SUMMER NIGHT

BLIND MAN'S BLUFF

HER UNWANTED PROTECTOR

REDEMPTION ROAD

THEIR SECRET SNOWBOUND CHRISTMAS

OWEN'S RETURN

THE REDEEMING LOVE SERIES

HER REDEEMING LOVE

HIS REDEEMING LOVE

REDEEMING US

MONTANA SKIES SERIES

HER MONTANA COWBOY

HER COWBOY SHERIFF

PROTECTING THE SHERIFF'S DAUGHTER

COWBOY MEETS HIS MATCH

MONTANA CHRISTMAS

SECOND CHANCE HERO

TENNESSEE TULANES SERIES

HER SNOWBOUND HERO

THE REBEL'S SECRET BARGAIN

HIS BABY PROPOSAL

THE DOCTOR'S NANNY

A HERO IN HIDING

OTHER BOOKS:

The Crash Before Christmas

Return to Eden

Ivy James is the alter-ego of Kay Lyons, who now focuses on sweet/clean and wholesome contemporary romance and romantic suspense. For more information about Ivy's slightly sexier novels (or to find Kay's clean and wholesome versions of them as well as her latest titles), please go to Ivy James Author/Kay Lyons Author. Or, find her at one of the following:

@KayLyonsAuthor (Twitter)

Kay Lyons Author (Facebook)

Author_Kay_Lyons (Instagram)

Kay Lyons, Author (Pinterest)

SIGN UP FOR KAY'S NEWSLETTER AND RECEIVE UPDATES ON NEW RELEASES, CONTESTS, PRE-RELEASE BOOK INFORMATION, EXCLUSIVES AND MORE!

AUTHOR BIO

Ivy James is the alter-ego of Kay Lyons, who now focuses on sweet/clean and wholesome contemporary romance. For more information about Ivy's slightly sexier novels (or to find Kay's clean and wholesome versions of them as well as more new titles), please go to Ivy James Author/Kay Lyons Author. Or, find her at one of the following:

@KayLyonsAuthor (Twitter)
Kay Lyons Author (Facebook)
Author_Kay_Lyons (Instagram)
Kay Lyons, Author (Pinterest)

Reader Note:

Dear Reader,

Thanks for picking up *Second Chance Hero*, one of the titles in my MONTANA SKIES series. Each book stands alone, so no worries if you haven't read the previous books; however as a fan of series myself, I want to let you know several of the characters featured in this book first appeared in my earlier releases.

Also, I'd like to ask your forgiveness in fudging the age of one of my secondary characters. If you read *Her Cowboy Sheriff* you'll note that Skylar is eight years older than her cousin Lexi, who is six at the time. In this story, I've taken the liberty of altering Lexi's age to better suit the issues she faces within these pages.

I hope you enjoy *Second Chance Hero* and invite you to take a look at all the other books in the series. Information on those can be found on my website Ivy James Author.

Ivy James is the alter-ego of Kay Lyons, who now focuses on sweet/clean and wholesome contemporary romance and romantic suspense. For more information about Ivy's slightly sexier novels (or to find Kay's clean and wholesome versions of them as well as her latest titles), please go to Ivy James Author/Kay Lyons Author. Or, find her at one of the following:

@KayLyonsAuthor (Twitter)

Kay Lyons Author (Facebook)

Author_Kay_Lyons (Instagram)

Kay Lyons, Author (Pinterest)